LESS DREADFUL
WITH EVERY STEP

# LESS DREADFUL WITH EVERY STEP

CLIVE WOOLLISCROFT

The Book Guild Ltd

First published in Great Britain in 2023 by
The Book Guild Ltd
Unit E2 Airfield Business Park,
Harrison Road, Market Harborough,
Leicestershire. LE16 7UL
Tel: 0116 2792299
www.bookguild.co.uk
Email: info@bookguild.co.uk
Twitter: @bookguild

Copyright © 2023 Clive Woolliscroft

The right of Clive Woolliscroft to be identified as the author of this
work has been asserted by them in accordance with the
Copyright, Design and Patents Act 1988.

All rights reserved. No part of this publication may be
reproduced, transmitted, or stored in a retrieval system, in any form or by any means,
without permission in writing from the publisher, nor be otherwise circulated in
any form of binding or cover other than that in which it is published and without
a similar condition being imposed on the subsequent purchaser.

This work is entirely fictitious and bears no resemblance to any persons living or dead.

Typeset in 12pt Adobe Jenson Pro Minion Pro

Printed and bound by CPI Group (UK) Ltd, Croydon, CR0 4YY

ISBN 978 1915603 678

British Library Cataloguing in Publication Data.
A catalogue record for this book is available from the British Library.

For Sue, Kirsty, Karen, Ian, Ben, and Luke,
not forgetting Bonnie

*Wade through mud,*
*Spill your blood,*
*'Victory!' your voices cry.*
*For a world that's fit for heroes*
*Brave men have to die.*

*Why?*

# ONE

# *Jarrow, August 1914*

I took the kettle off the hob. The water had boiled for the third time in the past hour. For the third time, I had been ready to warm the pot before making Fatha's cup of tea ready to place in front of him after a day working in his office at Palmers Shipbuilding and Iron Company Limited.

I could hear Mam tut-tutting away behind me.

'I can't think where your father can be, Emily. It's so unlike him to be so late,' Mam said. 'Tea will already have spoiled.'

I looked at the kitchen clock. It was nearly seven o'clock, long after my father should have returned home from work.

'So much for him constantly telling us that we could set the clocks by what he does each day,' I replied. 'Something must have cropped up at work. I'll go and look outside to see if I can see him.'

I left the kitchen, opened the front door and hurried down the path to the gate outside the house. No sooner had I arrived than Mam joined me.

'Where is he?' she muttered. 'Where on earth has he got to?'

We both looked along Albert Road.

'Shall I walk down towards the junction and look out for Fatha, Mam?' I asked.

'No, Emily, pet. Just in case you miss one another. Let's get back indoors and see what we can do to avoid a complete disaster in the kitchen,' Mam grunted as she started to walk back up the drive.

I followed her into the house and hurried back into the kitchen.

'The kettle's not long since boiled, Mam. Shall I make you some tea while we wait?'

'No, thank you, Emily,' she replied. 'At best these new potatoes will now end up as mashed potatoes and the vegetables are getting soggier and soggier. Perhaps the only thing for it will be to turn them into bubble and squeak. On top of that, the meat is in danger of being cremated.'

'Is there anything I can be getting on with, Mam?'

'Nothing, I'm afraid, pet – other than go and take another look to see if you can see Fatha.'

I headed for the front door, but as I reached it, Fatha walked in and made his way to the kitchen.

'About time, Percy,' said a relieved Mam. 'Where've you been all this time? You've had the pair of us really worried.'

Fatha took Mam's hand while he kissed her gently on the forehead.

'Sorry I'm so late, Matilda, pet,' Fatha said. 'It's been pandemonium at work today. Management has been running around like headless chickens. Finally, we were all called to a meeting late in the afternoon. It went on for hours. They told us that it seems likely that the Royal Navy will place new orders at the shipyard now that we are at war with Germany. It will be a case of all hands to the pump for everyone from now on. I fear this won't be the last time I'm late home of an evening.'

Fatha went into the kitchen, took his jacket off and placed it over the back of his chair at the kitchen table. He crossed over to the dresser, took his pipe from the pipe stand sitting on it and picked up the tobacco pouch lying next to the stand.

'To make matters worse, the town seems to have gone mad,' he continued as he filled the pipe bowl with tobacco and lit it. He sucked hard a couple of times, each time blowing out puffs of white smoke.

'There are crowds everywhere. As I walked down Ellison Street, I was pushed and shoved in every direction by a crush of men who had spilt out into the street in droves. It was worse than getting through the crowd at last year's FA Cup second replay at St James' Park.' He rolled his eyes, looked up at the ceiling, and took another puff of his pipe. 'It seems that all the town's young men are hell-bent on enlisting. They're hanging about the Drill Hall, singing all the patriotic songs imaginable.'

Fatha took his pipe from his mouth. His eyebrows came together in a frown.

'So, Emily, lass,' he sighed, 'I suppose this means that your young man will find himself right in the thick of things now.'

I gasped as the enormity of what Fatha had just said hit me. My fiancé, Alban, was in the Royal Navy. He was serving as an engine room artificer on board *HMS Achilles*. We were due to be married next Easter. The wedding plans had already reached an advanced stage – a necessity due to the very nature of Alban's job.

I sat down on the chair to the side of Fatha, for the time being, stunned into silence.

'But he's in the Navy. The last time he wrote, there were rumours they were about to sail to the Shetland Islands. If so, he'll be at sea. Safe,' I eventually spluttered, rather naively.

'Sadly, pet,' Fatha replied gently, 'it's inevitable that his ship will find itself in a naval battle at some stage – the Germans have a navy also.'

I knew at once how immature my reaction had been. Of

course Alban was likely to be involved in battles. Of course he would face danger. He could be killed. I shuddered at the thought of that. My eyes welled up, and I began to cry.

*

Frank Dawson was hurrying to work at the Ormonde Street branch of the North Eastern Banking Company. He was facing several busy days. Apart from anything else, Head Office had ordered the evacuation of all the bank's records from the branch. In addition, yesterday had been a bank holiday; today, there would undoubtedly be a great deal of catching up required.

As Frank reached the junction between St John's Terrace and Ellison Street and was about to cross the road, he stopped in his tracks. Outside Mr Morris' newsagent's shop, he saw the headline *War Declared on Germany*.

War had been brewing for some time. There had been a recurring topic of conversation ever since the assassination of Archduke Ferdinand in June, so the headline should not have surprised him, but it did. There was a world of difference between possibility and reality.

Frank scurried towards his office, sidestepping other pedestrians as he did so, and diving between passing carts as he crossed each road on his way. Finally, and with a film of sweat glistening on his face, he arrived at the main entrance to the branch. There he met an unusually flustered chief cashier.

'I guess you've heard the news, Dawson?' he said.

'Yes, sir,' replied Frank.

'All hands to the pump today, I fear. I wouldn't be surprised if we had a mini-run on the bank.'

As it turned out, the chief cashier had been unnecessarily pessimistic; business volumes were far less hectic than feared. In some ways, they were not much different from any other business day following a bank holiday. The net result was that the day seemed to drag on and on.

Shortly after finishing work, Frank left the bank and headed home, straight into a swirling maelstrom of people. He soon found that he had to battle his way through the crowd which had filled the streets. Everybody was excited. Some, though, had decided to engage in sinister practices.

Frank stared in horror at a mob gathered outside the shop of the German-born butcher. They had already daubed paint across the shop window and were hurling abuse at the owner. It only seemed a matter of time before they started smashing up the shop. Frank tried to push his way through the crowd to do what he could to help the butcher.

'What the hell are you playing at?' he shouted.

'Sorting out Fritz here,' came a reply.

'Don't be daft, man,' Frank called back. 'The owner's lived here for over twenty years. His son went to school with me. We play in the same football team.'

'So what? That doesn't alter the fact that he's a German – and, in case you don't know it, we are now at war with Germany.'

Others joined with Frank to help, and slowly the mob moved on, still shouting abuse – but at least words were all that they were now hurling.

As soon as they did so, Frank resumed his journey home. When he arrived, he went into the kitchen to find his mother, Grace, busy preparing tea for the family.

'Mam,' he said, 'have you heard the news? We're at war with Germany.'

'Yes, I heard it when I was shopping this morning,' Grace replied. 'What happens now, do you think, son?'

'Heaven knows,' replied Frank. 'But since the Declaration of War, some terrible things have already been happening in town – as I've seen myself.'

After finishing his tea, Frank fancied visiting the Ellison Arms for a few bottles of his favourite tipple – a well-known brown ale affectionately nicknamed "Dog". So, after a brisk walk along Ellison Street, he pushed open the door to the saloon bar and stepped in.

'Good grief,' he gasped. 'The place is packed. It's worse than it ever was for the Coronation in 1911.'

As Frank entered the bar, he walked into an almost overpowering wave of sound. The air was heavy with a thick fog of acrid cigarette smoke. Frank coughed violently as his lungs reacted with each breath he took. His eyes were stinging; they started to water.

'Howay, man, Frank, man,' shouted Frank's best friend, Jimmy Prentice. 'Over here. A bottle of Dog is waiting here for you, marra.'

Frank made out the figure of Jimmy standing up at a rectangular table by the bar window. Three other friends were sitting around the same table. When they weren't speaking, they were either puffing away at their cigarettes or downing the contents of a beer glass. Frank picked his way through the melee of bodies and sat down.

'What do you reckon then, Franky, man?' Jimmy shouted over the racket going on all around him.

Frank looked back at Jimmy, a little bemused. He could barely hear himself think for the noise.

'What do you mean?'

Jimmy stared back at Frank with a look of surprise on his face.

'The war, of course! What else?'

'I'm not sure,' replied Frank. 'I've not thought about it that much yet.'

'What's there to think about, Frank? We've all decided to enlist. We're all off to the Drill Hall first thing tomorrow.'

'That seems a bit sudden, doesn't it?' gasped Frank.

'We'll miss all the fun if we don't join up now, Franky, man. All the talk is that this war will be over by Christmas. You'll come with us, won't you? It has to be better than counting money behind your bank counter, bonny lad! Surely, even a bank teller needs a bit of adventure in his life before he croaks it?'

The war was the sole topic of conversation during the evening. Everyone around Frank seemed to have one reason or another to enlist.

*'Don't you see, Frank, man? It's a chance to explore and see the world!'*

*'But, Frank, it's going to be such an adventure!'*

*'At long last, Frank. It's the chance for me to escape from my boring job!'*

*'Frank, look at it from my point of view. You get paid a shilling a day – every day of the year – that's a real chance for us to escape poverty!'*

As glasses of Dog were filled and emptied, Frank went through a mental process of recrimination and self-doubt. On the one hand, there was the dichotomy between the inherent dangers of joining up and the inherent safety of staying at home. On the other, he had never been away from home before – or at least the area around his home. Now he had the opportunity to do something new – to visit new places. Then there was his career. He had a good job and was doing well in it. However, if the war was over by Christmas as Jimmy predicted, it could not prejudice his future if he joined up for three or four months. In any event, the bank would surely support his enlisting at this nationally critical point in time; support his contribution to the war effort.

'What about it then, Franky, man?' asked Jimmy, breaking into Frank's train of thought. 'Are you with us?'

By now, the jingoistic nationalist fervour swirling around

Frank, coupled with several more bottles of Dog than he was used to, had melted away his doubts.

'Aye – I'm with you, bonny lads,' he announced with a broad grin. 'I'm going to be a soldier, too!'

# TWO

# *Jarrow, September 1914*

I slumped down onto a chair and looked across at Mam in disbelief after she told me that something terrible had happened to Alban. 'Alban's missing in action, believed dead,' was what she had said, but I only heard the word *"dead"*.

I sat there bewildered. I was in a state of shock. Near distraught with sorrow. All the hopes and dreams Alban and I had shared now shattered.

'How...? When...?' I sobbed.

Mam came over, sat beside me, and put her arms around me. She pulled me gently towards her.

'Alban's mam told me that he was on *HMS Hogue* when it and two other ships were torpedoed by a German submarine while on patrol off the Hook of Holland,' she whispered.

My mind raced, trying to process Mam's words. What she had just told me didn't make sense. *HMS Hogue – the North Sea – that can't be right.*

'But...but... Alban is serving on the *Achilles*, isn't he?'

Mam kissed the top of my head.

'He was, pet, but it seems that he transferred to the *Hogue* a few days before the Declaration of War.'

My brain was working overtime, trying to glean even the faintest of hopes.

'But Alban is only reported as *"missing in action"*. That doesn't mean that he is actually dead, does it?'

Mam sighed.

'Ordinarily, no… Emily dearest,' she said softly, 'but not in Alban's case, I'm afraid. Before the *Hogue* finally sank, Alban jumped off the ship's side with a friend, another engine room artificer. As he did, he hit the bilge keel and badly damaged his legs. The friend swam over to Alban, clung to him, and kept him afloat. They were in the water for several hours, but the friend was too exhausted to hold on to Alban anymore; he had to let Alban go. There has been neither sight nor sound of Alban since. A Dutch vessel later rescued the friend. He wrote to Alban's mam to explain everything and the heart-breaking decision he had had to make. I'm sorry, pet, but there is no chance Alban is still alive.'

I sat staring at Mam for a moment; then, I gave myself up to grief with a flood of tears amid an anguished cry. She clasped me in a closer embrace.

'Oh, Emily, pet,' she said.

We sat there without saying anything more, me sobbing in Mam's arms. I just couldn't take it all in. Alban's loss had created such a massive void in my life. There would be no spring wedding, no future life to be spent together, and no sons or daughters as planned.

*What's left for me now?* I wondered.

\*

In the days that followed Alban's death, I took to sitting alone for hours in the parlour after I had had my tea. One evening, the lamp was unlighted, but the coal fire blazing in the fireplace reddened the farthest corners of the room. I was staring blankly at the fire, feeling particularly morose, when Mam and Fatha came in to join me.

'It will be three months and three weeks tomorrow,' I sighed, looking up at them both.

'Yes, pet,' answered Mam as she and Fatha sat on the sofa together, 'but, hard as it must be for you, you can't sit around moping the whole time. You have to move on with your life. It's what Alban would have wanted you to do.'

I knew Mam meant well, but I let pass what she said to me.

'If only he hadn't transferred from the *Achilles*...' I didn't finish the sentence, which faded away on my lips – useless and foolish conjecture. A long silence followed. Fatha lit his pipe while he stared into the fire. 'The only thing I can think of would be to somehow help with the war effort, but it's not as if I can join up as Alban did.'

For a moment, Mam did not move. Then, slowly, she lifted her head and looked at me; her eyes grew round and staring. I caught the look; it was one I had seen many times before. She had got an idea she wanted to share with me.

'Have you read this week's *Express*?' she asked, getting up off the sofa.

'Can't say as I have, Mam,' I replied, my curiosity aroused.

'Wait on, pet,' she said and hurried into the kitchen. Moments later, Mam returned with the latest copy of the local newspaper. She glanced towards me, went over to the lamp and lit it. 'I have an idea for you, bonny lass,' she said, facing me. 'You said you would like to do something to help with the war effort. Well, have a look at this.'

I moved over towards Mam as she spread the paper out on the sofa where she had been sitting next to Fatha. She pointed to an article in one of the columns.

'Here, pet,' she said. 'What do you think?'

I read through the article. The Saint John Voluntary Aid Detachment were to open a new hospital in Jarrow, and they wanted volunteers to work there. I began to smile.

'Oh, Mam,' I said. 'Perhaps this is something I could do.'

'Well, the secretary, Mrs Jarrett, lives just around the corner from us. Why don't you go and see her and find out what it's all about?' said Mam, smiling gently.

'I will,' I replied. 'I'll go round first thing in the morning.'

\*

I stood outside Mrs Jarrett's house and knocked on the door.

'May I help you?' asked a kind-faced, matronly lady as she opened the door.

'Are you Mrs Jarrett?' I asked.

'Yes, I am. Who is it that wants me?' replied Mrs Jarrett.

'I'm Emily Harland. I've come about the article in the *Express*,' I said. 'I understand that you are the person I should speak to about it.'

'Yes, that's right, Emily. Follow me.'

'Please sit down,' she invited once we reached her parlour.

'Thank you,' I replied.

I crossed the room and sat down on a two-seater settee in the bay window. As I did, I noticed a set of Gibbons' *The History of the Decline and Fall of the Roman Empire*, Macaulay's *History of England* and Pope's *Poetical Works* in the bookcase that lined one of the walls. There was an armchair to the side of it.

*This is a very cosy room.*

'Can I get you a hot drink?' said Mrs Jarrett.

'No, thank you, Mrs Jarrett.'

Mrs Jarrett moved to the armchair and sat down, leaning forward towards me.

'First of all, Emily, tell me a little about yourself and just why you are here.'

I explained about Alban and the conversation I had had with Mam the previous evening.

'Working at the new hospital seems to be the sort of thing I am looking for,' I continued. 'Although I know nothing about what it might involve.'

'All right, pet,' said Mrs Jarrett. 'Let's start at the beginning, shall we? The Saint John Voluntary Aid Detachment is opening a hospital to care for cases of sickness among the troops billeted in the town. We are looking for volunteers to train up to work in the hospital and help to run it. They would need to attend training courses in connection with this.'

'What exactly do the courses cover?' I asked.

'There are four in all – first aid, home nursing, hygiene and cookery.'

'What happens after the courses have finished?'

'Well, if you wanted to become a VAD, you would need to obtain certificates in first aid and home nursing and pass an exam.'

*This all seems to be getting a little complicated.*

'If I get the certificates and pass the exam, what will happen?'

'You would be invited to work at the hospital for a month on a trial basis. If you complete the trial period successfully, you will almost certainly receive an offer of a position as a full-time VAD.'

Mrs Jarrett finished speaking and sat back in her chair. I looked at her, not quite knowing what to say next.

'Well, having heard a little about things from me,' she said, breaking the silence that had developed, 'what are your thoughts now?'

'Well – I think that volunteering at the hospital as a VAD is something that I would like to do,' I replied, albeit a little hesitantly. 'I just hadn't anticipated the full extent of the actual process involved.'

Mrs Jarrett looked at me and smiled warmly.

'Yes, there are a lot of things that are required, pet – and it does take a bit of time to become a VAD. At the end of the day, it is not for everyone.'

'I can understand that,' I replied. 'I guess that the least I can do is to give it a try.'

'Tell you what,' said Mrs Jarrett. 'Why don't you take this in stages?'

Her suggestion struck me as being a little odd.

'What do you mean?' I asked.

'Well, I think that, as a first step, you should aim to get the certificates. If you successfully achieve those and are still interested, sit the exam. If you pass that, we could have a further meeting to discuss taking things further. How does that sound to you?'

I sat pondering for a moment or two.

'That does seem to make sense,' I replied.

'Would you be interested in setting the ball rolling at least, then?'

I looked at Mrs Jarrett.

'I think so,' I replied. 'No, I know so.'

'That's good to hear, Emily, pet. The courses have already started, but only a week ago. There's still a way to go yet. You shouldn't find it too difficult to catch up if you joined us at this stage and were willing to put in the effort.'

'Well, Mrs Jarrett, as Mam tells me, *a journey of a thousand miles begins with just a single step*. So when could I take my first step? Could it be next Monday?'

'Next Monday's fine. I look forward to seeing you at the Town Hall then, young lady, and I wish you the best of luck. Now, let me show you out.'

I got up and started to follow Mrs Jarrett. As we moved towards the door, I had a sudden thought.

'Do I need to bring anything with me?'

'No, Emily, not this time – but maybe after that.'

# THREE

# *France, Spring 1915*

Three minutes after the train from Aldershot drew up at the harbour station and five hours after leaving camp, Frank marched down the wharf and onto the gangways that led to the steamer taking him to France. Low dark clouds hung over Southampton, and it was raining.

The battalion filed on board, and the boat soon loaded up. The men put on life belts before the ship edged away from the quayside. It then slipped out of the harbour, bound for Le Havre.

Frank watched the lights of Southampton as they flickered and faded away. Now and then, he caught glimpses of destroyers as they went by and disappeared out of sight. Then, finally, the ship passed the last lighthouse and steamed out into pitch darkness.

Frank had never been on a boat before – let alone a cross-Channel steamer. He was filled with a mixture of trepidation and excitement. Despite the weather, he stood on the top deck. He clung to the rail, feeling every dip and dive of the boat as it headed towards France. Glancing around, he noticed others doing the same, but a forced sense of bravado hung about them. Frank steadfastly looked to the sea, avoiding eye contact.

*Mines! There could be mines!* Frank closed his eyes and prayed. When he opened them again, the ship was sailing onwards relentlessly. It knew where it was going. Frank caught the eye of Jimmy. A ghost of a smile crossed his lips. Frank quickly looked away to sea and turned and looked towards France, wondering what was in store for him there. As he did, it finally stopped raining.

Gradually, the French coastline became visible. The lights of Le Havre came into view, and Frank watched as they got progressively brighter. Finally, the steamer edged into the harbour and tied up at a quayside that was already a heaving mass of men, horses and equipment.

Feeling and probably looking very bedraggled, Frank put his pack on almost immediately after the steamer docked, and joined with the rest of the battalion as they slowly disembarked and formed up on the quayside. Eventually, they all moved off and crawled up a long, steep hill to a rest camp, where they were to stay overnight before setting off, bound for the front.

'Rest camp. They call this a rest camp,' exclaimed Frank as he looked at a line of tents standing in a muddy field.

'Howay, man, think of the money we're saving. It'd cost us each twenty-one shillings a week going to Canvastown Holiday Camp in Whitley Bay to stay in a tent,' joked Jimmy.

'What's more,' quipped Frank in reply, 'don't forget we actually get paid a shilling a day to stay at this camp!'

As it turned out, the camp offered little in the way of rest. The battalion arrived late at night and left early the next morning.

It all seemed surreal to Frank as he and his comrades marched out of Le Havre to a rousing send-off by the townspeople. One that stretched to the edge of the town. They came out of the houses. Adults were either trying to catch the hands of the soldiers or waving flags or handkerchiefs; children were running alongside the soldiers, cheering. All were crying out *'Bon chance!'* and *'Vive L'Angleterre!'*

As they did, it hit home to Frank that he was marching towards a great unknown – after months of training to become a soldier and practising at being a soldier. This was not another exercise. This was for real – as he was soon to find out.

\*

Frank had marched for nearly eighteen hours with barely a break. Most of the time, this was along cobbled roads that quickly took their toll on unaccustomed legs and feet. To make matters worse, it had rained almost continuously since leaving Le Havre. He was tired, wet and hungry. That, though, was of no consequence now. Barely three days after leaving Aldershot, he was about to go into action for the first time. His battalion was poised to attack.

Whistles sounded. *'Follow me!'* shouted Frank's platoon commander as he nervously edged his way over the parapet of the assembly trench and moved out into No Man's Land. Then, as one, the rest of the platoon followed. It had become instinctive in them all. It wasn't a question of what you could or could not do. When duty called, you went, even if it meant that you were going to your death.

A corporal stood up alongside Frank. As he did, he froze, as a rabbit does in that split second before being taken by a bird of prey. He fell backwards. Dead. Half of his face was missing. Shrapnel.

'Move on!' a voice screamed out. 'Leave that man there and get forward. There's sweet Fanny Adams you can do for him now!'

The men continued, stumbling across No Man's Land as the sky became a kaleidoscope of living fire, and a wall of sound hit them. Exploding shells sent up plumes of earth and black smoke. Earth and trees were constantly in the air.

There was the unmistakable sound of shrapnel: a bang, a strange whistling, swishing sound, and then another bang. As metal shards rained down on the advancing troops, smoke hung over the battlefield. Added to that, there was the incessant rattle of machine guns. Only heard. Never seen.

The carnage was fearful as the platoon advanced over open fields and came within range of the German machine guns and artillery. This was far worse than Frank could ever have imagined, but he briefly felt a strange calm taking hold of him.

Then, that calm was shattered. The head of the soldier in front of him evaporated. Frank thought his eyes were playing tricks on him. But in the next second, the soldier crumpled and fell to the ground. A warm mist of his blood settled on Frank's face as he did so. Frank gasped in horror. He was a religious man, but at that moment he began to question whether there was a God.

Moments later, Frank tripped and fell forward. He put his right hand down as he fell, rolled back to his right and tried to lift himself. But, as Frank did, he put his hand right through the abdominal cavity of a dead comrade whose body had been ripped open by shrapnel. Recoiling in horror, he suppressed the urge to vomit.

Looking around him, Frank scrambled to his feet. As he did so, a soldier fell face down into the mud, the back of his head gaping wide. His body slid back a few feet. Others followed. High explosive shells dropped in front of and on the advancing troops as they braved the barrage. Frank became indifferent to both the enemy shells and death. He no longer cared about the relentless and fearful curtain of machine-gun fire that swept backwards and forwards across the battlefield. He no longer cared where he went, just so long as it was towards the enemy.

Frank witnessed things too terrible to contemplate – or take in properly. He saw men fell backwards, some doubled over, while others danced like marionettes as they were pulled hither and thither by the rain of bullets. He advanced across a carpet of bodies lying motionless, some half-buried in debris. He saw wounded men who were lying on their own or in groups. Some were writhing on the ground. Some were trying to walk or crawl back to the trenches from where they had started. Some fell and rose silently. Some fell but did not rise.

Mercifully, with casualties rising with every passing minute, the battalion received the order to fall back, and Frank and his fellow survivors staggered, crawled, or were carried, back to where the attack had started. As soon as they safely could, they collapsed, exhausted. Frank was left wondering what the following day might hold for him.

*Already so many dead, so many wounded – and to no avail. Heaven knows why I have made it this far without catching a bullet! Will my luck hold? Will I make it through tomorrow?*

# FOUR

# *France, Summer 1915*

It was haymaking time. Groups of French women and children worked hard in the fields, tossing hay on wooden pitchforks. They were all taking full advantage of one of the hot sunny days between hot cloudy ones interrupted by frequent heavy downpours. That morning, the battalion had come out of the front line. Everyone was looking forward to a much-needed period of peace and quiet. Somewhere far away from a continual threat of danger.

Frank saw meadows on either side of the road that were edged with clumps of red clover and carpeted with yellow mustard flowers. The village where they were to billet came into view. There was palpable relief among the men in the battalion as it did so. Hedges around its outskirts were white with elderflower, the scent of which pervaded the air and further soothed their minds.

In truth, it was a beautiful village, more prosperous than most Frank had stayed at previously. It had a small church, thatched cottages, several houses, a few shops and two *estaminets*. There were several farms scattered around the outskirts. These, in turn, were surrounded by a mixture of recently ploughed fields and meadows. A stream that ran adjacent to the village meandered through the countryside. Some cows ambled around, calmly grazing. Others were lying down, contentedly chewing the cud. Although he was exhausted, Frank was glad of life for the first time in a long while.

The battalion was met on the outskirts by the billeting party, who led the various companies to their appointed places. Frank's company found itself on the right flank, centred on one of the farms set in the undulating ground. There was a small hill on one side and a wood on the other. A road rambled east of the farm, rolling on to the next village about a mile away.

The farm itself comprised a long, low building that stretched along almost one width of a rectangular yard. Bordering the other width and the rear length were a scattering of sheds and stables in varying states of repair.

A granary reached out alongside three-quarters of the front length. The remaining quarter formed the entrance to the yard. A steaming dunghill dominated the centre of the yard. Chickens were standing on it, several scratching at the surface with high expectations of finding worms. A reservoir abutted the dunghill.

The men were ordered to fall out and group together in their platoons. Frank's platoon formed up along the width opposite the farmhouse. The other platoons formed up along the rear and in front of the granary. All of them were to await further orders.

'Thank goodness,' gasped Frank as he dropped his pack to the ground.

Jimmy Prentice moved over to where Frank was standing.

'Have you got a cigarette, bonny lad?' he asked. 'I'm gasping.'

Frank reached into the breast pocket of his tunic, took out a pack of Woodbines and handed it to Jimmy, who took one out, lit it, inhaled deeply and exhaled slowly.

'God, I needed that,' he said, almost purring.

Jimmy handed the pack back to Frank.

'Thanks, Jimmy. What's next, do you think?'

Jimmy looked around.

'Who knows? But the officers and platoon sergeants seem to be having a pow-wow over there with the company sergeant major. All I know is that I could do with something to eat and a good night's sleep.'

Frank smiled, took a cigarette out of his pack for himself and lit it.

'You're not alone on that score, Jimmy, man.'

The two men stood together in silence as they finished their cigarettes and lit another. No sooner had they done so than their platoon sergeant moved towards them. He was a tall, burly, round-faced man with a greying moustache. He certainly looked like a man no one would want to tangle with – or be on the wrong side of.

'Hey up,' said Frank. 'Looks like something's about to happen.'

'Fall in!' shouted the platoon sergeant.

Frank and Jimmy hastily stubbed out their cigarettes, put their packs on again and joined the rest of the platoon.

'Right, you lot,' said the platoon sergeant. 'First things first. A defensive ring is to be established around the village. As part of this, an observation post will be set up on the hill. This platoon will man it in rotation. They tell me the view is lovely from there, so you can indulge in a bit of nature watching as you keep a lookout for any advancing Boche.'

'As long as the weather stays fine,' Frank whispered to Jimmy.

'Aye, man, and the operation of sod's law will ensure that it's pouring with rain when it comes to our turn to man the post!'

'You are to billet in the larger sheds and stables behind you,' continued the platoon sergeant. 'These may not be quite to the same standard as rooms at the Savoy, but the buildings are dry, and there is plenty of straw for bedding. Field cookers are by the road at the entrance to the village. A hot meal, and a brew, will be provided as soon as possible. When you are not on duty, you are free to go into the village, but the *estaminet* is out of bounds to everyone at all times tonight. Any questions?'

'Yes, Sarge,' a voice piped up. 'Are we going to be here long?'

'What is "long" in the context of war, laddie? As far as I know, we will be here for a bit yet – but anything can happen between now and whenever. So how long we actually do stay here remains to be seen. You can be sure that you'll find out about that when I do. Now fall out, get your sleeping arrangements sorted, and then get over to the cookers as soon as your grub's ready. After that, I suggest you get some rest. Reveille will be at six tomorrow morning, breakfast is at seven, and there will be a platoon commander's parade at eight o'clock sharp. Don't be late!'

After their hot meal and a brew, Frank and Jimmy decided to take a stroll into the village before turning in for the night. A mutual curiosity seemed to exist between them and the French women and children standing silently at the doors of the houses.

'What do you reckon they think about this war being fought in their villages, on their farms and in their fields – about us being here now?' Frank asked as he and Jimmy headed back to their billet.

'How would you feel if the war was being waged back home – say on the fields around Lake House Farm?'

'I see what you mean, Jimmy,' Frank replied. 'No small wonder, I guess, that these villagers didn't show the same enthusiasm that the people of Le Havre did when we left there.'

\*

Frank felt better than he had for a long time as he and the rest of the platoon paraded the following morning. A hot meal the previous evening, a good night's sleep and a full breakfast had worked wonders.

'Right, men,' said the platoon commander. 'The current plan is that we will be out of the line for a fortnight's rest period. You will be allowed three clear rest days, starting today. There will be nothing formal for you except for bathing and re-clothing during that time. From day four, there will be a mixed programme of company drill, musketry, bayonet training and sport in the form of inter-company and inter-platoon football and boxing competitions. Additionally, there will be intensive bombing training, at the end of which I expect you all to pass the usual bombing test. Any questions?'

Frank looked around, smiling inwardly. He and everyone else in the platoon knew that the question was rhetorical.

'No questions then,' said the platoon commander before continuing. 'Right. Mobile baths have been set up by the stream over there. As soon as I have finished here, you will march down to them for a bath, after which you will be issued with clean clothes. You are free to do what you like for the rest of today after that – within reason, of course. Everyone must be back in their billets by twenty-three hundred hours. Any questions?'

'Yes, sir,' a voice piped up. 'Are the *estaminets* out of bounds?'

'Good question,' the platoon commander chortled. 'The answer is "no" – that is, they're not completely out of bounds. You may use them between ten in the morning and two in the afternoon and from six o'clock to eleven o'clock in the evening.'

*You can bet your life we'll be visiting the estaminet as soon as we're washed and brushed*, thought Frank – a bet he wasn't about to lose, as he and Jimmy hurried into the village after their bath and change of clothes.

For a couple of hours or so, Frank forgot about the war. *Monsieur* served him and Jimmy with French beer, and *Madame* brought over plates of egg and chips. Other members of the platoon joined them. Frank smiled as he watched them trying out their language skills on *Madame*.

'*Erfs… s'il vous…* please, *avec…* chips… and *du pang*,' one man attempted.

*I'm afraid that the French "parlez" is not getting on very well "avec moi". I reckon that they might just as well be talking Chinese.*

The men's feeble attempts at speaking French did not stop the beer flowing or the eggs, *pommes frites* and bread coming before closing time.

Once the *estaminet* had closed, Frank headed back to the billets for a period of quiet contemplation and thoughts of Sybil – all the time trying to block out what he might next expect in two weeks' time.

\*

Frank enjoyed the luxury of a full night's rest before it was his turn to man the observation post. Time he spent in a period of fitful sleep followed by a full, if not entirely wholesome, breakfast. He couldn't have been given a more ideal time to man the post if he had asked for it; he was on duty shortly after breakfast and off duty at lunchtime.

Frank finished an entirely unremarkable stint in the observation post and returned to his billet. As he did so, and to his surprise, he heard the excited voices of children playing. A sound that seemed almost alien to him in all the circumstances.

He headed towards the voices and saw a dozen or so children playing a game of tag in a meadow about fifty yards away. He stopped to watch. There was normality when he least expected it and where he least expected it. Then, everything changed. High explosive shells fell on the village. The air was rent by the screeching whistle of shrapnel. It became opaque with smoke, earth, and dust tossed up by the heavy blasts of an irregular bombardment.

Everyone had started to run for cover when Frank caught

a sound that froze his blood: the pitiful low sobs of children wounded or dying from the hot flying shrapnel that had rained down onto the field where they had been playing.

Frank rushed towards the sobs. He scooped up two terrified little girls, frozen with fear, and carried them as quickly as he could to where he hoped they would be safe. He handed the girls over to a group of villagers sheltering near the church, and he rushed back to look for others still in the field.

Frank found a young boy whose leg had been shattered and picked him up as carefully as possible. He made his way back to where he had taken the girls. He handed the boy over and went back to the field for the third time.

This time, he found the broken bodies of two other boys and a girl – none of them aged more than about nine. One by one, he carried the bodies back to villagers becoming ever more grief-stricken.

Then, as suddenly as the bombardment had started, it ended. The air gradually cleared as the smoke drifted away, and the dust, earth and debris settled. Almost without thinking, Frank did not go back to his billet. Instead, he struck out across the fields around the village and was soon walking knee-deep in grass and weeds. He was hot and sticky with sweat froths from his efforts. A few sluggish clouds hung above, and there was a buzzing of insects swarming above the drying weeds and stubble.

Frank saw a large solitary oak tree on the far side of the field and headed over to it. Completely distraught, he collapsed face down on the ground in the tree's shadow, grazing his knees and elbows as he did so. He lay where he fell. He was exhausted and, for a brief while, neither cared for nor thought of anything.

Eventually, he turned slowly on his side and leant his head on his palm, his elbow resting on the ground. He looked back towards the village. A variety of insects buzzed hither and thither above the grass, every now and again attempting to swoop down towards his face. He could see people, villagers and soldiers milling around near where the main barrage had struck. And then a chilling thought struck him.

*What if someone saw me leave and thought that I was deserting?*

Frank knew he had to get back to the village, and quickly. There was no time to lose. Galvanised into action, he made his way back across the field and into the churchyard. He saw other members of the platoon going into the church itself and headed towards them. When he arrived, he could see that the church had escaped damage, apart from one hole in the roof. Frank opened the door, entered the church, slumped onto a pew and gazed towards the altar. It stood in front of a large arched alcove, in the middle of which hung a simple wooden crucifix. Frank had never before felt so helpless as he did at that moment. Nor as angry.

'How can men just drop shells so callously and so indiscriminately?' Frank whispered in anguish.

If he'd ever had any doubts about enlisting when being egged on by his friends in the Ellison Arms the previous August, they had now been dispelled, well and truly. What had just happened had provided him with a real purpose. Revenge.

*Inhuman German savages! This damnable war – I just need a chance to make them pay for all this.*

# FIVE

# *France, June 1916*

I took the train to London and from there to Folkestone before crossing the Channel to Boulogne. I was one of around 120 members of the Voluntary Aid Detachment who arrived in France in June 1916 and had met one of these, Sarah Nugent, when we crossed from Folkestone to Boulogne. She was from St Leonards-on-Sea in Sussex and, like me, had volunteered for military nursing duties following a year or so with her local VAD hospital.

When we arrived at Boulogne, the first thing that struck me was how the docks themselves resembled an arsenal, with ammunition cases everywhere. Outside the docks, the town had become one huge military base. I had never seen so much khaki. Men marched in long columns from the quayside. A continuous cacophony filled the air. Sarah and I stood and watched as soldiers landed from the transports which arrived, densely crowded with their human freight. Tentatively, they made their way from one boat to another to reach the gangways. Then, they came down inclined planks and lurched ashore before forming up and marching off.

'You get the impression that all of our youth is passing through Boulogne,' remarked Sarah.

'Yes, frightening, isn't it?' I replied.

'And it's both men and women,' said Sarah. 'See – the cafés and bun shops are filled with all kinds of women in uniforms – uniforms glinting with shoulder straps and buttons.'

'And, of course – there's us,' I replied. 'Come on then, Sarah. Let's go and find the hotel.'

Arrangements had been made for Sarah and me to meet the matron in charge at the Hôtel de Louvre and receive further instructions, but this meeting was not scheduled until the following morning. Consequently, we were to take a room at the hotel.

Sarah was not feeling well after the crossing from Southampton, and, even though it was still early in the evening, she went to bed almost immediately after our arrival. As the hotel only did bed and breakfast, I decided to venture out on my own to try and find a decent café where I could buy dinner. I walked past the Hôtel Christol, which I noticed was a makeshift hospital, crossed a bridge crowded with people passing on either side of me, and eventually happened upon Le Café des Amis, which seemed to be just what I was looking for. I entered the café and was shown to a table by the manager.

'Un moment, mademoiselle. Je vais vous chercher un menu.'

'Thank you,' I said when the menu arrived. I was surprised at just how decorative this was. A cream card decorated with a sprig of blue cornflowers that swept from left to right, partially framing the italic lettering of the menu itself.

*Menu card? It looks almost like a work of art. The trouble is, it's in French. I think I know what* hors-d'œuvres variés *are. Also,* saumon sauce mayonnaise. *I can also guess at* salade, petit pois à la française *and* desserts variés. *But I don't have a clue what* gigue de chevreuil, dindonneau rôti *or* glace panachée *could possibly be.*

I looked around the café, slightly panicking. As I did so, I saw someone approaching me.

'Forgive me, Miss, I'm not normally as forward as this,' he said, 'but if you're on your own and wouldn't mind some company, may I join you?'

I looked up, a little startled. Standing before me was a tall, slim, rather suave lieutenant with light-coloured eyes set in a ruddy complexion, a small black moustache and dark hair flecked with grey.

A pause.

'I'm not normally as forward as this either,' I replied, 'but some company would be very welcome – especially if you speak French.'

'Perhaps enough to get by,' he replied.

'In that case, please do sit down – I could definitely use some help with this menu.'

'Forgive me,' said the man. 'I'm Jack Miller.'

I allowed myself a grin.

'Nice to meet you, Jack. I'm Emily Harland.'

Jack sat down opposite me.

'How come you're here in France, then?' he asked, once he had made himself comfortable.

'I'm here as a VAD,' I replied.

Jack looked at me both quizzically and uncertainly.

'A VAD?'

'Sorry. I'm with the Voluntary Aid Detachment.'

'Ah yes – and that explains the uniform,' said Jack.

We studied the menu, which Jack explained to me.

'Are you ready to order yet?' asked Jack. 'I already know what I want.'

'I think so,' I replied.

Jack called a waitress over to the table and ordered for both of us. We each chose to start with the *hors-d'œuvres variés*. Jack chose the *gigue de chevreuil*, while I preferred salmon to venison or turkey and went for the *saumon sauce mayonnaise*. Finally, we would both finish with *glace panachée*.

'*Voulez-vous du vin, Monsieur?*' asked the waitress.

'Will you join me in a glass of wine, Emily?' Jack asked.

'Yes, thank you,' I replied.

'*Un verre de Bordeaux rouge pour moi et un verre de Pouilly pour la mademoiselle, s'il vous plaît,*' said Jack.

He looked back at me, smiling. His eyes sparkling.

'So, Emily, how do you come to be in Boulogne?'

'I only arrived in France today and will find out tomorrow which hospital I will be attached to. In the meantime, I'm staying the night at Hôtel de Louvre with another VAD I met on the boat from Southampton.'

Jack looked a little quizzical.

'So, what happened to your fellow VAD?' he asked.

'I'm afraid that the crossing was quite rough. I was all right, but my companion was not feeling well, poor thing, and went to bed as soon as we reached our room.' I paused before continuing. 'Well, I've given my story. What about you, Jack? How come you're here?'

Jack grinned. 'I've been back to Blighty on a course and am on my way to join my regiment. I am being collected from Boulogne early tomorrow morning. In the meantime, I'm staying at the Hôtel Folkestone. I didn't fancy eating there. It's full of officers of all kinds who are waiting for trains. All they do is spend hours over a meal, drinking red wine and talking "shop". Not for me, I'm afraid, so I decided to look for somewhere else to eat and arrived here – luckily, I found you here.'

He seemed to be making a pass at me with those five words. I could feel my face becoming increasingly hot.

*Good grief. I'm blushing!*

Fortunately, the waitress brought our *hors-d'œuvres variés* and I was able to use their arrival as the opportunity to steer the conversation to a general exchange of information about our home towns and families.

I thoroughly enjoyed my food. The salmon, in particular, was excellent. The wine, too, was very nice, but one glass was more than enough for me – as I explained to Jack when he suggested I have another. Though pleasant enough, the evening itself left me feeling a little embarrassed by Jack's attention towards me. An occasional comment here, a hint of innuendo elsewhere, reinforced my original thought that he seemed to be making a pass at me. Nothing that blatant or obvious, but if I'm honest, I did give the slightest sigh of relief when he announced that he would have to leave; he had an early start in the morning.

Jack called the waitress over and settled the bill before we headed out into the street. He accompanied me as we retraced my steps to the Hôtel de Louvre.

'Thank you for your company,' he said as we stood outside the hotel. 'It was nice to meet you. Good luck with the Voluntary Aid Detachment. Perhaps we may meet again – in a social capacity, of course, rather than nurse and patient.'

'You never know, do you, Jack?' I replied. But I wasn't sure whether I would want to meet him again – in "*a social capacity*".

I turned away from Jack and, without looking back, headed into the hotel and up to the room I was to share with Sarah.

\*

I woke early the next morning and crept out of the room and into the bathroom to ready myself for what lay ahead. I returned to the bedroom just as Sarah was waking.

'Good morning, Sarah,' I greeted. 'How are you feeling today?'

'Much better, thank you, Emily. So what did you get up to after I went to bed?'

I turned away, and Sarah began to chuckle.

'Aha,' she exclaimed. 'You're blushing. Come on, tell me all.'

I swallowed hard and looked back at Sarah.

'Well, actually, I had dinner with an army officer – a lieutenant returning to his unit.'

Sarah looked at me, perhaps a little surprised by my revelation.

'Tell me more!' she encouraged, 'and try and control all that blushing as you do.'

I told Sarah about the dinner.

'The food was delicious,' I concluded. 'In some ways, it was nice to be in the company of a man again. It has been a long time since I last was.'

'And…?' asked Sarah.

I thought about how I felt when Jack and I parted company outside the hotel the previous evening.

'In some ways, I think it might be nice to meet him again, but I'm not so sure in other ways,' I replied with a half-smile. 'Now, let's finish our breakfast and take a stroll around the area before meeting with Matron.'

After a short walk and taking in some fresh air, Sarah and I returned to the hotel and went into a large, rather austere room. Before the war, it had perhaps been a rather splendid dining room, doubtless adorned with all the usual trappings, like those at Mayfield in Jarrow before it became a hospital, but which had long since been removed. There was a trestle table in their place, with a large tea urn, cups and saucers, and a plate of biscuits. In the centre at the front of the room was a large desk, behind which sat Matron, looking every bit the queen bee. She was wearing an outdoor VAD uniform, her hat placed on the desk.

Five other VADs were in the room, nervously making small talk between themselves in the space between seven chairs set out in a semi-circle and the front of Matron's desk. A further chair stood to the left of the desk, close to Matron.

'Good morning,' said Matron as Sarah and I entered the room. 'I'm pleased to say that everyone is now with us, so if you'll all help yourselves to a cup of tea and a biscuit and then sit down on the chairs in front of me, I'll set the ball rolling.'

We all milled around the tea urn briefly before returning to the chairs, each carrying a cup of tea and a biscuit.

'Right, everyone, I expect you are all wondering what you've let yourselves in for,' she began. 'Well, I can only promise you that it will involve a lot of hard but, I hope, fulfilling work. You are all volunteers and have worked in hospitals before. But here, you are in a war zone. Accordingly, you will be working in a military environment, subject to military rules and regulations. The matrons at your allocated hospitals will give you the precise nature of your duties when you meet them. Today, I will work through a few formalities and tell you which hospitals you will be going to.'

One by one, Matron called the seven of us up to her. We each confirmed our details and learnt which hospitals we were going to. In my case and Sarah's, it was to one in Étaples. Then, rather excitedly, we went over to a waiting bus and climbed in. No sooner had we taken our seats and settled down than we were on our way.

'I hear that Étaples is an old fishing town and port at the mouth of the River Canche,' I said as we left Boulogne. 'I wonder if it will be like Alnmouth – a village near where I live.'

I was soon to find out that it was not. As the bus trundled onwards, I glimpsed flashes of the heaving mishmash of a training base, a depot for supplies, a concentration of hospitals and a network of railways, canals and roads, which hinted at what Étaples had become.

\*

The bus reached the hospital and stopped by the main entrance. Sarah and I got out and collected our cases. I felt apprehensive as an orderly came over to us.

'Good afternoon,' he greeted. 'Who have we here then?'

We introduced ourselves.

'Follow me, please,' said the orderly.

He led us to a vast tented area set out in neat rows and eventually stopped outside one of the tents.

'All the tents you can see are used for accommodation. The huts are a mixture of wards and offices… and the Mess. Hopefully, it won't take you long to find your bearings.'

A little bemused, if not overawed, the pair of us looked around and then back to the orderly.

'You two in here, then,' he told Sarah and me.

We went into the bell tent that was our new home and dropped our cases. At first, neither of us could think of anything to say.

'I can't believe just how tiny this tent is,' Sarah finally gasped. 'There's barely enough room to accommodate you and me, never mind our cases and the bits and pieces here already.'

Sarah was not wrong. The tent was claustrophobic.

'Good grief!' I exclaimed. 'It's a good job we're both small!'

'I guess we can store some clothes in the cases,' observed Sarah. 'But in the absence of any wardrobe, how will we hang our coats and uniforms?'

She stared at me with a troubled expression. She looked like a fish out of water. I racked my brain trying to think of a practical solution for what was indeed a problem for us both. Then I had an idea – I'm not sure where it came from, but it was an idea.

'Have you got a spare belt?' I asked.

'Yes… why?' replied Sarah, looking just a little puzzled.

'You'll see.'

I took her belt and one of my own and wrapped each around the top of the tent pole. Next, I fastened the buckles to create two loops that became hanging rails for our coats and outdoor and indoor uniforms.

'There you are, Sarah,' I announced as I stepped back from my handywork.

'Thanks, Emily. Nothing like a bit of practical ingenuity,' Sarah said admiringly.

\*

I couldn't sleep much on the first night after my arrival and was awake by five o'clock the following morning. I left the tent without disturbing Sarah and took a short walk around the tented area before joining her for breakfast.

As we were finishing our breakfast, a VAD approached the table.

'Good morning,' she said. 'I'm Florence Norgate. I'll take you to see Matron when you're ready to go.'

'I think we're all ready now,' said Sarah, as she got up from the table.

Sarah and I followed dutifully behind Florence. She stopped outside Matron's office and knocked.

'Come in, please,' a voice called out, and we all went in.

'Good morning, Matron. The two new arrivals,' Florence announced.

'Good morning. Thank you, Norgate. Please wait outside until I've briefed these two.'

'Of course, Matron,' Florence replied, and left the room.

'Welcome, both of you,' greeted Matron. 'Now, which of you is Harland, and which Nugent?'

We each introduced ourselves, after which Matron provided a broad overview of what would be expected from us.

'You will both start on the "day shift" while you find your feet. Every day starts at ten minutes to eight each morning when we have morning prayers. It finishes with evening prayers at eight o'clock in the evening. Where possible, you will have three hours off, usually taken during the afternoon between two o'clock and five o'clock. Any questions?'

As might be expected, neither of us had any.

'A few golden rules, then,' Matron continued. 'Make-up is not permitted, nor long nails. You must always look smart. You must always carry scissors, safety pins and a pencil. All qualified nurses are addressed as "Sister", all VADs simply by their surnames.' Matron paused before going on. 'If you have any problems, raise them in the first instance with the sister in charge of your ward, who is Sister Bettsworth. If she cannot help, raise them with me. Is that all clear to you?'

Sarah and I looked at one another. Neither of us replied. I just nodded.

'Off you go then, and good luck.'

Sarah and I left Matron's office and followed Florence to see Sister Bettsworth, who greeted us warmly.

'Welcome to the ward,' she said. 'For today, I want you to shadow Norgate. She will explain your duties as you help her. Listen carefully to what she tells you. I'm afraid there's a lot to take in and little or no time to do so.'

We took our leave of Sister and headed into one of the wards.

My initial duties were basic. I spent my time making beds, carrying food to the various patients, distributing and collecting bedpans and urinals, collecting pails containing discarded, often septic, dressings, and emptying and disinfecting these. I also gave bed baths to soldiers, chatted with them, cheering them up as best I could. I read letters from home to the men who could not do so because of their injuries. I also wrote letters home for them when asked to do this.

I already had some experience working in wards where there were wounded soldiers, some of them seriously wounded. However, they had already received medical treatment before arriving at the hospital. Any amputations necessary had already taken place. Wounds suffered in battle were already attended to, cleaned and dressed. I had also witnessed one or two soldiers die. I felt prepared for whatever faced me. Little did I realise, though, that I was not.

\*

The Somme offensives began that Saturday. We had been in France barely a week. I was doing everything I possibly could to help. Unfortunately, this was limited to undertaking the most elementary duties of a VAD. I lacked the experience to deal with newly arrived battle wounded, all suffering horrific injuries. Notwithstanding this, I was soon thrown in at the deep end.

'Harland, over here, please,' Sister Bettsworth called out. 'Help me clean this man's wounds. Bring a basin of hot water, a cloth and some carbolic soap!'

I collected the basin, soap and a cloth and, with a degree of trepidation, approached the bed on which lay a young soldier who looked little more than a schoolboy. He was deathly white and barely conscious.

'Come on, Harland. Quickly! No time for any form of dawdling.'

Sister had finished cutting through the bandages wrapped around the stump of the young man's upper leg.

'Wash the leg while I look to the man in the next bed. Then I'll come back and dress the wound.'

The stench of gangrene hit my nostrils as I placed the basin of hot water on the floor by the bed and knelt beside it. I gagged. Maggots were crawling over the wound. I forced back the revulsion as I washed the wound as gently as possible. Sister returned as I was finishing my task. She looked at the soldier, then took his hand and felt for his pulse.

'All right, Harland, you can leave things be now. I'm afraid this young man's gone. Go and attend to the soldier in the next bed. He's nowhere near as bad as this one was – just shrapnel wounds that will need to be cleaned ready for dressing.'

Soon, all beds were in use. To make matters worse, it was impossible to evacuate earlier arrivals. I found myself navigating an ever-increasing carpet of soldiers dressed in blood-soaked khaki. They were lying on the stretchers that had brought them to the hospital. The stretchers themselves were placed on the floors of the huts – wherever there was space for them.

Everywhere, there were torn and broken bodies. Limbs had been shattered or blown off. Men still conscious were in excruciating pain, some crying out, some whimpering, others suffering in eerie silence.

Every available staff member arrived to meet the influx and help the wounded, regardless of whether they worked on the day or night shift, whether doctor, nurse, VAD, ambulance driver or orderly. We continued to work to the point of exhaustion. Meals and rest periods were foregone in a collective effort to save lives and relieve suffering.

Still, the casualties arrived. I was by now increasingly required to remove blood-soaked bandages, never knowing quite what horror awaited me beneath each one. I also found myself having to take on more complex work.

'Harland,' Sister called out. 'Get over to the operating theatre, please. They're really up against it at the moment. They'll let you know just what they need you to do when you get there.'

I was thrown in at the deep end. Doing whatever I could do to help as surgeons used their saws to amputate arms or legs as a last resort.

It wasn't until Friday that things started to quieten down a little. The frequency of arriving ambulances finally began to abate. At the same time, increasing numbers of evacuations became possible, and several VAD reinforcements arrived, allowing me to be stood down that evening for a day's rest on the following day.

When I woke at half past five, the sun had risen, radiant in a delightful morning's pure sky. By the time I had finished my breakfast, white wispy cirrus clouds high in the sky promised a fine afternoon. My only thought was to get as far away from the hospital as possible. The recent rush of work had almost exhausted me. All I wanted was complete rest, somewhere where such things as bandages and iodine were unknown. I decided, therefore, to walk to Paris-Plage. The distance didn't matter.

Walking across green fields and through the woods was such great therapy. Spending an afternoon on the sands, enjoying the fresh air and the sea and delighting in the lights and shades as they played across the sand dunes provided additional relief. I even took off my shoes and stockings and revelled as I paddled in the cold seawater, feeling the wet sand slipping through my toes. It felt as if I was a child again. All thoughts of the recent horrors that I had experienced gently evaporated from my mind.

All too soon, though, I was making my way back to the hospital – and back to what had become my reality. As I was walking towards the Mess for supper, Sister Bettsworth walked briskly towards me.

'Thank heaven you're back. Come with me quickly. We've had a sudden influx of badly wounded infantrymen that need our immediate help.'

# SIX

## *Jarrow, Autumn 1916*

Frank's mother, Grace, opened the door. A wide smile spread across her face, then tears of joy welled in her grey-blue eyes. She stood there gazing at Frank in silence. At that moment, a mixture of pure happiness and joy washed over Frank. He moved his right foot onto the front step, put his right hand on her shoulder and leant forward to kiss her on the cheek.

'Hello, Mam,' Frank said, somewhat disguising his joy at being home again, before embracing his mother.

She kissed him gently on his forehead.

'Come in, son. Come in,' said Grace, barely containing her happiness at seeing her son again. 'I can hardly believe that you are back. I can't tell you how much we've all missed you.' Grace turned and led Frank into the hallway of the Dawson home. 'You've also got three very excited young ladies waiting for you.'

Almost immediately, Frank was surrounded by his three sisters. The eldest, Isabelle, stood back and looked him up and down.

'Good heavens,' she gasped, and then started to giggle.

'Look at our brother! He's got a moustache,' she called out, still laughing. 'Look, everyone, have you seen what's sprouting on Frank's upper lip?'

Frank could almost feel his face redden as he came under the close scrutiny of his mother and two other sisters. Grace hadn't taken in the fact that Frank had a moustache until that moment.

'Silly me, I hadn't noticed,' she said. 'The moustache suits you... I think... maybe... oh, I don't know. Fatha's reaction should be interesting.'

'It looks a bit like the product of stubble burning after a farmer has tried to clear the ground when he's finished harvesting his wheat crop,' Isabelle giggled.

'Comes with the territory, I'm afraid, Izzy, lass,' Frank replied, by now chuckling himself. 'We're not allowed to shave our upper lips.'

Grace helped Frank stack his kit in the hallway and then shepherded him into the front room.

'Sit yourself down, bonny lad, while I fix you a cup of tea.'

Frank started to make his way towards an armchair but then stopped dead in his tracks.

'What's up, pet?' asked Grace.

'I'm afraid that I will make everything filthy, Mam.'

'That's no problem, Frank. Sit yourself down.'

Frank looked at Grace and shook his head.

'No, Mam. I was lucky enough to get a bath and change of clothes a few days ago, but nothing by way of a wash since. I'm filthy. I'll dirty the chair covers – and there's a risk that my uniform will be infested with lice by now.'

Grace looked horrified at the mention of lice. She stood facing Frank, slightly open-mouthed.

'Sorry, Mam,' Frank continued. 'It's one of the horrors of serving in the trenches that we've all had to come to terms with. If you wouldn't mind, please fetch me a towel. I'll go into the backyard and get out of these clothes and leave them outside. Then I'll boil up some water and have a good wash for now. Later, I'll go to the public bath house for a proper soak and get something from the chemist's that I can use when I soak my uniform to make sure I get rid of any unwelcome passengers that may be hiding there.'

'If you're sure, son. I'm just as happy for you to get out of your uniform in the house.'

'No, Mam, really – but you could find something for the girls to do while I change.'

Grace laughed.

'I'm sure I can find plenty for them while you sort yourself out.'

Grace returned and handed Frank a towel.

'Here you are, son,' she said. 'I've laid out some clothes for you on your bed for when you've finished your wash.'

'Thanks, Mam. I shouldn't be too long.'

Frank went into the backyard and stripped out of his uniform. He wrapped the towel around his waist, returned to the kitchen and boiled some water. Once he had done this, he poured the water into a tub and carried this up the stairs and then along the landing to the dressing room. He put the tub down and went back along the landing to his bedroom, where he found a shirt, a pair of socks, a pair of dark brown trousers and a change of underwear laid out on the bed. A facecloth was hanging on the metal bedhead.

Frank picked up the clothes and facecloth and headed back to the dressing room. He placed the clothes neatly in one corner of the room and the facecloth next to the tub of hot water. Next, he unwrapped the towel from around his waist, before proceeding to wash as thoroughly as he could, making liberal use of the large bar of carbolic soap usually kept in the room. Once he had finished, Frank dried himself off, dressed and headed back down to the kitchen.

'Gosh,' he said as he entered the kitchen. 'That feels a whole lot better.'

Grace looked at Frank and smiled.

'Would you like a cup of tea and something to eat, bonny lad?' asked Grace.

Frank's face lit up.

'Please, Mam. I'm starving.'

Grace recognised instantly that something quick to prepare and filling was called for.

'How about some ham, egg and chips, with some bread and butter?'

'That'll do just fine, Mam. Thanks.'

Just then, Frank's sisters reappeared and began to bombard him with questions.

'What's it like in France, Frank?'

'Tell us what you've been up to, Frank.'

'How many battles have you fought in, Frank?'

'How many Germans have you killed, Frank?'

It seemed a never-ending onslaught until Grace came to his rescue.

'Girls, leave your brother in peace and let him eat. There's plenty of work still to be done around the house. For a start, you can bring the basin back from the dressing room and empty it. After that, you can put it in the yard for Frank to use this afternoon. Then get yourselves off down the shops. There's a list of things I need and some money on the hall table.'

Rather reluctantly, Frank's sisters left the kitchen while he sat at the table, faced with a plate piled with ham, egg and chips. Slices of bread and butter were stacked on another plate. Grace poured tea for Frank and herself and sat down next to him.

Frank attacked his meal. He hadn't realised just how hungry he was.

'How's your meal, Frank?'

Frank looked up at his mother.

'Champion, Mam, just champion,' he replied as soon as he had finished the mouthful of ham he had been eating.

'So, how was your journey?'

Frank looked at his mother and closed his eyes.

'Too long, I'm afraid,' he sighed. 'A good part of my leave's gone already. And I must do it all again in reverse next week.' Frank opened his eyes again and shrugged before continuing with his meal, savouring every mouthful as if it was his last.

'Still, you're back with us again, son. I can't tell you how happy that's made me.'

After Frank had finished eating, Grace cleared away the crockery and cutlery.

'All right, son,' she said. 'Go and sit down in the front room while I do the washing-up. I'll join you as soon as I've finished.'

As he sat in the front room, the sound of Grace busying herself in the kitchen, with water pouring into the sink, the scraping of plates and the clatter of crockery and cutlery was music to Frank's ears. How he had missed all this since he had enlisted! Once she had finished, Grace joined Frank and bombarded him with questions about his time in France until the clock on the mantelpiece struck two.

'If you're going to the public baths,' said Grace, 'you'd best go now so that you're back home before Fatha gets in.'

\*

That first night home, Frank couldn't sleep. When he finally managed to doze off, he had a nightmare; reliving an advance across No Man's Land, bombardment and machine-gun fire. Frank woke up in a cold sweat. After an hour or more awake, he finally started to fall asleep but was startled by a sudden jolt to his body and the sensation that he was falling. He buried himself under his bedclothes as if he was taking cover and lay there awake until his mother brought him a cup of tea in the morning.

'Frank, pet. Is everything all right?' Grace asked, her voice edged with concern.

Frank emerged from under the bedclothes. He looked at Grace, blinking profusely.

'Stop worrying, Mam. I had a nightmare and couldn't get back to sleep – perhaps because I'm out of the habit of sleeping in a bed, or maybe I've just become too used to sleeping in a dugout or on a pile of straw in a barn or somewhere.'

Frank sat up and took the cup of tea that Grace was offering to him.

'I'll get some breakfast for you, son, as soon as you've had your tea and a wash.'

'Thanks, Mam,' Frank replied. 'I shouldn't be too long.'

After breakfast, Frank felt that he had to try and clear his head.

'I've got to get out and about, Mam. So I thought I'd leave mid-morning, walk up to the park, wander around, and head off for a beer in the Ellison Arms around lunchtime.'

'But the weather isn't very nice today.'

Frank saw the look of disappointment that flashed across his mother's face, but he wanted, no, needed, a little bit of time on his own. The journey home and his disturbed night's sleep had taken a toll on him.

'I know, but I need a bit of time out and about.'

Grace hung her head before looking up at Frank.

'Will you be going to see Sybil today?'

'No, Mam,' Frank replied. 'I'm going over to see her the day after tomorrow.'

'Why leave it so long, pet?'

'I explained in a letter to her that I needed a bit of time to get things together in myself first. Fortunately, she seems to understand.'

Grace looked sad.

'I bet you really miss her.'

'Too right, Mam, and to think that we'd be married but for the war.'

'And maybe, I'd have been a granny by now,' replied Grace with a deep sigh.

Frank didn't reply at first, then he looked at Grace and started to laugh.

'And doubtless, you'd be a grandmother who completely spoiled her grandchildren,' he said.

Grace's face brightened. Frank kissed his mother gently on the top of her head and moved towards the front door.

'See you soon, Mam,' he said as he left the house and set off down Croft Terrace.

At first, Frank was a little concerned. He was aware that he still wasn't in uniform and had heard stories of soldiers who had returned home on leave who had been barracked or handed white feathers by women or "old timers" who thought that they had "*...failed to do their duty and answer their country's call*".

He needn't have worried. He was well known in the area. Those people he did meet gave him the warmest of welcomes. He was treated like a hero, especially when he went into the Ellison Arms for a lunchtime pint.

Frank pushed the door open and stepped into the gloomy public bar. As he did so, he was met by the all-too-familiar pall of thick smoke, the smell of beer, the sound of chinking glasses and the chattering of the seven or eight elderly regulars, either standing at the bar or sitting at the nearby round wooden tables.

'Howay, man, Frank, man, how are you doing, bonny lad? I wish I could have been there with you. Have a bottle of Dog with me, won't you?' chirped Alf Withers, one of the "regulars" sat at the bar.

'Thanks, Mr Withers, that's very kind of you.'

A bottle of Dog and a glass appeared on the bar in front of where Frank was standing.

'Here's to you,' said Frank as he raised the glass of beer once he had emptied the bottle's contents into it.

'Cheers, Frank,' replied Alf, raising his glass in salute. 'With what you must have been through and seen, I'm glad that I'm way too old to have been there with you. It was bad enough in South Africa when I was there during the Boer War.'

'Perhaps I shouldn't say this,' said Frank, 'but I'm glad that you are too old. I wouldn't wish being in France on you or anyone. You are out there knowing that, on the law of averages, you have no more than one chance in five of escape in your first attack. Next time, it's one chance in four, then one chance in three, then one chance in two, and then no chance at all. I've been in more than five attacks already, and half expect to meet my end every time I go into action now. It's a perpetual feeling of doom you can never shake off, only try and control – a hell on earth there's little or no escaping from.'

Reg Harper and Bill Armitage joined Frank and Alf.

'How do, Frank,' said Reg. 'We couldn't help overhearing what you were saying. Sorry to hear that things have been bad out there in France. Of course, we try and follow the news in the papers – but how are you in yourself?'

'I'm getting there again, thank you, Mr Harper,' replied Frank. 'I'm rather tired but glad to be back home again.'

'Have a tab,' said Reg, offering Frank a half-empty pack of Woodbines.

'Thanks,' replied Frank taking one and lighting it. He took a long drag at the cigarette, inhaled, and held his breath for a few seconds before exhaling. The smoke jetted upwards, adding to the thick cloud already hovering above and around the bar. Frank quickly emptied his glass and pointed at the glasses of Alf, Bill and Reg.

'Same again, gents?' he asked.

'Yes, please, Frank,' was the unanimous reply from Frank's drinking companions.

The barman, Harry Openshaw, obliged.

'Have one for yourself, Harry.'

'Thanks, Frank. I'll join you with a bottle.'

'I couldn't help but notice that the town now resembles a ghost town,' said Frank as he handed four bottles round while Harry poured the fifth bottle into a glass for himself. 'There is hardly anyone about.'

'That's true enough,' replied Alf. 'There are only old fogeys like us, young kids and women left these days – and Harry here, of course.'

'Yes, worse luck,' chuckled Harry.

Frank, Alf, Bill and Reg continued drinking, smoking and chatting for several hours. Harry joined them whenever he wasn't serving drinks or talking to the other regulars. By the time Frank left the Ellison Arms, he was feeling a good deal better.

*

The weather fully matched Frank's mood. Light clouds drifted across a deep blue sky, occasionally masking the late-afternoon sun. A gentle breeze blew from the northeast. Frank felt the mellow warmth of an Indian summer on his face. He was on his way to see Sybil. He was taking her for a meal and then to a concert at the Theatre Royal.

Frank reached Sybil's house, opened the gate set in low railings that ran the width of the house, walked the six feet or so to the door and rang the bell. As Sybil opened the door, Frank grinned.

'Goodness me – look at you!' he exclaimed.

Sybil blushed. She was wearing an ankle-length white satin

dress with a lace hem and elbow-length lace sleeves. Around her waist was a band of red silk tied in a bow at her side. For a change, her wavy auburn hair was down.

'You don't look so bad yourself,' said Sybil as she looked him up and down approvingly.

Frank slipped his arm around Sybil's waist and swept her to his breast. As he did, he caught the subtle notes of her perfume. He started to tremble.

'Frank – are you all right, Frank?' asked Sybil as she placed her left hand lightly on Frank's right shoulder.

'Just a little nervous, I guess. I've been in the trenches too long – and too long away from you.'

Sybil giggled. Frank gently lowered his head until his lips brushed against Sybil's. She lifted her face up to Frank and sighed. He kissed her again. Her mouth opened, and his tongue caressed hers. In that instant, Frank began to feel human again. He gently pulled his head back and gazed at Sybil and smiled. They stood together, saying nothing. No words were necessary.

Eventually, Frank broke the silence.

'We'd better go before we take root,' he whispered, taking Sybil's hand.

They linked arms and ambled away from Sybil's house and towards a rather smart, albeit slightly crowded, restaurant, close to the theatre, where they were shown to a table for two by a window looking out onto the road.

A menu was brought over to them, which they studied in silence. Neither quite knew what to say; both were looking to avoid any conversation about the war. In the end, they both ordered the same when the waiter took their order. Oxtail soup, followed by baked codfish, "Dutch style", with new potatoes and seasonal vegetables and, for dessert, fresh fruit. Frank also chose a bottle of Chablis to go with the meal.

'It's one recommended to me by Mr Henderson, the local

vintner and supplier to the restaurant,' Frank explained. 'And to be perfectly honest with you, I should add that he also recommended a Moulin-à-Vent in case our menu selection demanded a red wine.'

Sybil giggled at Frank's admission. She reached across the table and held his hand. Her lips quivered with a vain attempt to speak – she could only squeeze his hand repeatedly.

'We're a right pair,' said Frank, breaking the silence, 'sitting here saying nothing when there's so much to talk about – plans we have to make for our future together.'

*

Frank and Sybil had parted after a fond embrace and affectionate farewell the previous evening, each looking forward to being able to spend more time together before Frank returned to France. Today, they were planning to do just that. They were going to the weekly dance at the Village Hall. In the meantime, Frank wanted to revisit as much of his home town as he could in the time that remained of his leave.

Grace was disappointed. She wanted to spend more time with her son. But she was also concerned that Frank seemed to want to be on his own so much. Somehow, he didn't seem to be quite himself, despite being with his family and despite seeing Sybil again.

Frank turned his hand to his neglected bicycle that stood forlornly against the wall at the back of the house. He cleaned and oiled it and pumped up the tyres. Once done, he set off to ride around the town and the countryside. He wanted to reacquaint himself with places that were previously so familiar to him but had started to slip from his memory since he had gone away.

The weather was again fine, with glimpses of sun breaking through the light cloud from time to time. Frank left his house and headed off along Croft Terrace, passing the long terraces of red-brick houses that stretched along either side of the road. He headed in the first instance to the cricket ground – the scene of one or two feats of glory with the ball before he enlisted. Next, he cycled to Jarrow Park, where he dismounted and began to walk, pushing his bicycle alongside the woodland area that ran down to the railway line, the boscage of the elm trees diffusing the flickering shafts of light. Their pinnate leaves fluttered in the breeze, showing their warm autumnal colours. Some were fluttering down to form a golden brown carpet. This scene was wholly different from the shattered, splintered fragments of muddy woodland that littered the war zone he had escaped from, even if only temporarily.

Once he had left the park, Frank decided to take "pot luck" whenever he reached any junction on his way. Eventually, this took him to the Drill Hall, at which time he decided to stop off at the Ellison Arms for a swift bottle of Dog before heading up Ormonde Street. He was on his way to see Mr Parker and his other colleagues at what was now the Bank of Liverpool.

Just before he arrived at the pub, there was an almighty crash as a horse-drawn cart shed its load outside the furnisher's shop, which stood next door to the pub. Frank screamed and lost control of his bicycle as large, empty milk churns thundered, clattered and clanked along the cobbled street. He hit the kerb and was pitched over the handlebars, tumbling in a heap on the pavement. Bruised but not seriously hurt, Frank trembled uncontrollably.

Harry Openshaw rushed out of the pub to investigate the noise. He saw Frank and ran over to him. Reg and Bill followed.

'Are you all right, Frank?' asked Harry. Frank was conscious but gave no reply. 'Here, help me, lads,' he said, turning towards Reg and Bill.

Between them, they carried Frank into the pub and sat him down.

'Get him a glass of water, Harry,' said Bill.

A few moments later, Harry brought over a glass and gave it to Frank. Frank took a sip before putting the glass down and bursting into tears. At the same time, his arms began to twitch. He could hear and was cognisant of everything going on around him, but he felt detached from it all. As if he was outside of himself looking in.

'Come on, Harry,' said Reg. 'We'd best get Frank home.' He turned to Bill. 'Give us a hand, Bill,' he said. 'This is down to you and me. Harry won't be able to leave the pub.'

'Anything I can do?' asked Alf as he emerged from the saloon bar to investigate what was happening.

'Too right, Alf. Frank's not that big, but he's big enough – and we need to get his bike home as well.'

Alf and Bill stood on either side of Frank and helped him up. Reg collected Frank's bike, and the three men took Frank and his bike back to his house.

'I'll go and fetch the doctor,' said Reg as soon as they all reached Frank's home.

Alf knocked on the door, and he and Bill helped Frank up the stairs to his bedroom when Grace answered. Alf and Bill then took their leave as Grace began to make Frank as comfortable as possible. However, he was still crying, and his arms continued to twitch.

Grace sat by Frank, holding his hand as he cowered and twitched on the bed.

'Hush, pet – hush – it's all right,' she said soothingly, reaching up and stroking his head.

Grace continued to comfort Frank. Slowly, he began to calm down and stopped crying. That is until there was a knock on the door, startling Frank. Reg and the doctor came into the bedroom. Grace got up from Frank's bed and went over to them.

'Anything further I can do, Grace, pet?' asked Bill.

'I don't think so, Reg. Thanks for all your help. Undoubtedly, Robert will buy you, Bill and Alf a pint and let you know how things turn out later.'

Grace turned back to Frank, who had started to cry again. She caught her breath. A woman's tears are touching, potent; but a man's are terrible, like the cry of a lost soul.

'I'll stay with Frank while you're examining him, Doctor – if that's all right with you,' she said.

'That will be all right, but you'll have to give me space to examine Frank. Perhaps, you could move away to the side of the bed, but make sure that he can still see you, Mrs Dawson.'

Grace moved away from Frank's bed. He kept looking at her. As he did, his eyes were streaming with tears. Then, he started to twitch again as the doctor began the examination.

Frank cried intermittently throughout the examination. When not crying, he either muttered incoherently or stammered out his words. Finally, after what seemed to Grace to be an eternity, the doctor finished his examination. She looked at him nervously.

'How is Frank, Doctor? What can you tell me?' she asked in a half-whisper.

The doctor was silent for a moment or two, as if he was wondering what to say to Grace. Frank looked at him, then at Grace and then back to him.

'I have to be honest, Mrs Dawson,' the doctor finally replied. 'I am lost. I've not seen anything like this before – but just to help me try and pieces things together – am I right in thinking that Frank is home on leave from the Army?'

'Yes, Doctor, he arrived home from serving in the trenches in France three days ago.'

'Has he talked at all about his time in the trenches – you know, like being in action – fighting and so on?'

'Not really, Doctor.'

'How has he been while he's been home?'

Grace looked pensively at Frank.

'Insular, I would say – I was only thinking this morning about how much he seemed to be wanting to be on his own. He even took a day or so before he went to see his fiancée. That said, he did go out with her yesterday and was planning to go out with her again tonight.'

'Anything else unusual?'

'Well, yes, now you come to ask. I found him hiding under the bedclothes on his first morning home. He'd had a nightmare.'

'Did Frank talk about the nightmare itself to you?'

Grace looked at Frank again and then back at the doctor.

'No, he didn't, but I assume that it must have been about the war.'

Frank reached out and touched Grace's hand. He looked at her, smiled weakly and nodded.

'There's your answer then, Doctor,' said Grace.

'I see,' said the doctor before pausing again. 'That's all very helpful and seems to fit in with other factors. In addition to the crying and spells where Frank is incoherent, he has contractions in his pectoral muscles, rapid twitching in both arms and his head has started to nod uncontrollably. Given all this and what you said about Frank's general behaviour and demeanour since he returned home, I suspect that he is suffering from something that has been called "shell shock". I'm afraid it's not something I'm qualified to treat. For that, Frank will need to go to a specialist military hospital, probably in London.'

\*

Frank looked nervously across the ward as a doctor approached his bed, accompanied by an orderly. The doctor was a tall, grey-haired man with a long, pitted, weather-beaten face, perhaps fifty years of age. An aquiline nose fell over his full mouth, above which bristled a chevron moustache.

'Who have we here, then?' he asked.

'Private Dawson, sir. He arrived yesterday evening from Newcastle,' replied the orderly.

The doctor paused at the foot of Frank's bed, reading the notes on the clipboard hanging from the bed end.

'Good morning, Dawson. I'm Lieutenant Colonel Lewin,' said the doctor, after what seemed an eternity to Frank. 'How are you feeling today?'

'A little better, thank you, sir,' replied Frank.

'Good to hear it, Dawson,' replied Lewin. 'We're going to start your treatment today. In particular, we will focus on the head-nodding you've been experiencing.'

Frank began to stammer out an answer, but Lewin did not wait to hear what Frank had intended to say. Instead, he turned to the orderly who had accompanied him, saying, 'Let's get Dawson to the electrical room straight away.'

'Yes, sir,' replied the orderly.

Frank got out of bed and followed the orderly into the electrical room, where Lewin was waiting for them.

'Right, Dawson,' he said, looking straight at Frank. 'Before I begin to treat you, there are three basic principles that rule your treatment. They are simply this: *attention*, first and foremost: *tongue*, last and least: *questions*, never. So all you need to do is keep quiet and let me do my job – and ensure that you receive proper treatment. You are happy with that, I assume?'

'Yes, sir,' replied a slightly surprised Frank.

'Good. Take your shirt off and stand in front of me. Today, you will experience the real benefits of electricity,' said Lewin.

Frank's ears pricked up when he heard the word *electricity*, and he looked up at Lewin slightly wide-eyed.

'My father is an electrical engineer, sir,' said Frank, the pitch of his voice rising slightly. Then he lowered his head. 'But I'm afraid of electricity myself.'

'So am I,' Lewin replied with a smile that disappeared almost immediately after he spoke. 'But I have no fear of its power to stop your head from nodding and your stammering – and that is what you want, is it not?'

'Yes, sir,' Frank replied. 'I want to be cured – but won't the electricity be painful?'

'Remember what I just told you, Dawson: *questions*, never,' Lewin snapped.

Frank did not reply.

'For a start, I'm going to treat the nodding of your head by placing an electrode over your sacral spine. We call it "faradic treatment". In layman's terms, this means that I will simply use electricity to "exercise" the appropriate muscles. This will strengthen and firm them. At the same time, the treatment will stimulate your circulation to bring in extra nutrients and remove waste. You'll also find that the vibration caused by the treatment is extremely beneficial.'

'Thank you, sir,' replied Frank.

'Right, let's get started,' said Lewin as he picked up a roller electrode and showed it to Frank. 'This will produce an electric current as I apply it up and down each side of your chest. Are you ready?'

'Yes, sir,' replied Frank.

As Lewin began to use the electrode, Frank was surprised by the strength of the electric current that it generated. He gasped and his head jerked forward, then back, and then started to nod. Lewin lifted the electrode and glared at Frank.

'Remember the first principle, Dawson – *attention!*' he snarled. 'In the case of this treatment, that means that you must make every effort to keep your head still.'

With that, Lewin placed the electrode on Frank's chest again, but no matter how hard he tried, Frank was not able to control the movement of his head.

'Drat it,' muttered Lewin. 'It's quite clear to me that you need a much stronger current. The strength will be increased from time to time. Is that clear?'

'Yes, sir.'

'Now make sure that you hold your head back when I do so.'

As the current was gradually increased, Frank began to experience even more excruciating pain. Eventually, it reached the point where the pain finally became intolerable. He tottered forward and fainted.

Frank came out of his faint almost immediately to see Lewin standing over him.

'Get up, Dawson, for Pete's sake!'

Lewin made no effort to help Frank as he struggled back to his feet. However, once Frank was upright, his head began to nod more violently than ever.

'Good grief, Dawson! How long have I got to keep this up? The current must be applied again, but this time over the upper fibres of your trapezius. For heaven's sake, man, keep your head still.'

'Sorry, sir,' mumbled Frank.

'I shall continue to apply the current until you show some improvement. Are you ready to show me that you have better control of the movement of your head?'

'I'll do my best, sir,' Frank spluttered.

'I very much hope so!' barked Lewin.

Fortunately for Frank, his nodding soon ceased, and the electrode was removed.

'That's better, Dawson. Now, let's try and make some progress. I want you to pace up and down the room – at the same time, keep your head erect.'

Frank set off, but as soon as he began to walk, he began to nod again in a series of very fine movements.

'Right, Dawson, hold it there,' said Lewin after a short while. 'We're now going to try and kill two birds with one stone – treat the nodding and your stammering at the same time.'

Lewin applied an electrode to Frank's neck, placing it over the larynx.

'You will continue to walk up and down the room as before – with your head thrown back. I want you to recite the *Lord's Prayer* as you do.'

Frank set off again, reciting as he went. Powerful shocks were applied to the area around his larynx as he repeated each word. Frank summoned every ounce of his inner strength.

*I've got to keep my head still… I've got to keep my head still… I will… I will…*

Gradually, Frank's mental efforts to overcome the pain and discomfort caused by the electric current enabled him to take control of both his head movement and stammer. With each improvement he made, Lewin reduced the strength of the current. Eventually, Frank could talk without the slightest stammer. The movements of his head finally seemed to stop. The electric current was switched off; the treatment and the pain it caused ceased.

'That's great, Dawson. It looks like we've got there at last,' said Lewin. 'Now, put on your shirt and return to your ward.'

'Thank you, sir,' replied Frank, exhaling a deep and relieved breath.

Once back in the ward, he flopped down onto his bed.

'I'd have been better off if I'd gone straight back to the trenches rather than come here,' he muttered to a private in the Buffs, who occupied the bed next to him.

'Me too,' came the reply. 'The doctors here don't know what the fuck they're doing. They don't understand what we've been through and what we're going through now. They think that we're all malingerers. Ones like that bastard Lewin are sadists,

I'm sure. They've read in a book somewhere that electric shocks are the way forward. They haven't a clue how. Nor do they realise that it causes us so much discomfort and pain that we will do anything to deliver the result they are looking for just so that the treatment will be ended.'

'That's true enough,' replied Frank. 'It took all the willpower I could muster to stop my head nodding so that I could get away from Lewin.'

'Trouble is, he thinks that he's cured you by his method, so there'll be no stopping that fucker now, or his barbaric practices.'

'Perhaps,' Frank replied dolefully. 'Well, I'll soon find out if he has cured me – I'm returning to my regiment tomorrow.'

The private looked at him and winked.

'Time will tell, eh, matey?'

## SEVEN

# *France, Autumn 1916*

It was a cold, chilly day, and the smell of autumn hung heavy on the air as Frank's battalion approached its final destination of Guillemont, completing the latest route march across France. Frank was horrified by what he saw. No sign that a town had existed there remained intact. Virtually all buildings had been reduced to piles of rubble. No recognisable tree was standing, just shattered stumps. No part of the ground surface had escaped. All that Frank could see was mud pockmarked with shell holes resting edge to edge with other shell holes. Many of these were brimming with stinking slime, often littered with the bodies of dead soldiers left lying where they fell. Now rotting, these became powerful magnets for swarms of flies and hordes of rats.

Frank caught sight of the platoon sergeant, Sergeant Bishop, approaching to lead the platoon sections to their allocated part of the line. Frank pictured him as transformed Virgil in Dante's *Inferno*. He was the platoon's guide as they reached the entrance to the fire trench – the entrance to hell.

*Abandon all hope, you who enter here.*

Frank was stunned by the scale of the desperation he was witnessing. All around lay grenades, stick bombs, shell cases, unexploded shells and a whole variety of other detritus. The floor of the trench itself was covered with fallen earth and mud that was two feet deep. The paradoses and communication trenches had fallen in, and the going was terrible.

'Right, men,' Bishop called out as Frank's section came to a halt when they reached their dugouts, 'stow your kit where you can find a place for it and fall in back here sharpish. Bring your trenching tools with you. There's plenty to do and not much time to do it.'

'He's not joking about there being plenty to do,' Frank said as he looked about him. 'These trenches have taken a right hammering!'

'Nothing like stating the obvious, Franky, man,' gasped Jimmy. 'What needs to be done here would challenge the whole of the company – not just us few lads.'

Frank looked at Jimmy, nodded towards No Man's Land and sighed.

'Yes, Jimmy, man – and you can just imagine the state of the wire in front of the trenches. I'll lay a pound to a pinch of salt that'll need replacing as well. The German artillery bombardments will have shot it to pieces.'

Frank claimed one of the dugouts, undid his webbing and placed it behind him. He then took off his jacket and helmet and piled these behind him also. He removed his trenching tool from its pouch and, carrying his rifle and trenching tool, went back to where Sergeant Bishop was waiting.

'Follow me,' ordered Bishop as soon as the men had all returned to him. 'There's no time to lose.'

As Frank's section moved along the fire trench, Bishop allocated them with a "stand" each at six-foot intervals.

'First things first – dig out the trench floor and use the soil to repair the parapet,' he ordered. 'While you're at it, the parados needs shoring up and sand-bagging. My granny could finish it in ten minutes on her own and with her eyes closed, but she's not here. Still, it shouldn't take strapping young lads like you very much longer. So, get on with it.'

As Frank started to dig, he shot back in horror as a rat, disturbed by him, jumped out. Then another. They scurried out over the top of the trench before disappearing into the darkness. In truth, there were rats everywhere. The stench pervading through the trench was brought directly into the lines by a light breeze that blew across No Man's Land. To make matters worse, a direct hit by a shell on the latrines had thrown up a large quantity of human waste, scattering it in all directions.

'Heaven help us,' gasped Frank, barely holding back a reflex bout of retching. 'This place is vile. Worse than if we were digging straight into a midden.'

By degrees, as the men continued to work, they each began to uncover broken rifles, bayonets, webbing and other pieces of equipment. Finally, to his horror, Frank uncovered a hand, then an arm, then further evidence of a buried body.

'Sarge,' he called out. 'Sarge, see here, please.'

Bishop hurried over to look at Frank's discovery.

'Hold your horses, lads,' he said. 'I'm afraid that you'll have to stop digging. There may be other dead in this part of the trench. So you'll have to use just your hands until you're sure there are no more bodies buried here.'

A feeling of despair flooded through Frank. An unpleasant job had just become almost intolerable.

'Over here, lads,' he called to the two section members closest to him.

Inch by inch, they uncovered the corpse.

'Jesus,' gasped Frank as he realised the extent of the injuries suffered by the dead man. There were ugly wounds to his face, chest and abdomen, with parts of these ripped away. Trench debris and dirt had embedded into gashed flesh.

'Oh, God,' cried out one of Frank's comrades as he finished uncovering the man's lower body. 'His right foot is missing.'

Moments later, another body was found. Working together, the section gradually cleared the earth from around the dead man. Then, as Frank and Jimmy began to lift the body holding the arms and legs, these became detached from the torso. A further body was found, with lice crawling over it in legions. All three were carefully removed from the trench and placed just behind it.

'Here, bonny lads,' said Frank as he found some blankets. 'I'll use these to cover the bodies. After that, we can get on and finish clearing the trench.'

In the meantime, Bishop left to inspect another part of the trench, before returning soon afterwards.

'You'll have to stop what you're doing. Bring your shovels and rifles and follow me,' Bishop ordered.

'For fuck's sake, what now?' muttered Jimmy.

The men followed Bishop to a trench ladder resting against the end of a sap.

'Get up that ladder and move half left. Stay on that line, and you'll find a large shell hole. It's full of dead and wounded soldiers that you must bring back here. Keep your eyes peeled at all times. There may be other dead and wounded in other, smaller, shell holes between here and there. It should go without saying that you need to bring them back also. You'll have to get a move on, however. It'll be dawn before too long.'

*Is this the moment I pass through the gates of hell, and enter Limbo?*

Frank ascended the ladder, slithered over the parapet and edged across No Man's Land. His five comrades followed. A star shell looped across the sky. Then another. The balls of light rose into the darkness, suffusing the sky with a lurid glare that faded about forty seconds later. The six men in the patrol dropped instinctively to the ground. Motionless and feigning death, they waited until the flares finally flickered out and darkness resumed.

Frank and his comrades began to edge forward again.

'Help me,' a voice called out weakly.

As far as Frank could tell, it came from his right. He stopped still and crouched down.

'Jimmy, man, did you hear that?'

At first, Jimmy heard nothing until the voice called out again.

'Heard it that time, Franky.'

'It sounded to me as though it's someone to our right. Do you agree?'

'Aye, man,' replied Jimmy. 'Come on. Let's find whoever's there.'

It took the pair a little while, but Frank and Jimmy eventually found a wounded man lying in a heap in a shallow shell hole. They positioned themselves on either side of him, but as they were about to lift him to his feet, another star shell burst above them, followed by a sustained burst of machine-gun fire. Frank and Jimmy dived into the mud and waited for darkness to return.

When it did, Frank and Jimmy set to work immediately. They brought the wounded man to his feet with one mighty, united heave and held him there. Frank faced Jimmy.

'Let's get out of here,' he said, and they began a slow, tortuous return journey. Eventually, they clambered down the trench ladder and made their way to their dugouts. As dawn broke, Frank uttered a silent prayer of thanks. They would not be going out again – at least not until darkness fell again.

\*

Frank readied himself. He was to be part of a raid on the German front line. The raid was to be short and sweet. No longer than ten minutes in duration. A party of one officer, a corporal and eight soldiers were to go over the top. They would cross No Man's Land and enter the enemy trenches. Once in the trenches, they were to do as much harm as possible. They were to return immediately a green flare was fired from the right flank of the British front line, bringing back as many prisoners as possible.

Frank and Jimmy were to go out across No Man's Land five minutes before the raid started. They were to cut a gap in the German wire for the raiding party to go through. Hopefully, the task would be much easier than might otherwise have been the case. The British artillery had recently pounded the German wire as effectively as the German artillery had pounded the British wire.

Both Frank and Jimmy knew that much of the raid's success rested in their hands. However, they also knew their lives were very much on the line. The slightest noise, cough or sneeze on their part would inevitably cost them their lives and result in the raid's failure.

No packs were to be worn, or rifles carried. The raiding party could arm themselves in any way they wanted. Jimmy, the officer and some others carried revolvers. Several carried billhooks, fascine knives or maces. Frank went armed with a trench knife he had crafted from a shortened and sharpened bayonet. He also took a knobkerry, which he carried on his belt. Everyone carried several Mills bombs.

Precisely at zero minus five, Frank and Jimmy began their crawl out to the wire. When they reached it, Frank grabbed a strand with both hands and held on tight while Jimmy cut the wire. They repeated this process until they had opened a gap wide enough for the rest of the raiding party to pass through and on towards the German fire trench. Once they were through, Frank and Jimmy followed behind them.

Eventually, Frank slid down into the trench on his back, hitting the fire step as he did so. He stumbled forward a little before reaching out with his left hand to steady himself on the back wall of the trench.

The party split into two groups of five. Frank and Jimmy's group moved to the right, quickly and purposefully down the zigzagged trench. Then, as Frank came round the corner of a fire bay, he found himself face to face with a German soldier.

The German lunged at Frank, forcing him back against the trench wall. The German's rifle moved upwards and under Frank's chin, pressing into his throat and causing him to drop his trench knife. He kicked out sharply with his right foot, connecting with the German's left kneecap. The German yelled in pain. He momentarily dropped his right shoulder just enough to allow Frank to push him back.

Frank was then able to reach down and grab his knobkerry, raise it and strike the German on the shoulder. The German screamed and let go of his rifle. Frank took this opportunity to push the German further back to create the opening for him to strike out again, causing the German to drop to his knees. By now, devoid of any feeling or emotion and pumped full of adrenalin, Frank delivered a final blow to the side of the German's head to finish him off. All he could think of at that moment were the children he saw slaughtered a year earlier.

There was no further time to do anything. Green flares had been sent up from the British lines. The raiding party beat a hasty retreat and picked its way back across No Man's Land. Frank skipped from one shell hole to another as bullets buzzed and zipped above his head. Flares were set up regularly from the German front line, and every time one did, Frank froze till it went out again. Every now and again, a shell dropped near him. Somehow, though, Frank and the rest of the raiding party returned safely to their dugouts to await further orders.

When those orders came, they were unexpected; the battalion was to withdraw to billets in a small town located away from the front for a three-day rest break.

*Thank fuck for that. I'm just about done in!*

\*

The moon was nearly full, partially obscured by fleecy clouds at first, but these soon passed and the town became bathed in soft moonlight. At that moment, for all Frank cared, the heavens could have opened, pouring the foulest weather imaginable on everything below. He was away from the front line. Out of harm's way for three days at least. All he was concerned about was spending an evening enjoying himself with his friends.

'C'mon, Franky, my friend, let's go down the *estaminet* and get something decent to eat. Something that's not bully beef or worse,' said Jimmy as he and Frank left their billet. They wandered up and down a few streets and eventually found a crowded *estaminet*. There, over a meal, they drank several glasses of *vin blanc*.

Jimmy liked a drink and had enjoyed a string of girlfriends, often boasting: *'I've never been to bed with an ugly woman, but I've certainly woken up with a few.'*

Jimmy seemed at home in the *estaminet*. He was full of a self-confidence that came from living a far less sheltered life than Frank.

Jimmy had picked up a smattering of French and was in conversation with Marie, one of the young women who had been serving beer and food to the soldiers. He had persuaded her to sit between him and Frank.

Jimmy looked along at Frank, smiled and whispered into Marie's ear. Marie looked a little puzzled at first, then burst out laughing. Frank looked at her, wondering what was going on.

Jimmy whispered something else. Marie looked at Frank and smiled gently before turning back to Jimmy.

'*Mais bien sûr* – but of course, *Monsieur*,' she said, chuckling.

Marie, looked at Frank, and ran her tongue across her lips. Chuckling, Jimmy looked at Frank also.

'Howay, man, have you got two francs?'

'Aye,' replied Frank, 'why do you want to know?'

Jimmy winked.

'Fancy becoming a "six minuter" then, bonny lad?' he asked.

Frank looked confused.

'What do you mean?'

'Why don't you go with Marie. She'll soon show you,' Jimmy chortled.

He turned to Marie and nodded at her. Then, giggling, she turned to look at Frank.

'*Viens avec moi* – come with me. Don't be shy,' she said invitingly.

Marie gently took hold of Frank's left hand and pulled him after her. She worked her way towards a flight of stairs by wriggling past numerous tables and the throng of soldiers sitting at or around them. Finally, she reached the stairs and began the climb to the upper floor of the *estaminet*. Jimmy shouted after them as they went.

'Howay, man, marra. She's right in what she says, don't be shy. So off you go now – and don't forget to put the lock on the door!'

Guided by Marie, Frank reached the landing at the top of the stairs and hesitated. He felt apprehensive and embarrassed but was just drunk enough not to resist Marie when she pulled him into a shabby bedroom. It was the first time Frank had found himself alone in the bedroom of a strange woman – any woman for that matter, let alone a woman he had just realised was not someone who merely served drinks. She was also a prostitute.

Frank stood in front of the bed and stared wide-eyed at it as

Marie closed the door and moved back to him. He was trembling. He did not know what to do.

'Come to me, *mon petit*,' Marie whispered, taking Frank's hand. She pulled Frank towards her. 'Sit down next to me,' she said as she sat down on the edge of the bed and patted the area next to her.

Frank took a deep breath and sat down. Marie began to fondle him. Frank froze. Sobering up in a flash, his mind was filled with thoughts of Sybil.

*I can't do this! I can't do this!*

He looked down at the floor – at the bed – around the room. He looked at Marie. He took a deep breath.

'No... I'm sorry... no,' he mumbled as he stood up, gave Marie a pat on the shoulder and put her aside with a mechanical gesture.

Marie gave a raucous laugh.

'It will still be two francs, *mon petit*,' she said.

Frank rubbed his eyes with the base of his palms, grunted incoherently, and then thrust his right hand into his trouser pocket, fumbled around, and pulled out two one-franc coins and handed them to Marie.

'*Merci bien... et bon chance.* Thank you... and good luck,' Marie said with a wry smile.

Frank turned without looking at Marie and fled the room. He descended the stairs a little sheepishly and sat down next to Jimmy, who looked immediately at his watch.

'Welcome back, Franky man,' Jimmy declared triumphantly. 'Six minutes from start to finish – and you're no longer a virgin. A real "six minuter" if ever there was one!'

Frank was too afraid of losing face to admit that he was not a "six minuter" – or even a "six seconder" for that matter.

'Just grand, thank you, marra,' he mumbled softly.

'Now, you must excuse me, my friend. My turn,' Jimmy chuckled loudly.

Jimmy left Frank, climbed the flight of stairs and entered the bedroom.

'I'll see you back at the billets,' he called back cheerfully. 'Don't wait up for me!'

\*

Frank felt awful. His head was splitting, he was sweating, he had a terrible cough, and his mind was racing.

*Is this down to feeling ashamed or guilty about what happened with Marie last night? Or is it down to too much to drink before then? Or is it simply a case of spending too long in a room full of acrid tobacco smoke?*

Frank suffered another fit of coughing, but when he removed his hand from his mouth after he stopped coughing, it was covered with bloody mucus. Frank put it down to a heavy cold or perhaps a mild case of influenza. He had assumed that a day's bed rest would suffice, but he started showing signs of fever and decided to report sick.

'Sorry to trouble you, sir,' he said to the medical officer. 'I don't think I have anything more than a heavy cold but thought I'd better just check.'

The medical officer took Frank's temperature and pulse.

'Your temperature's up a little, Dawson. Almost a hundred. And your pulse is up also,' he said. 'I suggest that you rest today. I'll see you again tomorrow – unless you start to feel worse.'

Frank's condition worsened quite quickly. He was sweating profusely, coupled with chills.

'I don't like where this is going, Dawson. Your temperature is now over a hundred and one, and your pulse rate is up again. I fear it could be pneumonia. We need to get you away from here and back into a hospital.'

# EIGHT

# *France, Autumn 1916*

I could hear a weary, raucous, rasping cough as I entered the ward and headed towards Sister Bettsworth.

'Harland,' she called out. 'Please help this man and get him settled. His name is Dawson, Private Frank Dawson. He's just been sent to us… a possible case of pneumonia.'

'Yes, Sister,' I replied, and moved towards Frank.

'Let me help get you comfortable,' I said.

I helped him to undress and put on a pair of pyjamas and then helped him get into bed, turning the sheet and blanket down as I did.

'Thank you, Miss,' he croaked, his voice foggy and distant.

Then with a listlessness that portrayed great physical effort, Frank leant against me, swayed unsteadily towards the edge of the bed and sat down. I placed my arm around his shoulder and helped him ease himself into bed, and then pulled the sheet and blankets over him. Frank's breathing was rapid and shallow, and he was gasping for breath.

He pressed his hand to his chest.

'Have you a pain there?' I asked.

'Yes.'

'Where is the pain?'

'Here,' and Frank pointed to his sternum.

'Does it hurt you there when you cough?'

'Yes.'

And at that moment, Frank was seized with a violent fit of coughing. I helped him to sit up, which seemed to help, and positioned a pillow behind his back to support him. Gradually, the coughing fit eased. He lay still, bathed in perspiration.

'Have you ever looked at what comes up when you cough?' I asked.

'Yes, about a day before I reported sick.'

'Was there blood mixed with it?'

Frank nodded.

I didn't bother him with any further questions and started to take his temperature, pulse and respiration.

'Sister, please come over here,' I said as soon as I had finished. 'His temperature is a hundred and three, his pulse is a hundred and twenty, and his respiration is thirty-five.'

'Thank you, Harland. The doctor needs to see him urgently. Go and find him for me. He's doing his rounds – he should be in the next hut by now, so try there first.'

I found the doctor and told him about Frank. He came immediately with me back to the ward and quickly confirmed that Frank had pneumonia – and a severe case at that.

'Obviously, we can't give up on this man, but I'm not sure that there is a lot we can do for him,' the doctor told Sister and me. 'Perhaps, Harland, you can stay with him to make him as comfortable as possible until his time comes. You know what I mean – keep him cool, and make sure he is cleaned up immediately if he's sick. Also, give him plenty to drink to ensure that he does not dehydrate.'

Frank soon dozed off after the doctor left, but he vomited several times and became increasingly confused as the night wore on. I remained close to his bed throughout the night, keeping him comfortable and clearing up after him as soon as he was sick.

*

Frank woke with a start; someone was wiping his forehead with a cool cloth. He grasped the hand holding the fabric and pulled it down to his chest. Clearing his mind of confusion, which appeared to have wholly fogged it, Frank remembered that he was in a hospital. He realised that the hand must belong to one of the nurses caring for him. He looked up, trying to make out who was wiping his face. No matter how hard he tried, though, he could make out nothing more than her eyes looking intently at him, surrounded by pale mist. Gradually, his sight grew turbid again, and he drifted back into a blankness until this was succeeded by a restless sleep fractured by visions of his war. Visions of the horrors he'd seen and experienced intermingled with memories of reading *War of the Worlds*.

A violent thunderstorm erupts. Frank is advancing along the road in a horse-drawn milk cart during the height of the storm. He has his first terrifying sight of a fast-moving body of grey-clad soldiers in the distance. His milk cart crashes. He somersaults forward from the cart to discover that the Germans have assembled three-legged fighting machines – tripods armed with some sort of death ray. Elsewhere, chemical weapons spew out poisonous yellow-brown smoke that has a mustardy smell. These tripods wipe out most of the platoon as they advance towards a crater. Then they attack and destroy most of the front line. He cannons against Jimmy as they race back to the British trenches, and a moment later, the two are gyrating and twirling in the air like a sycamore key before crashing onto the fire step. Then everything goes black.

Sometimes, while in his semi-comatose state, Frank grasped words spoken by various people close to his bedside, which seemed to come almost from another world.

*'I think that we are losing him…'*

*'Nurse, wipe the sputum from that soldier's face and chest.'*

*'He's become delirious… almost maniacal on occasion…'*

Somehow, though, Frank doubted that the words could be directed towards him. It could not possibly be him that was near to death – or who had coughed up phlegm or vomited. Inwardly, he felt so well. It could not be him who behaved maniacally in any way. Inwardly, he was entirely sound of mind.

Sometimes, he would awake from a nightmare for long enough to find himself sitting in bed, his arms pinned down by other arms, which endeavoured to hold him. Then he would sink back into that world of horrors from which he had emerged, yo-yoing between that world and a progressively less troubled consciousness.

\*

Although Frank came close to succumbing to pneumonia more than once, he somehow clung on. Then, very slowly, his condition started to improve. Much to my delight, he was sitting up in bed one evening as I approached him at the start of my rounds.

'Hello there, Frank,' I greeted. 'I'm delighted to see that you seem to be on the mend at last. You really did give us a fright. So many times, you opened your eyes, but you did not recognise anyone – and you raved like a madman from time to time! But it's all over now. Hopefully, we have given you the best of care then, and will continue to do so now. In which regard…' I chuckled '…are you ready for me to give you your evening bed bath now?'

A look of surprise crossed Frank's face, which gave way to a look of horror. He sat there open-mouthed as his face turned bright red. Then it dawned on me that he had not realised before that moment that a woman had given him the bed baths he had received.

'Oh, my goodness,' he spluttered. 'I guess so. But if you're going to, I can't keep calling you "Miss". May I call you by your Christian name?'

I felt a little flustered at first.

'Er... well...umm... you shouldn't really... but... whey aye, pet, as long as you only do so when no one else is around, you can. My name is Emily.'

Frank looked at me a little quizzically, and then he laughed.

'Well, I never, Emily. You sound like you're from the same part of the world as me.'

'Jarrow?' I questioned.

'Yes, Jarrow!'

For a brief moment, I was speechless.

'I live in Croft Terrace,' said Frank, breaking the brief silence.

'Good grief,' I spluttered. 'I live in Albert Road – five minutes' walk away!'

'Small world, eh?' laughed Frank. 'Now, we've really got something to talk about, you and me!'

As Frank's recovery continued, we swapped stories about Jarrow until he was eventually transferred to a convalescent depot in Étaples before returning to his unit. It never ceased to amaze either of us how little we knew about one another's friends or family, even though Jarrow is not that large – and we lived so close to one another. When Frank left, we arranged to spend some time together on the Sunday afternoon before he was due to head back to the front.

Luckily, we were blessed with a dry, fine, albeit cool day for our meeting. I attended church in the morning before walking down into Étaples for my rendezvous with Frank. As I had done a number of times previously, I left the hospital and walked past the motor ambulance depot and some farms before entering the town. I walked past the Hôtel Loos on the Grande Place d'Étaples. I couldn't help reminding myself that it had been a haunt of the Étaples art colony before the war – but it didn't look so special now. I headed towards the small, quaint café where I had arranged to meet Frank and sat at a table inside to wait for him.

When Frank arrived shortly afterwards, the first thing that struck me was how much better he looked from the young man I had first cared for when he arrived at the hospital. He cut a fine figure. He seemed to fill his uniform. The once haunted and gaunt look I could remember had well and truly gone. Instead, the colour was back in his cheeks. There was a distinct shine to his light brown hair and his blue eyes sparkled with renewed life.

'My, someone looks fit and well,' I said.

Frank looked at me briefly before holding out his hand.

'That's nice of you to say so,' he replied. 'I owe most of it to you and the care you gave me in hospital.'

'It was the least I could do for someone from Croft Terrace,' I joked, taking Frank's hand and shaking it. 'Now sit down, and let's order a coffee and a *pain au chocolat*.'

We sat drinking our coffee while watching a seemingly never-ending stream of soldiers marching by. At first, I wasn't quite sure what to say to Frank. Should I talk about the war, his thoughts, and any concerns he might have about returning to the trenches? It would be all too easy to do so. But would that be the last thing he wanted? The one thing I did know was that I had to say something to try and break the metaphorical ice that had formed.

*Here goes*, I thought. *The easiest way forward is to ask him about the war.*

'How long have you served in France? Have you been away from Jarrow long?'

Frank smiled. It looked as if he was pleased that I had been the first of us to say something.

'I came out here about eighteen months ago with a few friends from the Ellison Arms. One or two are still with me, including my best mate – Jimmy Prentice. He's from Lime Street. Do you know him?'

I thought for a while. I knew of Lime Street, but Jimmy Prentice's name meant nothing to me.

'I'm afraid not, Frank,' I replied. 'I do know the Ellison Arms. My father occasionally drinks there on the way home from his work at Palmer's. I can't say I've ever been there myself, though.'

Frank laughed.

'Chances are then that I've been in the Arms at the same time as your father.'

'I guess that that is a distinct possibility,' I replied. 'Just think, you and Fatha might have stood at the bar together – the old and the new.'

'My mates and I usually occupied one of the tables in a corner. Well away from all the grey and silver-headed locals,' Frank joked. He took a sip of his coffee. 'I hope you don't mind me asking. Is anyone waiting for you back home?' he continued.

I choked slightly. It still hurt thinking about Alban.

'There was. I was engaged, but my fiancé died when his ship was sunk two years ago.' I knew that I needed to change the subject quickly. 'What about you, Frank? Do you have someone waiting for you?'

'Yes, Emily. There's my fiancée, Sybil.'

'I bet you miss her,' I said.

'Oh yes,' he sighed. 'A ray of life and light enters the room whenever she does.'

I was touched by Frank's all-too-clear feelings for Sybil.

'Have you had the chance to go back and see her since coming to France?'

A strange look passed across Frank's face. He seemed seized with a stupor of despair before he regained his self-possession.

'Sorry,' I mumbled. 'I didn't mean to pry unnecessarily.'

'No… forgive me, Emily. Let me explain. It's not been long since I returned to France from leave. I was only at home for two or three days when the war took its toll on me. I was outside the Ellison Arms when I suffered an attack of shell shock. I had been out with Sybil the previous evening. We made new plans for our wedding – we should have been married at Easter in 1915, but the war ruined those plans. We were supposed to see one another again the following evening, but I was in no fit state. I ended up in a London hospital before returning here to France.'

I really empathised with Frank. I knew only too well what it felt like to have one's hopes and dreams shattered and to be separated from a loved one.

'And now, just a few weeks later, I'm back in a hospital – here in Étaples,' Frank continued.

Then a flicker of a smile crossed his lips. 'But at least it meant that I got the opportunity to meet a fellow Jarrow *émigré*.'

I cracked a grin towards Frank and wrung my hands together.

'Well, let's make the most of what remains of that opportunity. It's still nice outside. I'll give you a guided tour of the joys of Étaples. First, I'll try to avoid as much of the military invasion as possible, but that won't be easy. After that, I'll take you to a café I know – my treat.'

Frank put his hands behind his head and leant back in his chair before slowly getting up and looking at me.

'Let's go then, but on one condition, Emily. I get to take you to a café the next time I see you in Jarrow – and that time it will be my treat.'

'You're on,' I replied. 'Here's to today and our next meeting in Jarrow – in that case, sooner rather than later, eh?'

# NINE

# *France, Late Spring 1917*

As spring was in the throes of giving way to summer, I decided to take a trip to Paris-Plage for the day. I felt that I needed to spend a bit of time relaxing on my own, time to be spent not working or doing things for others. An opportunity to restore my energy. An opportunity for a little bit of self-indulgence.

I set off from the hospital and walked down to the tram stop. It was a pleasant day, warm but not too warm. White cumulus clouds drifted across the deep blue sky, occasionally obscuring the sun. Now and then, I lifted my head to allow the sun's warmth to caress my cheeks.

The tram to Paris-Plage was waiting, and I climbed aboard, paid the ten centimes fare, found a seat about halfway down the car and sat down. I looked forward at the driver, resplendent in his cab, surrounded by a large glass windscreen.

*He certainly would stay dry on a wet day, even if he would appear to any onlooker that he was sitting in some form of a goldfish bowl.*

I looked around me and saw a man in a uniform that aroused

my curiosity. The uniform looked like an army uniform, but it didn't quite seem right. Furthermore, he was sporting a full beard.

Trying to avoid staring, I noticed that the top pockets of his jacket were triangular. The man's jacket also sported a Red Cross badge sewn on the left sleeve. It had twisted cord shoulder straps. His cap had no regimental badge – instead, there was a sewn-on red cross on a white background. I felt the urge to satisfy the curiosity welling inside me.

'Forgive me for appearing nosy,' I said. 'I couldn't help noticing your uniform and wondered which unit you're serving with.'

The man's grey-blue eyes twinkled.

'I'm with the Friends' Ambulance Unit.'

'I thought that must have been something like that!' I exclaimed. 'But how come you are with the Friends' Ambulance Unit rather than serving in the infantry?'

When the man did not respond immediately, I sensed that my question had made him a little uncomfortable.

'Well – I'm a Quaker,' he finally said. 'I strongly oppose war. I had no wish to enlist when—'

I didn't allow him to finish his sentence.

'You mean to say that you were a conscientious objector?'

'Yes,' the man replied.

I looked at him, not quite knowing what to say.

'Oh dear!' I eventually blurted out.

'Does that bother you?'

'A little – if I'm honest,' I replied. 'You have to understand that my fiancé was in the Royal Navy – an engine room artificer. He was killed in action only seven weeks or so after the war started. Also, many people I know at home willingly enlisted immediately after the Declaration of War. But I'm curious as to why someone opposed to war is here in France. Wearing a uniform. Actually participating in a war.'

The man looked sad.

'I'm sorry to hear about your fiancé. It must have been awful for you.' He hesitated before continuing. 'When I was conscripted last year, I appealed for exemption on the grounds of conscience. That appeal was granted – but only with the proviso that I joined the FAU in France. The alternative was imprisonment. Some conscientious objectors chose prison. I chose to join the FAU. To me, it seemed an acceptable compromise. As for my uniform: we have to provide our own uniforms. I couldn't afford a tailor's bill but was lucky enough to have an uncle who had been in the yeomanry just after the Boer War. He still had his uniform, which he let me have. Of course, he's shorter than me and somewhat stouter, but the uniform fits more or less.'

'But I still don't understand why you wear a military uniform, given your beliefs and convictions.'

A faint smile hovered on his lips.

'Simple,' he said. 'We don't stand out too much when we're working alongside "real" soldiers, do we? But there are no hard and fast rules about the uniform itself.'

'Does that explain the beard as well?'

'Yes,' he replied, laughing this time. 'Just as well. I've had my beard for a good few years now. I would have hated to have had to shave it off.'

'I guess it must have been difficult for you back at home, given your beliefs,' said Emily.

His shoulders slumped.

'Yes,' he replied.

'Was life hard?'

'Friends and family ostracised me and called me all sorts of names – "coward", "scrimshanker", "shirker", "pansy", and worse. I was given numerous white feathers – some by people I knew. It was not nice, but I tried not to react and to move on from them as quickly as possible.'

As we continued to speak, I was drawn to him – notwithstanding my initial misgivings.

*This man has something about him.*

I didn't quite know what to do or say next. I looked towards but not directly at him. I looked away. I swallowed.

'Here we are in a tram and chatting away…' I said '…and we don't know one another's names. I am Emily Harland.'

'And I'm Edward Bennion.'

'So, how come you're heading to Paris-Plage?'

Edward smiled.

'I could ask you the same question,' he replied. 'But… since you asked first… I'm working on an ambulance train. We arrived in Étaples earlier today. I've been allowed a bit of time away before we set off again tonight. I saw this tram and decided to see just where it was going. So here I am.'

The tram reached the Place de l'Hermitage and stopped. Almost instinctively, I turned to Edward. He intrigued me. I felt that I needed to find out more about him.

'Fancy walking from here?' I asked.

A look of surprise dashed across Edward's face. Then he looked at me and smiled.

'Why not?'

We alighted from the tram, crossed the road, picked our way through the carriages, and headed towards the sea at Le Touquet. Neither Edward nor I said anything as we looked around, taking in the sights and sounds as we walked.

'I never thought I would see so many fine buildings and shops here,' said Edward, finally breaking the silence. 'This place must have been something special before the war.'

I turned to look at Edward.

'Yes, I think it was,' I replied. 'It's certainly a world apart from Étaples – I often wish I was working here in the Duchess of Westminster's hospital rather than the one where I do.'

'Have you been in Étaples long?' asked Edward.

'Coming up for a year in June. I arrived just before the slaughter at the Somme.'

'That can't have been easy.'

I bowed my head.

'It wasn't. One minute, it was a case of finding my feet; the next, I was pitched into the midst of my worst nightmare, but I'm sure neither of us wants to think about life in a hospital – or life on an ambulance train just now. So tell me about your interests, ambitions, and what you'd be doing if it wasn't for the war – if there's anybody special waiting for you in Blighty.'

Edward burst out laughing.

'Steady… steady… steady, Emily… one thing at a time.'

It was my turn to laugh.

'Well, let's start with your interests.'

'That's easy. Music,' Edward replied.

'Ah… but "music" covers a multitude of things. I love music. I play the piano; Chopin, Beethoven, Schubert and Brahms — and Scott Joplin. I also enjoy Irving Berlin's music.'

Momentarily silenced by my response, Edward's face lit up.

'Well, I'll see your six composers,' he laughed, 'and raise you two: Verdi, Puccini – and, while I'm at it, let's not forget Gilbert and Sullivan. I don't play a musical instrument. I believe it's a great mistake for anyone to waste time learning to play one with no ear for time or tune—'

'Why do you say that?' I interrupted.

'It's because they only make their attempts an intolerable nuisance to others,' he guffawed. 'But I am a dab hand with the spoons, especially when accompanying my father, who does play an instrument – the accordion.'

'All right… all right, Edward. I give in… I give in,' I laughed back. 'But you still haven't told me anything about Edward Bennion.'

'No – you haven't told me much about Emily Harland yet, so tell me a little about yourself. What about you? Have you found anyone since your fiancé was killed?'

I hesitated a little. I hadn't wanted to talk about Alban beyond what I had already said.

'Well,' I began, 'with everything that's been going on since Alban died – volunteering as a VAD, being here in France caring for the victims of all the sickness and injury I've faced most days – I've not thought about anything else. I did briefly meet an officer when I first arrived. I recently met a soldier brought to Étaples with pneumonia who also came from Jarrow. He lives only about five minutes' walk from me – a nice, decent chap but someone who could only ever be a friend. Other than those two, there's been nobody other than work colleagues and patients.'

At that moment, I saw a rather pleasant-looking café I'd seen before but never visited.

'How about we continue our mutual interrogation over a coffee?'

Edward agreed and we went in, sat down and ordered coffees.

'Now it's my turn,' I said. 'What about you? Is there, or has there been, anyone in your life?'

'Well, there have been a few, I have to confess, but none were serious, and none were permanent. Nevertheless, I often wonder what it would feel like to find the one I might dream of in this life.'

'And what sort of person is the one you might dream of?'

'Forgive me if this sounds forward of me, Emily – but I think that it could be someone like you.'

I could feel the blood flooding into my cheeks. I gasped but said nothing. For once in a long time, I couldn't think of what to say. At that moment, I realised that despite everything I had just said, I was still looking for someone to be in my life. Someone like Edward.

*I hope that we will meet again*, was my silent wish.

# TEN

# *France, Autumn 1917*

It was teeming with rain. All was still deathly quiet as word passed down the platoon line in whispers. '*Get ready*.' Frank looked nervously around him. Moments later, his platoon edged over the parapet and, as silently as they could, inched out towards some derelict houses to the south of a strong point they had been ordered to attack.

Frank could scarcely see anything in front of him, but it was as much as he could do to remain upright in any event. He tentatively picked his way over ground littered with myriad fragments of barbed wire and other battle debris and pockmarked with small shell holes and pitted with large craters full of water, slimy with chokingly stinking mud. Frank was slipping and sliding everywhere as he went.

'So far, so good,' Frank whispered to Jimmy Prentice as they reached the first derelict house. 'Let's hope that our luck holds.'

'Too right, Franky, man,' Jimmy replied.

One by one, each of the other derelict houses was searched and found to be deserted. The platoon then edged forward into position about twenty yards further forward. The Lewis Gun team made its way to the left flank. It was to provide covering fire. Finally, the platoon was ready.

Frank looked at his watch and shuddered. His hands started to tremble. The attack was to begin in two minutes.

Precisely on cue, an intensive artillery barrage bombarded the German position: one that set the earth and air quivering. Bursting shrapnel filled the sky over the enemy. High explosive shells smashed into the German front line.

'Let's go, men!' the platoon commander shouted.

Instantly leaping forward, the platoon hurled themselves towards the strongpoint, their bayonets flashing. They swept forward like the crested foam of a wave. The Lewis Gun chattered loudly, bullets sweeping the earth around the enemy machine-gun positions.

The platoon commander moved deeper into the strongpoint trenches. He headed towards machine-gun positions that had caused so many problems previously. Six men from the platoon followed. Frank was the seventh, providing cover at the rear.

As the seven men worked through the trenches, the air resonated with the usual crash of steel on steel during bayonet fighting, intermingled with rifle fire and screams of terror and pain. Every German soldier they saw was either shot or bayoneted.

Frank moved past the entrance to a communication trench. As he did so, an enemy soldier rushed forward with his bayonet at the ready, just as Frank had his. Frank felt the fear of death for a split second, knowing that the German was intent on killing him. The German made a lunge at Frank's chest, but Frank was quicker. He thrust his bayonet out and ran the enemy soldier through the chest. The German screamed, dropped his rifle and brought his hands to where Frank had struck, clutching at the bayonet with both hands. Frank twisted his rifle and pulled his bayonet out, its blade dripping with blood. He thrust his rifle forward again, driving his bayonet into the German once more, the blade sinking to its hilt. For good measure, Frank also pulled the trigger. This was trench fighting in its most basic form.

Frank was filled with mixed emotions: fear, excitement and, perhaps for the first time in a while, remorse. It struck him that killing a man by shooting him from across No Man's Land was one thing. Doing so "up close and personal" was something entirely different. Somehow abhorrent.

*But a good soldier kills without thinking of his adversary as a human being – the very moment I see him as a fellow man, I will no longer be a good soldier. It's a case of kill or be killed. I must be the one who gets in the fatal blow. I must be the one who survives.*

The battalion came under heavy machine-gun fire from the area around the derelict houses that Frank and the platoon had investigated earlier. At the same time, shrapnel and high explosive shells began to pound the battalion's newly taken position. The battalion's casualties were climbing. The men were becoming increasingly demoralised, while incessant heavy rain and a bitingly cold wind added to everyone's misery.

None of the men could get any rest. They had to remain on the fire step, prepared to meet any enemy counterattack. Furthermore, there was to be no let-up from the weather for anyone. The men could not shelter from the elements even after they stood down. There was no chance of getting any sleep – the dugouts had all been rendered useless. There was no alternative other than to stand around in the trenches in the pouring rain. But these were filling with water. There seemed to be nothing more the battalion could do other than to pull back.

Withdrawing, though, was easier said than done. The ground was churned up badly by shell fire and was as slippery as ice. All around, Frank could hear men crying out around him as they splashed down into shell holes. He also fell into a hole. Struggling to stand up one minute, he was plunging face down into a shallow shell hole filled with stinking mud, and water the next. To his horror, two khaki-clad bodies were floating in the scummy water. Covered from head to foot with thick, smelly mud, he scrambled back to his feet and continued to move back. However, he had only gone a few yards further when an artillery shell exploded behind him, throwing him and another private into the air.

The private's body returned to earth and disappeared as a mountain of mud, first lifted by the explosion, now returned to the area where it had lain initially. Frank also fell back to earth, landing on his front just below the lip of a deep shell hole.

Somehow, he managed to prevent himself from slipping back into a dark, muddy morass below him, which seemed to be reaching up to clutch him, drag him into it, and drown him. Frank had to remain as still as he could. Any struggle on his part would surely see him slip downwards into the gaping mouth of the shell hole to an almost inevitable death. It took all his self-control to remain still. His heart was racing, and he was very much in danger of hyperventilating.

'Franky, man. Franky – where are you?' a voice called out.

It was Jimmy.

'Here, Jimmy,' Frank called back. 'I daren't move. I may just slip back into this shell hole. If I do, there's no way I could get out, nor could anyone get down to pull me out.'

Jimmy crawled to the edge of the shell hole and leant in.

'Hang on, Franky. I've got an idea.'

Moments later, he lowered his webbing towards Frank, holding onto the shoulder straps as he did so. The belt was buckled up.

'Try and grab this, Franky, and I will pull you out.'

Frank's heart skipped a beat. Any false move on his part would inevitably result in an irrecoverable slide downwards.

Jimmy manoeuvred the webbing to ensure that the belt was under Frank's chin and resting on his thorax.

'Whenever you're ready, Franky, man,' he called down.

Frank took a sharp intake of breath and quickly moved his right hand to grab the left-hand strap of the webbing. He held on tight and grabbed the right-hand strap with his left hand. Then, dangling down dangerously, he felt himself being slowly pulled upwards by Jimmy.

Frank heaved a sigh of relief as he was finally pulled out onto the ground in front of the shell hole.

'I don't know how to thank you enough,' he gasped.

'No problem, Franky, man. It's what friends do for one another,' replied Jimmy cheerily. 'Now, on your feet, man. Let's get back to our lines – ASAP.'

The two men scrambled back to the front-line trench and dropped to relative safety.

'Thanks again, Jimmy, man,' said Frank as they did so. 'You saved me from every soldier's worst fear – drowning in a shell hole.'

'Howay, man! You're a proper lucky bugger an' all!' Jimmy replied, putting a comforting arm around Frank's shoulder. 'Let's get back to the dugout, have a quiet smoke and a clean-up. They'll not need us to do anything more for a few hours.'

Frank and Jimmy made their way through the lines to their dugouts. They sat together without a word passing between them for the next ten minutes before Frank broke the silence.

'Have you got a cigarette, marra?' he asked.

Jimmy took out his pack of Woodbines, took out two cigarettes and lit them both before handing one to Frank. Frank drew smoke into his lungs before sending a long stream upwards. He finished the cigarette and got up slowly.

'I think I need to get my head down for a little while,' he said.

'Sounds like a good idea,' replied Jimmy. 'You do that. I will have another Woodbine and may well join you afterwards.'

Frank lay down and drifted off to sleep. But only very briefly before waking up screaming. He had dreamt that he was lying on the ground next to a mass grave. A voice was ringing in his ears.

'This should have been the day you died,' Frank heard the voice say.

He lay in the dugout troubled, his sleep shattered.

*Was that a premonition I've just had? Have I been spared? If so, is it once and forever – or just for the time being?*

\*

Frank was on the march. He was heading away from the front line and towards a town more than three miles behind the lines. The battalion had been taken out of the line. They had been given a period of rest. Reorganisation and training would inevitably take up some of that rest period, but there would be time to do nothing other than relax. More importantly for Frank, there was the prospect of the luxury of a bath and change of clothes.

He had not had a bath or a change of underwear for six weeks and felt filthy and disgusting. He knew that he must have stunk. Every single man on the march around him did. None of them would have wanted to stand downwind of any others.

Frank had become the victim of fleeting pangs of despair, but he felt his spirits lifting as the battalion approached its destination. A billeting party met them and led the various companies to their appointed billets.

Frank found himself billeted in a large, empty barn that was part of a farm about half a mile from the centre of the town. The sun was beginning to set, and a cooling breeze had sprung up. Weatherwise, a pleasant evening was in prospect. But, unfortunately, for Frank and his comrades, there was little immediate chance for them to enjoy the evening weather, given the state of the barn. Much work would need to be undertaken before any degree of comfort could ever be afforded to Frank and his comrades. But while the barn may have been dirty, it was well away from artillery barrages.

As he set to work on his billet, Frank looked to where the field cooker was standing and watched the cooks prepare the evening meal. But what he watched could never be said to be an exercise in *haute cuisine*. First, one of the cooks used an axe to bisect some fifty tins of bully beef. Then, devoid of finesse, several cooks scooped the meat out of the bisected tins. Finally, they tossed it into one of the cookers, adding potatoes and vegetables before exercising the alchemy that would transform these into an edible, if not visibly appealing, stew that they would serve out into dixies in the first instance and then the men's mess tins.

Frank's platoon cleared up the barn as best they could. At least there was plenty of dry straw to manufacture mattresses that offered some small degree of comfort, albeit, in all probability, the straw was infested with all manner of parasitic wildlife. Soon, there was also the prospect of a hot meal and drink.

'Every man, go and get his mess tin,' Sergeant Bishop shouted. 'Get a move on. Grub's ready – and there will also be a rum issue.'

Frank and Jimmy headed over to the area where the field cookers stood, with mess tins and spoons ready. Mess tins filled, and with a chunk of bread in hand, they made their way to an area near the cookers and sat down to eat their meal.

'How is it?' Jimmy asked.

Frank sniffed his mess tin. The stew seemed to smell all right, albeit there was a faint smell of burnt meat. He tasted it.

'Not like Mam makes it,' he said with a grin. 'But I'm that hungry I could eat most things.'

Cleaning up the last of the stew in his mess tin with the remains of his bread, Frank went to the cooking area again to partially fill it with tea before returning to wait for the promised rum issue, which arrived almost as soon as he was back. Then, still relishing the warm glow of his rum and tea, Frank paraded with the rest of the platoon to be given the orders for the following day.

Frank didn't listen too closely to these, registering only that there was to be a typhoid vaccination parade, a pay parade at 10:30, some free time and a march into the town to a building that housed the divisional baths. The vaccination parade was not something to look forward to, but the pay parade, the free time and the baths were.

To Frank's immense relief, the platoon was one of the first to arrive at the baths. He quickly shed his uniform; tunic, shirt, puttees, trousers, socks and, finally, his undergarments, foul with perspiration and dirt. The only items he remained wearing were his boots. The rest were heaped on individual piles to be removed and laundered eventually. Frank was handed a towel, which he wrapped around his waist to preserve his modesty, before joining the queue at the foot of a short flight of stairs leading up to an outbuilding that once formed part of a brewery but now housed the baths.

Frank inched up the stairs before finally entering the outbuilding, a cavernous space housing large round wooden tubs which held twelve men each. Frank was handed a bar of soap and went to a tub close to a wall of the building. He hung his towel on a large nail hammered into the wall, took his boots off and moved back to the tub. He climbed the wooden steps next to it and joined four other men already standing in the waist-deep water. Others followed Frank. The water was hot, not lukewarm or cold, to the relief of all. It flowed into the tub through a large bore metal pipe.

Frank knew that his time in the tub was limited, but there was just time enough to bathe in luxurious languor. He submerged under the water and soaped himself as he resurfaced. As Frank did so, he looked across the tub and saw a grinning Jimmy; his face streaked brown with the mud and dirt once caked around his head that now flowed down from his hair. Frank knew that he must look the same. He ducked back under the water and soaped himself again before looking back and returning Jimmy's grin.

A whistle blew, the signal to Frank and his comrades that they had reached the end of their allocated time in the bathtubs. Frank hauled himself out of the tub and returned to his towel. He dried himself, put his boots back on and made his way outside to an area where he received brand-new underwear and socks, a clean, ironed shirt, and a uniform, supposedly decontaminated by baking it in an oven. As luck would have it on this occasion, both the shirt and the uniform fitted him.

Frank felt better than he had done for many weeks as he finished dressing. And things were about to get better.

'Dawson – show yourself,' a voice called out.

It was Sergeant Bishop.

'Here, Sarge.'

Frank hurried over to Bishop.

'Ah, Dawson, report to the platoon commander as soon as we get back to the billets.'

'Anything I need to know, Sarge? Have I done something wrong?'

'I'm sure you'll find out soon enough,' Bishop replied curtly.

*Thanks for being so helpful*, thought Frank.

Frank marched to the platoon commander's office, halted in front of him and saluted.

'I was told to report to you, sir,' he said.

'Ah, Dawson. Yes. At ease, please.'

Frank stood at ease, fearing the worst and trying to think why he was where he was.

'Tell me, Dawson, am I right in thinking you have only been granted home leave once since enlisting?'

'That's correct, sir.'

'And am I right in thinking that that leave was cut short for medical reasons.'

'Yes, sir, that's correct.'

*Where's this going?* Frank wondered.

'So, am I right in thinking you might welcome it if you were granted a further period of home leave?'

Frank was dumbfounded and struggled to put the words together to reply. He couldn't quite comprehend what he had been asked.

'Begging your pardon, sir, but are you joking with me?'

'No, Dawson. This is something I could not and would never joke about,' the platoon commander replied with a smile. 'If you'd like it, I can grant you ten days' home leave. Transport is available to take you to the railway station tomorrow.'

Frank was trembling. He couldn't quite believe his ears and couldn't speak.

'Well, say something, Dawson, even if it's only "bollocks".'

Frank regained his composure.

'Sorry, sir… thank you, sir. That's the best news I've had in ages. I would truly welcome ten days of home leave.'

'Good, Dawson. A travel warrant will be ready for you at eight o'clock tomorrow morning. Your transport will depart at eight-thirty. Enjoy your leave.'

\*

The leave train at Fréchencourt was supposed to depart at midnight. Frank arrived there well before then. Fearful of somehow missing the train, Frank had had no wish to stray from the station. He was content to simply sit and wait. The decision to do so was to reap dividends for him from about one minute past ten when several hundred men scrambled into the half-lit entrance hall that contained five seats only. Frank occupied one of these immediately after climbing out of the lorry that had brought him to the railhead. All French cafés and other haunts in the town frequented by men on ticket-of-leave were required to close at ten o'clock in the evening, and it was precisely then that hordes of muddied soldiers began to crowd the station.

Despite the prospect of a long period of waiting and discomfort, everyone seemed content. An atmosphere of jolly expectancy was comparable to that at Jarrow Station on the morning of the August Bank Holiday. Little groups gathered to swap stories of their exploits in the trenches all around Frank. At the same time, a few officers, who seemed acquainted with the somewhat corpulent but affable railway transport officer, made their way to his office. Frank sat quietly in his own little bubble of thought, imagining being back home again, patiently awaiting the arrival of the train and the order to board it.

The train was very late, but eventually, it crawled into the station well after midnight. Hissing and puffing, it came to a halt. Frank's initial advantage of arriving early at the station vanished immediately as those around him rushed towards the train and began jostling for seats, albeit in a good-natured manner. Somehow everyone was eventually shoe-horned into carriage accommodation barely sufficient for two-thirds of the number attempting to travel, and the train pulled out of the station.

Frank managed to squeeze into a compartment with eleven others, and all twelve somehow sorted out their legs, arms and luggage before attempting to rest. The chattering voices of his fellow travellers first became lost amid the loud rumbling of the wheels of the carriage. Then they faded away as the train rolled on and on without a pause. Finally, they gradually drifted off to sleep. There was, though, no chance of any respite for Frank. He was consumed with thoughts of what lay ahead. A day of his leave had already gone, and an additional day would be lost making the return journey, but the bright prospect of the remaining eight days' freedom in Blighty remained undimmed.

The sapper who was sitting on one side of Frank and who reeked of alcohol passed into a deep sleep, snoring incessantly. The head of a lance corporal in the Buffs on the other side of Frank kept flopping onto Frank's shoulder. Others sat opposite him and wriggled and turned continuously in a near vain attempt to get comfortable. In the meantime, the train chugged slowly, making frequent halts to enable more urgent trains to wend their way.

Frank finally managed to doze off after a few hours of tedious and excruciatingly uncomfortable travel, sleeping fitfully until just before the train pulled into Boulogne Railway Station and came to a halt. Almost as soon as it did, the carriage doors were flung open, and a mass exodus of soldiers began.

Relieved to be free from the constraints of the train, Frank eagerly made his way to the docks and onto the steamer that would take him to Southampton, taking no notice of, and showing no interest in, anything else.

In the end, Frank's boat was late leaving Boulogne. It was no comfort to him when he found out there was a good reason for the delay; his steamer had ceded the right of way to a hospital ship and waited while a procession of ambulance cars drove along the quay and unloaded their stretcher cases. Eventually, the hospital ship moved slowly out of the harbour, with Frank's boat following discreetly behind.

Frank was more than happy to remain on the top deck throughout the crossing. He couldn't face the prospect of occupying space in one of the claustrophobic lower decks, where there was scarcely room to move. He was happy to just walk around from time to time, taking care not to tread on passengers lying asleep on the deck and to avoid small groups of men sitting and talking of fighting as if it were a thing of the half-forgotten past.

As the steamer neared its destination, a shadowy view of the English coastline drew a crowd to the boat's starboard side, who gazed long and admiringly at the cliffs. It all seemed so subdued. There was no outward sign of excitement; the deep satisfaction felt by all was too intimate to prompt any cheering and cap-throwing or other forms of exuberance. The starboard deck remained crowded as the shore loomed larger, and on entry into Folkestone Harbour, everyone prepared to disembark.

For Frank, the front seemed remote as he walked down the gangplank onto a quayside now raucous with the bustle of departure, the thump of trunks dropped down skidways, and the shouts of passengers calling for porters. It seemed remoter still as he gazed out of the carriage window as the train sped towards his home town. Finally, the train rumbled into Jarrow Station before it came to a halt.

As it did, all he could think about was spending time with his family again. Seeing Sybil, making plans with her. At that moment, he realised how much he missed her and how much he was looking forward to being with her again. If that couldn't be tomorrow, it would be the day after.

# ELEVEN

## *Jarrow, Autumn 1917*

I stood looking out of the open carriage window as the train bringing me on the final leg of my journey moved slower and slower into Jarrow Station and finally, with a rasping of brakes and the hissing of released steam, it stopped. I could scarcely contain my excitement. I leant out of the window, turned the handle and pushed the door open.

'Need any help, Miss?' a female voice asked as I did so.

It was a woman porter. Not much older than me and slighter in build, she was wearing a long black skirt, a spotless white blouse, a jacket neatly fastened with four brass buttons and a peaked cap.

'Yes, thank you,' I replied. 'I have a suitcase here if you wouldn't mind fetching it down for me. It's not that heavy, just a bit awkward to manoeuvre through the door.'

I stepped onto the platform, and the porter reached into the carriage and pulled my case out.

'Is anyone meeting you?' she asked.

'Yes, my parents. Doubtless, they'll be waiting in the ticket hall.'

'I'll help you with this then,' she said, and started to head down the platform with me following.

We reached the exit, and I handed my ticket to the ticket inspector and glanced in my purse for a threepence coin. Then, having found one, I gave it to the porter.

'Thanks very much for your help,' I said. 'I can manage by myself from here.'

I picked up the case, went out into the ticket hall and stood scanning the people milling around.

*I wonder if Mam and Fatha are here yet.*

'Emily... Emily, pet,' a rather excited voice cried out.

I looked around. It was Mam and a beaming Fatha standing to the side of her. I was so happy to see them that I could hardly bear it. I dropped my case down onto the floor and ran over to them. Sobbing tears of joy, I embraced both. The three of us stood there, pulled together as one during the long silence that followed.

'Come on, Matilda, lass,' Fatha said, seemingly finding words to say at last. 'Best we get this young lady home.'

He picked up my suitcase and set off towards the station entrance. Mam and I followed, her arm linked with mine.

'How was your journey home?' asked Mam.

'Mostly uneventful, Mam, but it was pretty special when I caught sight of England again. The green hills looked fantastic in the early-morning sun. The only other thing of any real note was when we passed a wooden training ship for cadets. Hundreds of them were clustered on the masts and rigging, shouting and cheering as we passed. It made us feel a bit like we were royalty.'

We emerged from the station hall to face a very light drizzle that had sprung up from virtually nowhere but was scarcely noticeable. The sky was grey, but the clouds drifted high above. It looked like it was likely to brighten up through the afternoon.

We quickly made our way along Railway Street and into

Albert Road and then home. Relieved and very happy, I hurried to the front room and sank into an armchair. Finally, for the first time in a long while, I could relax and begin to unwind.

*

After experiencing the deepest sleep for a long time, I awoke feeling fresh and well rested. The sunshine was streaming through the open curtains in my bedroom, flooding it with dancing, golden dust. The light rested in soft yellow shafts upon the wall and lit up the side of my wardrobe. I climbed out of my bed and stood discreetly at the side of the slightly open window. Outside the house, Albert Road was already heralding the clamour of the coming day, waking up to its busy life. A milk cart bearing the legend, "Red House Farm", was being drawn along at a leisurely pace by a sedate skewbald pony, its harness adorned with horse brasses and sparkling bells that jingled lightly as the horse moved. The milkman whistled tunelessly as he worked. He was in no hurry as the cart stopped outside one house and then another before turning down towards the nearby rectory.

As I watched, I could smell bacon cooking. Just then, Mam knocked and put her head around the bedroom door.

'Good morning, pet', she said. 'Fancy some breakfast?'

'Yes, please, Mam,' I replied.

'Fatha has already set off for work, so just put a gown on and come down. It's just you and me at home for now.'

I looked at Mam and smiled.

'Thanks, Mam, I'll follow right behind you.'

I went downstairs and into the kitchen. Mam was already pouring me a cup of tea.

'Sit down, bonny lass,' she said.

Moments later, she handed me the cup.

'Here you are, pet,' she said. 'Breakfast is ready. Bacon, eggs and fried bread – I hope that's all right.'

'Thanks, Mam,' I replied. 'Just what's needed.'

Mam sat at the kitchen table and poured herself a tea. We sat silently while I tucked into my breakfast and Mam sipped her tea.

'Mam, do you know a Dawson family?' I asked as I positioned my knife and fork neatly on the cleared plate and pushed it a few inches away from me.

'Dawson... Dawson... I can't say as I do, pet. Why do you ask?'

'About a year ago, I looked after a Frank Dawson who had pneumonia. We talked, and he told me he lived in Croft Terrace—'

'Croft Terrace?' Mam interrupted. 'Do you mean the Croft Terrace near us?'

'Yes, Mam, small world, eh?' I continued. 'This Frank Dawson joined up with a few friends from the Ellison Arms at the start of the war. One was a lad called Jimmy Prentice from Lime Street – does that name ring any bells with you?'

Mam looked thoughtful for a moment or two.

'No, pet... I don't know anyone called Prentice. But, of course, Fatha may know him. After all, he's sunk a beer or two in the Ellison Arms over the years!'

'I'll ask him when he gets home tonight,' I replied.

'So tell me about Frank Dawson.'

I stifled a giggle. I knew precisely where Mam was coming from.

'Oh, Mam,' I said. 'Nothing to get yourself excited about. Nothing to get your hopes up over. We chatted occasionally, walked around Étaples together once, and had a cup of coffee and a chocolate pastry. Nothing more. He's a very nice lad, but he's no Alban. In any event, he's got a fiancée.'

'All right, pet, but you can't blame me for asking,' Mam replied, her eyes sparkling mischievously. 'So, now… and to change the subject, anything you've got planned for today, pet?'

I laughed.

'I was looking to spend a bit of time with you.'

'Then maybe we could kill two birds with one stone, although what I'm about to suggest might be too close to what you've been doing since you went to France.'

I looked at her, a little puzzled.

'What do you mean, Mam?'

'I help at the station for a couple of hours once a week. I meet trains arriving with wounded soldiers with a few other women from Albert Road and Caroline Street. We provide them with tea, buns, and some kind words before they are taken to the hospital in Pine Street – or elsewhere around Jarrow. We could go together if you felt up to it.'

I didn't need to think twice.

'Of course I'll come, Mam. We can do our bit, and you and I can have a good natter on the way to and from the station and back here again afterwards. What time do we need to leave?'

'I usually leave around ten – back again around twelve-thirty.'

'Time to let breakfast settle before we go then.'

\*

Even though I'd seen many wounded soldiers brought into the hospital, watching them being unloaded from a train in Jarrow seemed even more sad and sobering. Stretcher cases were lifted off and laid down along the platform before being picked up by stretcher-bearers and taken to waiting ambulances. The walking wounded moved slowly from the train. Some were relieved and pleased that they had returned with "a Blighty". They happily tucked into the buns and downed the mugs of tea offered by Mam and me. Others seemed bowed and listless as they shuffled past to the ambulances, taking little or no notice of either of us. They had become pale shadows of the undoubtedly keen, eager and alert young men who had left for France not so long before.

I had mixed feelings when we left the station. I had enjoyed being with Mam at the station, but it was a bit too much like being in Étaples, and I did need a break from being around sick and wounded soldiers.

'Mam, may I ask you a question about you and Fatha?' I asked as we turned into Station Street.

'What do you want to know, pet?' she asked.

'When did you know that Fatha was the one for you?'

Mam stopped and looked at me, a puzzled look on her face. Then a shadowy smile swept over her face.

'What sort of question is that – why do you ask?'

I could feel my heartbeat start to increase.

'Curiosity, I guess,' I replied, half whispering, half spluttering. 'Was it a gradual thing, or was it… love at first sight?'

'Now there's an interesting question, bonny lass,' she said, taking my hand and stroking it gently, 'especially since it's been a while since Fatha and I first met. I think that it was something that came about over a long time. I've known Fatha nearly all my life. We grew up in the same street, went to the same school – the same church. I don't think I could say it was love at first sight, but there again, there's never been anyone else for me.'

As we stood there, Mam's eyes widened and lit up.

'Have you met someone in France?' she asked. 'Is that what's behind this?'

I felt a hot flush spread from my throat to the roots of my hair.

'My, my, Emily lass – your face has turned quite crimson. Do tell me more.'

I tried to regain my composure, taking a couple of deep breaths before answering.

'Yes, Mam, I have met someone – a very nice man. He is working on an ambulance train in France with the Friends' Ambulance Unit, but I've only been out with him once. Since then, I haven't been able to stop thinking about him.'

'Aha… your question about *"love at first sight"* makes sense now.'

I knew what to expect during the rest of our walk home – and beyond. Mam would fire questions at me non-stop. Doubtless, Fatha would do the same as soon as Mam told him after he got back from work. However, what I didn't expect was Fatha's reaction when I told him that Edward was a conscientious objector.

Fatha started to his feet with an angry exclamation, which died as he looked at me and then around him in bewilderment and amazement.

'What do you think you're playing at?' he spluttered.

He stormed out of the kitchen and returned five minutes later with a couple of old newspapers.

'Look at this,' he said as he handed me a page from the *Echo*. Printed on it was the joke:

*Grocer to a customer:* 'How do you get out of rationing, sir?'
   'Oh, no problem for me,' came the reply, 'it doesn't apply to me. I'm a conscientious objector.'

'And this,' he said as he pointed to an article in another copy of the *Echo*, which reproduced an open letter from the president and secretary of the Durham Miners' Association condemning conscientious objectors – 'and I agree with the man.'

He sat down again and looked at me in a way I had never seen before.

'Have you forgotten Alban's sacrifice so soon?' he continued. 'He died doing his bit for all of us.'

At first, I just didn't know what to say. How to reply to Fatha. I could feel the colour drain from my face. I felt hurt and angry.

'Of course I haven't forgotten Alban, Fatha. I'll never stop thinking about him – *but he is dead. I am not*. Should his death and how my life has developed since mean that I must remain a spinster for the rest of my life? Edward is out in France. He is doing his bit. He's not in prison like those men who won't do anything. He may not be in the trenches but is often under fire. He is also a decent man, and I like him.'

'That's not the point, Emily. Nothing he's doing takes away from the fact that he's not giving his all for King and Country. So, please have nothing more to do with him, for heaven's sake.'

I sat in silence. I couldn't think of what to say at that moment. Then Fatha's face softened. He stood up again and gently put his arms around me. I looked up at him.

'Who knows what might happen when I return to France, Fatha?' I said. 'It may be that he doesn't come back to Étaples. But, on the other hand, it may be the case that he simply doesn't want anything to do with me even if we do meet up again. Yes, I like him, but I can't say that we know each other well. We write to one another regularly, but we've only spent a few hours together; walking, talking and having a cup of coffee. Only time will tell – but that doesn't change how I felt about him when I was with him. It hasn't changed since.'

\*

Typical of some days you can get in autumn, the morning had been dull and grey. Clouds of mist and fog had dropped on the River Tyne, sending out long, ghostlike arms writhing through the town's streets. Mam, Fatha and I left the house to visit Mam's eldest sister.

We were approaching the junction with Bridge Street when I heard someone call out my name. Someone behind me. I stopped and looked back to see who it was. I was somewhat surprised when I realised that it was a soldier. He was hurrying towards me from the direction of Albert Road Post Office.

'Heavens above,' I gasped when I recognised who it was. 'Mam, it's the soldier I was talking about the other morning – it's Frank Dawson.'

Frank caught us up. He took a minute or so to catch his breath.

'So, it is you, Emily,' he said, panting slightly. 'I caught sight of you as I was leaving the post office. I wasn't one hundred per cent certain at first, I must say. Especially as it's been a while since I saw you in Étaples.'

'Who have we here then?' asked Fatha.

'Forgive me, sir,' replied Frank. 'I'm Frank Dawson. Emily cared for me while I was in her hospital.'

At that moment, a young lady arrived and stood next to Frank.

'And I'm Sybil Oakes,' she said, announcing herself. 'I'm Frank's fiancée.'

Frank looked slightly embarrassed and blushed.

'Sorry, pet,' he said, turning to her and taking her hand.

'Hello, Sybil,' I said, jumping in. 'Frank, Sybil, let me introduce you to Mam and Fatha – Percy and Matilda Harland. As I discovered when I last saw Frank, we are near neighbours of his – without knowing it until we met in Étaples.'

'Where are you going?' Frank asked.

'We're heading to Howard Street,' I replied, 'and you two?'

'We're off to High Street,' replied Frank. 'Were you planning to go down Edward Street to get to Howard Street?'

'I think so, Frank.' I looked at Fatha. 'Is that right, Fatha?'

'Yes, pet,' replied Fatha.

'Mind if we join you until then, sir?' asked Frank.

'Not at all – and while we're on the way, may I talk to you about something?' said Fatha. 'Doubtless, Matilda and Emily will take good care of Sybil.'

*What's Fatha playing at?* I wondered.

Before I knew it, Fatha and Frank had passed under the railway bridge, crossed the road and were heading northeast towards the junction with Henry Street.

*

'I bet Matilda, Emily and Sybil are all wondering what we're doing, Frank,' said Percy as he and Frank strode away.

'Well, if they're not, I am,' replied Frank.

Percy chuckled.

'Sorry about that, bonny lad. It's just that I need the opinion of a serving soldier about something Matilda told me originally. Something I didn't take particularly well. Something that later caused a heated discussion with Emily.'

Frank was puzzled.

*I've met Emily previously, but I've never met or spoken to Percy before. So what could he possibly want my opinion on?*

'Forgive me, Mr Harland, but this all seems rather odd. How may I be of help to you – especially where it might somehow concern Emily?'

Percy stopped, reached into his jacket pocket, pulled out a packet of Woodbines and opened it.

'Cigarette?' he asked.

'Thanks,' replied Frank, taking one out.

Percy took one for himself, closed the packet and put it back in his pocket. Next, he produced a box of matches from the same pocket, took one out and struck it.

'Light?'

Percy lit Frank's cigarette before lighting one for himself. He inhaled, looked away from Frank and sent out a stream of smoke.

'When did you join up, Frank?' asked Percy, setting off along the footpath again.

'In 1914 – just after the war started. I went out to France in 1915.'

'Have you been back home since then?'

'Yes, I came back on leave in 1916, but that leave was cut short when I had a bad turn – outside the Ellison Arms, funnily enough. When I returned to France, I was in the trenches for a while before getting pneumonia and ending up in hospital. That's how I met Emily. About a week ago, they gave me some more home leave – and that's how I come to be here now.'

'When you were ill in France, did you come across men serving with the Friends' Ambulance Unit on ambulance trains?'

'Not personally, but I am aware that many of the men serving in the Friends' Ambulance Unit are Quakers – invariably conscientious objectors – "conchies" as we call them. But why do you ask?'

'Well… Emily told me that she had been out with a chap in the Friends' Ambulance Unit who is a "conchie". It was on account of that that I had a falling-out with her.' Percy stopped again and turned to Frank. 'Do you have any strong views about "conchies"?'

Frank took a long draw on his cigarette and exhaled.

'I can't say that I am bothered or concerned about "conchies" serving in France. I've met a good few while I've been out there; all of them in the Medical Corps – all doing their bit. You know, stretcher-bearers and the like. I have a problem with those who refuse to serve and end up in prison. At least the lad you're talking about is out there in France – if that's any comfort to you.'

*

I looked in surprise as Fatha and Frank headed off away from us. I turned and looked at Mam and Sybil.

'Where on earth are Fatha and Frank off to?' I asked.

'Beats me, Emily,' Mam replied. 'Seems a bit rude of them, in any case. But perhaps they'll enlighten us in due course.'

We also passed under the railway bridge, crossed the road and followed Fatha and Frank as they continued to outpace us.

'I gather, from what Emily told me the other day, Sybil, that you and Frank had to postpone your wedding when the war started.'

Sybil looked at Mam and sighed.

'Yes, we were meant to have been married at Easter in 1915. Heaven knows when we will eventually have the wedding. If Frank had warned us that he was coming home on leave, perhaps we could have arranged something for now.'

'Frank's leave was a surprise, was it?' I asked.

'Yes, he just appeared back home a week ago. More's the pity he has to return to France again in a couple of days.'

We walked on in silence for a short while until Sybil turned to me.

'Frank told me you looked after him for a while in France,' she said.

I noticed a slight, nevertheless noticeable, edge to her voice as she spoke, and hesitated slightly before answering.

'Yes, he was very poorly for a while. At one stage, we thought that we would lose him. Fortunately, though, he eventually came through.'

'Frank tells me you sat with him through the night on one occasion.'

'Yes, but that's not uncommon for us when caring for patients. I've lost count of the number of nights I've spent in a ward after my day shift ended.'

Sybil looked at me and frowned, her lips compressed in distaste.

'I daresay that you would spend time with Frank and your other patients while in their care, but didn't you see Frank again after being discharged from the hospital?'

'Yes, we met up at a small café when he was at the convalescent depot – a couple of fellow Jarrow *émigrés*, as we called ourselves, drinking a cup of coffee and eating a chocolate pastry. We talked about you and my fiancé, Alban, who had been killed in action in September 1914. So you can imagine my surprise when he called after me as Mam, Fatha and I had gone past the post office.'

Sybil glanced briefly at me and then away.

'And you can imagine my surprise when Frank chased after you as he did.'

*Oh, dear – I don't like the way this is going.*

'Come on, Sybil. Come on, Mam,' I said. 'We'd better catch the men up quickly and get off to Aunty's before we're late.'

*

Frank and Sybil crossed the road and began to walk along Market Street. Sybil had barely spoken to Frank since they had parted company with the Harland family at Exeter Street.

When they had gone about a hundred yards, Sybil shot in front of Frank and stopped dead in her tracks. Her eyes flashed. The colour drained from her face.

'What on earth was going on between you and Mr Harland, then, Frank?' Sybil demanded. 'Why the sudden urge to rush off and leave me?'

Frank stopped, wondering why Sybil seemed to be in such a mood.

'Oh, sorry, pet, he just wanted to ask about my views on conscientious objectors. He was concerned that Emily had gone out with one and was writing to him.'

Sybil grimaced. Her face was now contorted and flushing crimson.

'Since you mention Emily, what on earth has been going on between you and her?'

'What do you mean, pet?' Frank sputtered.

'What do *I* mean...?' Emily snarled. 'The way you ran after her from the post office – not sparing a thought for me. That's what I mean.'

Frank was stunned. His eyes opened wide. For a moment, he was struck dumb as a feeling of panic started to engulf him. He struggled to find the words to answer Sybil.

'I was just so surprised to see Emily,' he sputtered. 'I just didn't think... I just—'

Sybil didn't allow Frank to finish what he was saying.

'You just couldn't wait to see her again, I know,' she mocked.

'No, Sybil, it wasn't like that. If you'd let me finish, I just wanted to say "Hello" to her – someone who looked after me when I had pneumonia – someone I hadn't expected to see again – and certainly not someone I expected to see while I was back at home on leave.'

Sybil didn't wait for Frank to finish. She spun round and started to rush away as soon as she had heard '*...I just wanted to say "Hello" to her.*'

Horror struck; Frank chased after Sybil. He caught up with her and gently took her arm. She turned to look at him, tears streaming down her face.

Frank's lips quivered in a vain attempt to speak – he could only embrace Sybil repeatedly. Then, finally, he pressed her to him.

'Sybil. Sybil. Don't be daft, pet.'

She did not answer but stood silently in his embrace. Then, lifting her head to his at length, she looked at him. Frank stopped for a moment and moistened his lips with the tip of his tongue. He was silent for a few moments, letting his thoughts just wander.

'There's been nothing going on, pet. There never could be,' Frank finally said, and turned away. His voice sank lower and lower. 'It's you I love, Sybil. That's all.' His head slumped forward; he trembled as if he might fall. 'I love you; I love you… and you alone!' he murmured, trying to kiss away her tears and hoping to make her consoled and happy once more.

*

The decision I had taken to see my cousin who lived in Ellison Place gave me the opportunity to walk with Fatha as he made his way to work. Something I hadn't done since just before leaving for France; a little bit of father and daughter time.

We hadn't gone very far when Papa raised the subject of him and Frank breaking away from Mam, Sybil and me and walking away together.

'I owe you an apology, lass,' he said, taking me completely by surprise.

'An apology, Fatha, whatever for?'

'What I said to you about the young man you met who is in the Friends' Ambulance Unit.'

'Edward?'

'Yes, Edward. I realise now that I was out of order. I allowed *my* prejudice to try and interfere in *your* life. It's not for me to act as judge and jury about Edward. Only you are entitled to do that. Whether you see him again is nobody's concern but yours – and certainly not mine.'

'Thanks, Fatha, I appreciate that. Time will tell, eh?'

'Yes, indeed,' he replied with a grin.

'What did you think of Frank?' I asked.

'He struck me as a decent young man. Seems to have his head screwed on, too – not like some of the lads around here the same age as him. Stayed on at school until he was eighteen and got a good job at the bank in Ormonde Street. I think that his Sybil's got a good one there. Hopefully, you've found a good one also.'

As we continued towards Palmers with arms linked, I was feeling quite heady. I was happier than I had been since Fatha and I had had words about Edward. We had seldom been at crossed swords with one another before.

\*

After seeing my cousin, I headed back down Ellison Street and reached the junction between Ellison Street and Grange Road. Then, who should I see but a very smartly dressed Frank walking along Grange Road? I waited for him.

'Hello, bonny lad,' I said. 'Fancy seeing you again. I thought that you might have returned to France by now. Sybil had said you were due to go back there when we met the other day.'

'Hello, Emily, lass. Not yet. I leave for France first thing tomorrow morning. Where are you headed?' he asked.

'Back home,' I replied.

'Me, too, so we're heading in the same direction. Fancy a cup of coffee? We could go to the restaurant at the Ben Lomond Hotel – it's only just down the road. There's no chance of a *pain au chocolat*, but they do serve very nice cakes. Oh – and let's not forget what I said the last time I saw you: "*I get to take you to a café the next time I see you in Jarrow – my treat.*"'

It was a nice gesture on his part, but I remembered Sybil's slightly odd behaviour when we met.

'What about Sybil, won't she mind?' I enquired.

'I'm sure she won't. Why should she?'

I wondered if I should mention what Sybil had said when we had spoken a few days earlier but decided it might be better not to; better to simply let things pass.

'Well, make sure you tell her you saw me – and pass on my congratulations.'

We entered the restaurant, found a window table, sat down and ordered coffee and a cake each when the waitress came over to take our order.

'Now, this is champion,' Frank exclaimed. 'This is really champion, Emily. Rather odd, too – coincidence and that sort of thing, I mean. I had wondered whether I'd meet up with you again before I returned to France.'

'A coincidence indeed – like our meeting up in Étaples, eh? Two people living barely half a mile apart for our entire lives but never having met before, and yet recently, we've had two chance meetings. First in Étaples, and now in Jarrow. So, how come Sybil's not with you?'

'Oh, she's at home,' replied Frank with a beaming smile. 'Doubtless, she's getting ready for our big night out this evening.'

'Big night out?'

'Yes, after I met you the other day, we decided to get wed the next time I get home. We've even settled on a house we want to buy in Victor Street. It's just around the corner from Mam and Fatha. It's one of the houses my grandparents own, and they've said they'll sell it to me as soon as I need it. So I've just been to the bank – killing two birds with a single stone, saying "Hello" to everyone I worked with, and setting the ball rolling with getting a mortgage – one of the perks of working for them.'

If I'm honest, I envied Frank at that moment. Alban and I would have been married for more than a year but for the war which had taken him from me so cruelly. By now, we could have had a house of our own. We could have already started a family.

Fortunately, Frank broke what could have become a rather morose train of thought.

'Your father mentioned that you had been out with a chap in the Friends' Ambulance Unit you met in France.'

I looked at him, slightly open-mouthed. At that moment, Fatha's words to me earlier became clear.

'Is that what you and he were talking about when you shot off under the railway bridge together?'

Frank smiled.

'He didn't say anything to you at the time then?' he asked.

'Not then, but what you've just said explains something he said this morning. I have a sneaky feeling that I've got you to thank for it.'

'All he asked me was whether I had any strong views about "conchies", and I told him that "conchies" serving in France didn't bother or concern me. I only had a problem with those who ended up in prison because they refused to serve at all.'

At that moment, I could have hugged Frank.

'Thank you, Frank, for what you said. I think it really put Fatha's mind at ease.'

'No problem, Emily, I only told him what I believed. Sounds to me that the lad he was talking about means something to you?'

'Well… yes… he does, but, as I told Fatha, apart from writing to each other regularly, we're still pretty much strangers. Only time will tell, of course, but nothing's changed about how I've felt about him since I first met him. The fact of the matter is I like him – and would very much like to see him again.'

Frank reached across the table and placed his hand on mine. He looked at me and smiled.

'Well, here's hoping that you do,' he said gently.

The coffee and cakes arrived. As they did, I saw Frank look out of the window.

'At least we can look out at Jarrow folk from here and not at a never-ending stream of soldiers,' I laughed.

'Too right,' Frank replied, laughing also, 'and one of them is my sister Isabelle.'

'Where?' I asked, slightly catching my breath.

'That's her over there,' said Frank, pointing towards the other side of the road. 'The one who is waving at us and looking demented.'

I looked up – but saw no one.

'Where?' I asked.

Frank pushed his chair back, stood up and leant towards the window.

'I wonder where she's gone so suddenly,' he said. 'It's all very odd – I would have thought that she would have come in and joined us. Doubtless, I'll find out soon enough.'

## TWELVE
# *Étaples, Late Autumn 1917*

The weather had been unseasonably warm while I had been at home on leave, and many nursing staff throughout Étaples had developed a gastric bug, which became known as "Étaplitis". My new hospital had been particularly badly hit, necessitating my transfer there.

My duties didn't change, but I was surrounded by new colleagues; for the time being, all strangers. I felt very lonely, especially when I thought about my time at home and Frank and Sybil in particular. How I envied them; planning to get married, planning a home together. My life, in comparison, seemed to centre uniquely on work. Outside of that, it was empty, especially as I hadn't heard from Edward for weeks.

*Nobody wants to be on their own. Everyone needs to know they're not alone,* I thought. I hadn't, though, abandoned a natural optimism. *If Edward and I are not meant to be together, there has to be somebody else out there for me.*

That optimism remained with me as I left the hospital one afternoon to walk down to see some of my friends in the Mess at my old hospital. It was a typical late November day. Cold, grey and overcast. But at least it was dry, and I was well wrapped up in my long cape of grey blanket wool. I heard someone behind me call out as I walked past the motor ambulance depot.

'It's Miss Harland, isn't it?'

I looked back, my eyes widening, to see a tall, slim army officer. I vaguely recognised him but couldn't put a name to his face. So I stood there staring at him a little vacantly.

'Clearly, you don't remember me,' he laughed. 'It's Jack – Jack Miller – the Café des Amis in Boulogne.'

I looked at him but maintaining minimal eye contact. I glanced away briefly and then towards him. Then it all came back to me.

'Ah yes,' I replied with a smile. 'The penny's just dropped. Please forgive me. But how come you're here? Now.'

Jack grinned and tilted his head back.

'I was posted to Étaples in the aftermath of the mutiny at the Bull Ring – you know, the training centre here. I came out this way for some fresh air away from the camp and am just on my way back into town. Is that where you're headed? If so, may I join you?'

'Yes, of course,' I replied, turning my head away and maintaining eye contact. 'I could use some company.'

I started to walk towards the town, and Jack skipped forward beside me.

'So, how are things with you?' he asked.

'Fine, thank you, Jack. I returned from home leave a month or so ago. I've been temporarily transferred to another hospital thanks to a gastric bug doing the rounds throughout Étaples. I have a few hours off, so I thought I'd have a look in on some friends at my old hospital.'

We chatted until we reached the hospital. Then, I stopped outside the entrance gate and turned to face Jack.

'Well, here I am, Jack. It was nice to meet you again.'

'Yes, it was,' he replied.

He was about to move off again towards the town when he stopped and faced back towards me.

'Any chance I could see you again?' he asked.

Taken slightly off guard, I paused.

*It would be nice to have a bit of male company again.*

He looked at me a little anxiously.

'That would be nice, Jack,' I finally replied in a half-whisper. 'We'll have to be discreet, however. It's a strict rule in the camp that a VAD and an officer may not go out together.'

Jack burst out laughing.

'Of course. Rules are rules,' Jack said. 'But how does that saying go? Ah yes! *Rules are for the guidance of wise men and the obedience of fools.* While I am sure that neither of us is a fool, I am certain that both of us are wise – and I am the soul of discretion.

'When shall we say? When do you next have some time off? Perhaps we might go to Paris-Plage. It would be nice if you could make it sometime next week. It's my birthday next Monday, and you could help me celebrate it.'

I stood slightly open-mouthed momentarily, flummoxed somewhat by the barrage of questions.

'That would be nice, Jack,' I eventually spluttered out. 'I'm free on Sunday after church at ten o'clock.'

'Shall we say we'll meet up at the tram stop in Étaples at eleven-thirty and head into Paris-Plage for lunch?'

\*

I set off from the hospital and walked down to the tram stop. It was another cold day. The sky was overcast, and there was a short, sharp rain shower every now and again. Jack was waiting when I arrived.

'Hello, Emily,' he said as I reached him. 'Good to see you.'

I raised my hand in greeting.

'Hello, Jack,' I replied.

'Not the nicest of days, I'm afraid,' he said, 'but, if it's all right with you, I've taken the precaution of sending my servant into Paris-Plage to arrange a table for us for lunch at the Hôtel l'Hermitage. At least we'll stay warm and dry there.'

'That sounds nice. I look forward to it.'

The tram to Paris-Plage arrived, and we climbed aboard. I found a seat while Jack paid the fare. Afterwards, he made his way down the tram and sat next to me. Outside, a dash of rain beat against the windows.

'I think we made it just in time,' Jack said. 'Here's hoping the rain ceases before we get to Paris-Plage.'

The tram reached the Place de l'Hermitage and came to a halt, and we alighted from the tram and headed towards the hotel. As soon as we arrived, we were greeted by the manager, who seemed to know Jack very well. He showed us to a private dining room just to the side of the hotel's restaurant. We sat down at a beautifully dressed round walnut table.

'Champagne, please. The 1914 Pol Roger,' Jack ordered.

'*Oui, Monsieur*,' replied the manager.

'I hope that champagne is all right with you,' said Jack, propping his head up on one arm and looking straight at me.

I tilted my head up, slightly open-mouthed.

'I've never had champagne before, Jack,' I whispered.

'Well, Emily, there's a first time for everything,' he chuckled.

The manager reappeared and poured a flute of champagne for each of us. Jack raised his glass towards me.

'Here's to you, Emily,' he said, leaning forward, his eyes fixed on mine.

I looked down and away.

'Thank you, Jack,' I replied, looking back at him, raising my flute towards him. 'And here's to you.'

I put my mouth to the edge of the flute and felt the bubbles tickle my top lip. I sipped the champagne while I looked at Jack and smiled.

'How is it?' he asked.

'It's very nice, Jack, thank you.'

'Then drink up,' he said, grinning broadly. 'In the meantime, I have a confession to make. I've already ordered our meal for today.'

'Really?' I gasped.

'I know I've taken a liberty, but if I remember correctly from the Café des Amis, you might have ordered *hors-d'œuvre variés, saumon sauce mayonnaise,* and *glace panachée* if you had a choice.'

I burst out laughing.

'How on earth have you remembered that?'

'I never forget a pretty face – and what she likes to eat,' replied Jack, his face lighting up.

'And what are you having?' I asked, the scarlet heat of a blush warming my cheeks.

'The same,' he replied. 'And I have ordered a bottle of Pouilly to go with our meal. But first, let's refill our flutes and drink a toast to a most enjoyable lunch.'

As we chatted, I realised that Jack was good company. I remembered the reservations I had held then but now began to feel that I may have misjudged him. It also crossed my mind that Fatha had been right – maybe Edward was not the man for me.

As the afternoon flew by, I realised that I was getting more than a little tipsy as I burst out randomly in fits of giggling. Internal alarm bells started to ring in my head. It was getting late, and it would soon be dark. I had to get back to the hospital.

'Sorry, Jack,' I spluttered. 'I have to go. Will you see me back to Étaples, please?'

Jack leant in towards me, moving into my personal space. A look of anger flashed across his face.

'Why do you have to go?' he asked sharply.

I gasped. Jack's manner scared me.

'I'm sorry, Jack, I just want to get back.'

'Yes, but you're not on duty tonight – are you?'

I started to panic. The whole atmosphere of the afternoon had changed dramatically for me. Very much for the worse.

'Not tonight, no. Tomorrow morning at ten,' I said in a voice increasingly becoming a tremble. 'But I must get back now. I was only coming out for the afternoon.'

I got up from the table and started to move away.

'But I've booked a room for us at the hotel tonight!' Jack announced.

I spun around.

'You've done what?' I gasped in disbelief.

He looked straight at me with a supercilious grin spreading across his face.

'I've booked a room for us at the hotel for tonight,' he repeated.

'Why on earth would you do that?' I said, spitting out each word.

'Why not? I thought that you would want me to,' he sputtered.

I stared at Jack in disbelief. I could think of nothing to say. He was treating me as if I was a prostitute. I could only think of getting away.

'Have you any idea how much I have spent on you here today – the meal – the room?' Jack squealed.

He stood up, pulled me towards him and kissed me violently on the lips. Then, I felt him try to push his tongue between my lips. Horrified, I immediately thrust him away from me and slapped him across the face.

'Don't do that!' I snapped.

I retreated several steps and covered my mouth with my hands. I felt numb. The whole world seemed to be moving in slow motion. I felt like I had been transported to a dream world, a horrific, nightmarish dream world. Inwardly, I tried to make sense of what had happened, to find a rational explanation. Finally, I turned and started to hurry out of the room. As I did so, Jack leapt forward behind me. He wrapped his arms around my waist, moved his hands up to my breasts and pulled me back towards the table. I struggled free of him.

'Get off me,' I hissed, 'or I'll scream the place down.'

Jack stepped towards me, stopped, and threw back his arms with an air of submission.

'Your loss,' he whimpered, his voice cracking. 'You'd better go then.'

'Yes, I will – and quickly,' I snarled.

I ran out of the hotel with tears streaming down my face, not stopping until I reached the tram stop. It was raining, but I didn't notice. I didn't care.

It seemed to take forever before a tram lumbered towards the stop. All the time, I continually looked back towards the hotel. I was constantly on edge – as though something could happen at any moment.

The tram came to a halt, and I scrambled on board. I felt as if I was watching myself from the outside. Wide-eyed, my heartbeat racing, I looked along the tram and saw the very welcome face of Sarah Nugent. Relief flooded through me. I almost ran along the tram and sat down in a heap next to her. I felt dirty. I felt abused.

Sarah put her arm around me and pulled me into her.

'Emily,' she whispered, 'what on earth has happened?'

I couldn't find the words in reply. We sat together in silence as I tried to recover my composure, but thoughts flashed through my mind all the time.

*Have I imagined what has just happened?*
*Was it my fault?*

*Why else did I allow myself to be alone with Jack if it wasn't?*

The tram finally reached our destination, and Sarah helped me out and guided me to the Mess. She sat me down and went to get me a cup of tea. When she returned, I was finally able to tell her what had happened and my fears for the future.

*Would I ever be able to trust a man again?*

# THIRTEEN
# *France, Late Autumn 1917*

Frank eagerly opened the letter he had been handed. He used his bayonet to slit open the envelope, pulled out the letter and started to read it. It was from Sybil. Her hand, so firm at first, was straggling and faint at the close. Frank could scarcely believe what he was reading.

*Dear Frank,*

*I think back to that horrible moment when we had to say goodbye at Jarrow Station as you started your journey back to France. I wept bitter tears of anguish as your train pulled away. You promised me that I was the only one for you. That when you returned, we would never again part.*

*Only days before, you had told me that you loved me – me, and me alone. You assured me that nothing was going on between you and Emily Harland. But it seems that what you told me was a load of baloney.*

*If nothing was going on between you and Emily Harland,*

*why were you with her in the restaurant at the Ben Lomond Hotel the day you went to the bank?*

*Don't try and deny it. I know you were there. Your sister Isabelle told me yesterday that she saw you with a young woman – a young woman who could only have been Emily Harland, I am sure. She saw you take hold of her hand.*

*If nothing was going on, why didn't you tell me that you had been in that restaurant and why you were?*

*The fact of the matter is that you didn't and I'm left with the feeling that the trust that should be there between us is gone.*

*I'm sorry that things have turned out the way they have, but I can't think of any plausible explanation that you might be able to give me. And without that, I cannot see how we can be married or why we should marry.*

*Yours in disappointment,*

*Sybil*

With tears welling in his eyes, he reread it. So, it seemed to him, Sybil had more or less announced that their engagement was off; she no longer seemed to want to marry him.

'Dear God, no!' Frank called out despairingly, feeling a deep despondency.

Jimmy heard Frank's cry and rushed over to him.

'Howay, man, what's up, Franky, man?'

'It looks like Sybil has finished with me – but there's nothing to what she's saying – no reason to end things between us,' Frank replied, passing Sybil's letter to him.

Jimmy read the letter.

'You're a daft bugger, man. Why in heaven's name didn't you tell Sybil? Sure, she'd have had a right go at you but she wouldn't have been left feeling like she seems to be now.'

Frank looked down at the ground. He couldn't look Jimmy in the eye.

'I know you're right. The daft thing is that Emily had said that I should tell Sybil about our meeting again in Jarrow. Indeed, she asked me to pass on her congratulations. But I forgot.'

'Who is this Emily, anyway?' asked Jimmy.

'She is a VAD who looked after me when I had pneumonia. She's from Jarrow, too – from Albert Road. I saw her again when I was at the convalescent depot. She bought me a cup of coffee and a *pain au chocolat* after we met one another in Étaples. I promised her I would reciprocate if I saw her back home.'

'Doesn't alter the fact that you're a daft bugger. As I read the letter, Sybil is looking for you to explain everything to her. Get writing, man. That's assuming, you still want her.'

'Of course I do, Jimmy. She means everything to me.'

'Then, for God's sake, Frank, tell her – and quickly. No – do it now.'

Frank grabbed a pencil and paper and wrote to Sybil, pouring his heart out to her. For good measure, he also wrote to Emily, pleading with her to write to Sybil and explain why he and Emily were in the restaurant at the Ben Lomond Hotel together.

When he had finished, he passed the letters to Jimmy.

'Tell me what you think, Jimmy.'

Jimmy shook his head.

'No, Franky, man. Those letters have to come from you alone. It's between you, Sybil and Emily. I'm your friend, but whatever I may think or say is irrelevant. Send the letters off immediately. After that's done let's take a walk into town and sink a few beers.'

Frank sealed the letters, and posted both at the regimental field post office as he and Jimmy headed on their way into town.

Unfortunately, a few beers became too many beers. Frank drank much more than was good for him, especially after Jimmy took his leave and headed back to his hut. In a moment of madness, Frank lost his head and gave himself up to a prolonged drinking bout. He became blindly, stupidly, senselessly drunk. But it seemed to drape a veil between him and Sybil's letter. It became the anaesthetic for his body to numb the barbs of anguish torturing his mind. There were, though, consequences for that moment of madness.

\*

Frank stood in front of the three Members of the court-martial, an escort standing on either side of him. They were in the largest bedroom of an *estaminet*, Les Coquelicots, in Liéramont. The Members sat at a table with their backs to the bed. The summary of evidence of the two witnesses for the prosecution, Sergeant Bishop and Private Ralph Holt, lay on the table. Frank had been present at Battalion Headquarters when they gave their evidence and had not challenged them at the time. Not that he could have if he had wanted to.

The sworn summary of evidence of Ralph read:

*I was returning from Hendecourt-lès-Cagnicourt when I saw the accused about fifty yards outside his hut. He appeared unstable and was wavering. It was evident to me that he was drunk. I saw him totter and fall. I ran over to him and saw that he had his rifle. He pulled the bolt back and loaded it as he lay on the ground. I asked him: 'What the hell are you doing?'*

*He said something along the lines of: 'What's that to do with you, Ralph, man?'*

*I said: 'Steady on there, bonny lad. Come along with me. Let's go back to your hut.'*

*He mumbled: 'Whey aye, me marra. Let's go then.'*

*I helped him to his feet, but he wouldn't let go of his rifle when I tried to take it from him. We started to walk back to his hut.*

> *Suddenly the accused yelled out: 'Let's go and get us some Germans, Ralph, man. There's some over there.'*
>
> *He pointed to his left and fired a shot in the direction of where he was pointing.*
>
> *I said: 'Don't be daft, man, there are no Germans here. So you'll only shoot one of our lads.'*
>
> *He said: 'Oops, sorry, man. Better be careful, then. No more bullets.'*
>
> *We walked on until we met Sergeant Bishop, running towards us. I went to Sergeant Bishop and told him what had happened. He then approached the accused and persuaded him to hand over his rifle.*
>
> *Sergeant Bishop placed the accused under arrest and ordered me to escort him to the guardroom.*

The sworn summary of evidence of Sergeant Bishop read:

> *At about 15:40 hours on the thirteenth of December 1917, I was off duty and just leaving my hut to go into Hendecourt-lès-Cagnicourt when I heard a shot fired. I rushed towards the sound and saw Private Holt approaching me with the accused. Private Holt came over to me and told me that the accused was in a state and had just fired his rifle.*
>
> *It was clear to me that the accused was drunk. I approached and asked him quietly to let me have the rifle. He handed it over without any fuss, and I placed him under arrest.*

The first of the two charges Frank was facing was read out: 'Private Dawson, you are charged with an act to the prejudice of military discipline and good order; wilfully discharging a rifle at Hendecourt-lès-Cagnicourt on the thirteenth of December Nineteen Seventeen, pursuant to Section Forty of the Army Act Eighteen Eighty-One.'

He was then asked: 'Are you guilty or not guilty of the charge against you that you have heard read?'

'Guilty,' replied Frank, his head hung down, his eyes fixed on the ground.

The second charge was then read out: 'Private Dawson, you are further charged with drunkenness pursuant to Section Seventeen of the Army Act Eighteen Eighty-One.

'Are you guilty or not guilty of the charge against you that you have heard read?'

'Guilty.'

Frank called no witness as to his character and made no statement in mitigation. He was sentenced to undergo twenty-one days' Field Punishment Number One.

Frank's punishment began at dawn on the following day as he was tied to a post. He stood with his back to the post while his wrists were tied behind him. His feet were tied twelve inches apart. The ropes used for these purposes were of sufficient width that they did not inflict bodily harm and left no permanent mark on Frank.

It was bitterly cold throughout the first two days of Frank's punishment. It snowed, then froze solid on the third. Fortunately, it was only permissible for him to remain tied to the post for one hour twice a day on three days in any four during his sentence. Frank was required to undertake fatigues when not tied up to the post. This invariably meant latrine duty and any other unsavoury job going when the battalion was not serving in the trenches on the front line.

The weather did not let up as Frank's period of Field Punishment continued. It was bitterly cold again during the next three days. It rained on the seventh day. A slightly warmer day followed before a day of snowstorms. Frank still had twelve days left of Field Punishment to serve – twelve days where the battalion was back in the trenches.

# France, Late Autumn 1917

\*

A bombardment along the whole of the battalion's front and support lines had been ongoing for two days, increasing in intensity with the passing of every hour. The noise of bombardment was deafening. The ground shook with each explosion, and earth, wire and more besides were sent into the air. Frank began to tremble; at first slightly but the trembling became increasingly uncontrollable – especially so as the bombardment lifted.

'Eyes peeled,' shouted Sergeant Bishop. 'Expect a Boche attack any time now!'

A temporary semi-silence was broken by a spatter of machine guns and the spit of enemy bullets striking the parapet, sending up spurts of earth.

German infantrymen loomed out of the half-light, braving a fusillade of rifle and Lewis Gun fire. Some of them fell down and did not get up again. The rest kept coming and started to drop into the trench. One rushed forward towards Frank with the obvious intention of bayoneting him. Frank stood there, paralysed with fear. Then, just when he thought he was to meet his end, he was jerked backwards by someone grabbing his webbing. He fell sprawling on the trench floor. Two loud bangs just behind him nearly deafened him. The German soldier fell, dead. Feeling somewhat disorientated, he looked up to see Jimmy and Ralph standing over him.

'Come on, Frank!' shouted Jimmy.

'What happened?' Frank asked, pulling himself to his feet.

'Jimmy pulled you clear of Fritz,' replied Ralph, 'and I shot the bastard. Now let's get the fuck out of here, man!'

As more Germans poured down into the trench, the three disappeared into a communication trench. Then, they ran down into the support trench where they rejoined other platoon members who had also made it back there.

'Good of you to join us,' Bishop shouted to them as they arrived. 'We are to hold this trench in anticipation of launching a counterattack to get our fire trench back again.'

'Typical of everything we are doing,' muttered Frank. 'We take some ground; they take it back – and vice versa. Nothing changes other than an increase in the number of dead and wounded. So what's the purpose of all that?'

At that moment, the Germans began a short but fierce bombardment of the support trench before launching a full scale, and ultimately overwhelming, infantry attack. Within minutes, Frank, Jimmy and Ralph were forced to scramble out of the support trench onto the ground behind it. They began to zigzag from one piece of cover to the next before dropping into a shell hole about halfway between the support and reserve trenches to escape the heavy machine-gun fire that began to rake across the whole area.

All three lay in the shell hole breathing heavily.

'What do we do now, man?' Frank asked, weakly.

'We wait,' replied Jimmy. 'In the meantime, hoy us a tab, Ralph, marra. I'm gasping.'

'You crazy bugger!' exclaimed Ralph, looking open-mouthed at Jimmy. 'Oh, what the heck,' he guffawed, reaching into his jacket and pulling out his pack of Woodbines. He took one out and handed the packet to Jimmy, who also took one out.

'Tab, Franky?' asked Jimmy, offering the pack.

Frank didn't reply; he just looked vacantly at his friend.

'Suit yourself, marra,' chirped Jimmy, handing the cigarettes back to Ralph. 'Thanks, Ralph, man.'

Both men enjoyed a long slow smoke.

As Frank, Ralph and Jimmy lay there, shells of all sizes began to blow up above them and fall in steely splinters all around. The noise was deafening. Frank was becoming increasingly agitated. Finally, notwithstanding the enemy bombardment and the fact that bullets were still zipping overhead, he edged up to the lip of the shell hole and tried to raise his head over it.

'Frank, man, you daft bugger. Don't do that. What the hell are you playing at? Are you trying to get killed?' shouted Jimmy as he pulled Frank back into the shell hole. 'For heaven's sake, man, keep down. You idiot!'

Frank sat there staring blankly, first at Ralph, then at Jimmy, saying nothing.

'Do you think HQ will launch another counterattack?' Frank heard Ralph ask Jimmy.

'Maybe – maybe not,' replied Jimmy. 'Whatever else, though, we can't just sit here forever – although we should be all right for now. If the Boche have taken both the fire trench and the support trench, they should follow through to the reserve trench via the communication trenches and leave us be.'

'For the present, then, it looks like we're stuck,' said Ralph. 'We'll be sitting ducks the moment we show ourselves while it's still light.'

'In that case, time for another tab,' Jimmy laughed.

After what seemed like an eternity, it started to get dark again. Elsewhere, things were still relatively quiet, apart from the occasional rifle and machine-gun fire exchange.

'If we stay any longer we'll likely take root,' said Jimmy as he carefully peered over the lip of the shell hole before easing himself out of it. 'Looks like we still hold the reserve trench,' he reported to Frank and Ralph. 'They're firing towards the support and fire trenches taken by the Boche. As I see it, we have a clear choice. Either we somehow contrive to get taken prisoner, or we crawl back to the reserve trench. Personally, I have no desire to be taken into a Boche prisoner of war camp.'

'I'm with you there, Jimmy,' said Ralph. He looked towards Frank. 'Come on, Franky, lad,' he called out. 'Let's go.'

Frank said nothing, but with Jimmy and Ralph on either side

of him, he inched back, crawling with his stomach low to the ground until he finally dropped down into the reserve trench.

Frank squatted on his haunches, breathing heavily. A worried Jimmy went over to him.

'Are you OK, Frank?' he asked.

'I'm not feeling so good,' replied Frank, looking up as he did so, but without making eye contact.

'You wait here while Ralph and I report us all back at HQ,' said Jimmy.

Frank stood up and watched as Jimmy and Ralph made their way along the reserve trench. As soon as they were out of sight, he started to feel dizzy, then nauseous. Next, his heart rate started to accelerate. Finally, he began to experience a choking sensation. He thought he had to get away and began to wander along the trench, following the direction taken by Jimmy and Ralph.

It seemed to Frank that he had been walking for ages when he saw Jimmy and then Ralph heading towards him.

'Where the heck do you think you're going, you daft bugger?' asked a concerned Jimmy when he reached Frank. 'I told you to stay where you were.'

Jimmy went over to Frank and put his arm around Frank's shoulder. Frank started to shiver, and his whole body began to shake. He tried to speak but could only manage incoherent grunts and mumblings.

Ralph approached both of them.

'Is Frank micey?' he asked.

'Don't be daft, Ralph, man,' chided Jimmy. 'There's no way he's mad. He's just shaken up. The war's got to him. He'll be all right again soon, you'll see. Just make sure you don't shoot your big mouth off to an NCO or officer about this. Here, take Frank's rifle and helmet while I sit him down with me for a short while so that he can pull himself together again.'

Ralph did as he had been asked and watched as Jimmy and

Frank sat down side by side on the trench floor. Jimmy took out his pack of Woodbines, took out two, placed them on his lips and lit them. He handed one to Frank before passing the packet and matches to Ralph.

'Tab, Ralph, man?'

Ralph took a cigarette, lit it, and also sat next to Frank and Jimmy. The three men were sitting and smoking in silence when Corporal Dale approached them.

'Well, well, well,' he said. 'What have we got here then?'

'Everything's all right, Corporal,' answered Jimmy. 'Dawson's just a little bit out of fettle. I think he fell awkwardly as he jumped down into the trench.'

'Oh, really?' replied Dale, unconvinced by what he had heard.

'Yes, really, Corp,' said Jimmy. 'Why would you doubt me?'

'All right, I'll believe you, but thousands wouldn't,' Dale sneered. 'No more fucking about having a cosy little smoke together... Platoon Commander's briefing for everyone in ten minutes, so look sharp about it... or face the consequences.'

\*

The battalion was in reserve. It had moved back to allow it to rest and reorganise and enjoy the luxury of being in billets in a village some miles from the front line. They were to be there for four days before going back into reserve.

After Frank, Jimmy and Ralph had settled into their billet, Sergeant Bishop entered the barn. 'Time to get ready for all the *mademoiselles* in the *estaminet* tomorrow. Get fell in outside. Mobile baths are available for all of you. You will find them behind what's left of the large house standing at the entrance to the village. By the stream. You get to enjoy a bath and change clothes, but you must be on your best behaviour.'

'What do you mean by that, Sarge?' asked Ralph.

'You'll find out soon enough – but be warned, I shall be watching you all very closely,' he replied.

As Frank and his platoon marched towards the house at the entrance to the village, they soon realised what Bishop had meant.

'Good grief!' exclaimed Jimmy. 'Lasses are working the baths.'

A Daimler motor car, converted for its present purposes, was parked close to the stream. Its engine was running. A hosepipe connected to a hand pump ran from this to the stream.

A stout woman of about thirty years of age was working the pump. She was wearing a FANY's uniform. While she was somewhat red-faced and sweating from her efforts, she radiated nun-like calm and respectability. Water flowed into a cistern in the car's interior as she pumped. The heat from the car's engine warmed the water.

Two tents were set up next to the Daimler, each containing five collapsible baths. A tap protruding from each side of the car's body was connected to the cistern by a pipe. Another pipe ran from each protruding tap to one of the tents to fill the baths it contained.

Another lady in a FANY uniform was sitting in the Daimler, watching over the cistern.

Jimmy turned, looked at Frank and laughed.

'I don't fancy yours,' he said as he disappeared into the tent.

After his bath and feeling almost human again, Frank had his first hot meal in four days. Horse-drawn field cookers stood close to the centre of the village and provided all the men with something rather more appetising than cold tinned bully beef and biscuits. Now, both clean and fed, it was time for Frank and his friends to get "watered".

*

That evening, Frank, Ralph, Jimmy and the rest of their platoon strode off to drown their sorrows in the town. As they wandered down the street, Frank could see women working or gossiping at the doorsteps. Outside one house, a child was hugging a loaf of bread. Outside another, an old man sat blinking in the sunshine. The *estaminet* doors had been flung wide open but it was not yet overcrowded. Nevertheless, it was shrouded in a cloak of thick tobacco smoke and reeked of body odour, albeit this was mitigated by the sickly sweet smell of third-rate cologne. They sat down around large rectangular tables. Yvette, the daughter of the *estaminet* owner, took their orders for a meal, served it when it was ready, and willingly brought a steady stream of bottles of beer over to them. Very briefly, all thoughts of the war abated.

Gradually, the number of platoon members who sat around Frank's table dwindled until just he, Jimmy and Ralph remained. Jimmy got up, went over to the bar and chatted briefly with Yvette before returning. After he sat down again, Yvette joined the three men, easing herself into the chair next to Frank. She edged in closer to him. He could feel her press up against him and gulped as she placed her right hand on his knee.

Yvette moved her hand slowly up Frank's leg to his crotch. He froze.

*Whoa – what the – There's a time and place for all things, but not this – not now.*

He gently moved Yvette's hand away and eased himself out of his chair. Then, he stood up rather sheepishly.

'I have to use the netty,' he said, and quickly left the room.

As he did so, he heard Jimmy and Ralph chuckling.

'I win,' said Jimmy. 'I knew Frank would bottle it. That's three francs you owe me, Ralph – give one of them to Yvette for playing her part.'

Frank returned several minutes later and picked up his glass of beer.

'Time to make my way back to the billets,' he said as he drained the glass. 'I've had enough to eat and more than enough to drink.'

'Wait on, bonny lad,' said the others. 'You can see us safely home.'

All three got up and left the *estaminet*.

Frank, Jimmy and Ralph passed the town brothel reserved for officers on their return to their billets.

'I wonder if the platoon commander's dipping his wick in there,' joked Ralph. The others burst out laughing.

They walked on a little further down the road and passed two brothels serving other ranks, each displaying a red lamp outside it. There was a long queue leading from the front door in both cases. As Frank passed the second brothel, he came face to face with Corporal Dale.

'My God, Corp!' exclaimed Frank. 'Careful. You don't know what you might catch in that place.'

'Whey aye, man,' Dale replied. 'That's as maybe, but in the meantime, I will enjoy myself.'

\*

'Well, lads, do you fancy another night out in the town?' asked Ralph the following day. 'I think that we should finish off our break in style. I fancy having a few beers first and then joining a queue under one of the red lights we passed yesterday. Who wants to join me?'

At first, Frank was a little reluctant. He looked questioningly at Jimmy, who shrugged and nodded. Frank hesitated still.

'Come on, Frank, man,' encouraged Ralph. 'The Three Musketeers and all that.'

Frank still wavered. His mind started to churn.

*Maybe I should go. What if I'm killed tomorrow? I've still never been with a woman – I'm still a virgin. I don't want to die one – that I do know.*

'Come on, Frank, man,' Jimmy chirped in. 'What's the

problem? Surely, you're not saving yourself until the next time you get to see Marie again. That may never happen, bonny lad!'

'But, Sybil—'

'Oh, Frank, man,' Jimmy interrupted rather impatiently. 'She's given you the heave-ho, hasn't she? You've not heard back from her since you wrote to her, have you?'

Frank still procrastinated, half wanting to go, half scared to do so.

'I'd like to join you, Ralph, but I'm almost skint,' replied Frank.

'Well, that's soon sorted, Frank, man. I'm up a couple of francs from Ralph thanks to you last night,' said Jimmy. 'Happy to treat you if needs be.'

'Looks like I will be the one who will have paid for it,' laughed Ralph.

Frank realised that there was little he could do. Peer pressure was a very powerful persuader.

'All right then,' he said. 'The Three Musketeers it is.'

'Hurrah – all for one and one for all, then!' exclaimed Ralph. 'Let's get on down to town after tea. We need to get to the knocking shop early. It opens at half past six, and judging by what we saw last night, there will be a great long queue well before opening time.'

The three young soldiers returned to the *estaminet* they had visited the previous evening. They had a glass of beer each, after which they made their way back to the *maison tolérée*.

When they arrived, around fifty men were already waiting for opening time, singing raucously outside the front door.

> "*Three German Officers crossed the Rhine, parlez-vous*
> *Three German Officers crossed the Rhine, parlez-vous*
> *Three German Officers crossed the Rhine*

*To fuck the women and drink the wine,*
*Inky-dinky parlez-vous…"*

'Good God!' exclaimed Ralph as the three men joined the queue. 'It's like finding yourself in the crowd going to a match just before kick-off at Roker Park.'

'Hey, Franky, you're a clever man,' said Jimmy in a break in the singing. 'Why do you think that the lasses came to work here? For sure, none of them will be "amateur girls". It beats me why they do what they do when they're likely to end up with the pox, or pregnant.'

'I guess that most of them are there out of financial necessity. You know what I mean. Their husbands are dead, they've got children to feed, and no possible chance of other employment. The truth is that where there are soldiers, pimps quickly follow. Some of the locals took up prostitution. The pimps brought others in.'

'Whey aye, man,' Ralph chirped. 'This is all a bit too deep for me. I just need a bit of female comfort in more ways than one.'

The red lamp over the doorway lit up precisely on time. That was the starting signal for a near stampede by sottish-faced soldiers who had been waiting. They whooped and shouted as they charged through the door.

'Steady on! Steady on!' shouted Frank as he was caught somewhat off balance by the surge forward of the soldiers and almost knocked over.

By the time Frank had recovered his balance and found Jimmy and Ralph again, they were in another queue that stretched across a dimly lit hallway, up the flight of stairs leading to a landing. A huge pall of tobacco smoke was already forming, and the whole area was starting to take on a powerful whiff of body odour and bad breath.

'At the rate of six minutes at a time, Frankie, man, we'll be meeting our ladies in about an hour and a quarter,' joked Jimmy as he produced a bottle of red wine that he'd brought from the *estaminet*. 'Have a swig while we're waiting.'

'Thanks,' replied Frank.

He took a drink from the bottle and handed it back before taking out a pack of Woodbines and offering it to Jimmy.

'Tab?' he asked.

'Thanks, Frank,' he replied, taking a cigarette from the pack and lighting it. He inhaled the cigarette smoke deeply, giving his lungs the nicotine they had been craving.

'Drink, bonny lad?' he said, offering the wine bottle to Ralph.

A group of soldiers behind them resumed their song from earlier.

A rendition followed of *When This Lousy War is Over No More Soldiering for Me* and a never-ending selection of trench songs until Frank finally walked through the second of four doors facing the landing.

He found himself in a gloomy room lit by a single small lamp on a bedside table. It stank of a mixture of body odour, garlic, smoke and intimacy, only very partially masked by cheap perfume.

'*Je m'appelle Françoise*,' a voice called out.

Frank could make out Françoise sitting on the edge of a bed in the middle of the room. As he got closer, he could see that she was probably in her mid-forties. She looked emaciated – but Frank reckoned that he must have looked far worse to her.

'Let me help you,' she said.

Françoise stood up, reached forward with her right hand, grasped Frank by the wrist and pulled him towards her. She took off his belt, undid the five buttons of his tunic top, took this off and placed it on a chair in the corner of the room. She then slid his braces over his shoulders. They fell to his waist.

'*Mon chéri*, how would you like me? On top? Underneath? From behind?'

Frank was speechless.

Françoise gave a cackle of a laugh.

'Ah... *oui... je sais... un vierge*! You are a virgin, yes?'

Frank remained speechless.

'*C'est bien*... that's good, *mon chéri*... my first one today,' Françoise said as she gently pushed Frank down on the bed. 'On top then... *Je crois.*'

Frank lay on his back and nervously manoeuvred himself back so that his head rested on the pillow. As he did so, Françoise undid his waist button and fly and eased down his trousers and underpants. She climbed onto the bed and knelt astride Frank before guiding him inside her as she lowered herself back onto him.

Once Frank was inside Françoise, she placed her hands on his shoulders and gently rocked backwards and forwards. Frank groaned as he came shortly afterwards.

'Oh! *mon chéri*, you are such a wonderful lover,' she lied. 'I shall look forward to you coming back to me soon. For now, though, you must give me two francs, please.'

Frank dressed as quickly as he could, took two francs from his trouser pocket and paid Françoise. Afterwards, filled with pangs of guilt and remorse, Frank went back down to wait for his friends. Once all together again, the three men returned to their billet. Jimmy immediately went to his kitbag and took out a small box.

'Here, Frank,' he said, handing Frank a small tub of calomel ointment. 'Go and have a good wash and make sure you use this.'

'What is it, Jimmy?' he asked.

'It's ointment – a disinfectant for use after sex,' was the reply.

'But I thought that places like that knocking shop were inspected regularly by the RAMC and permitted to work only if pronounced clear.'

'Yes, Frank, but a lot can happen in between inspections, can't it? Better safe than sorry, eh?'

\*

Frank was feeling better than he had done for a while as he held in his hand a letter that he had received from Sybil.

*Dearest Frank,*

*Thank you for your letter.*

*While thinking about how to reply to you, I received a letter from Emily. A letter prompted by you writing to her as well as me, but no matter.*

*I am still angry that you did not talk to me about meeting with Emily, especially since she asked you to – as she has explained. However, I do realise that I over-reacted after Izzy told me what she had seen. A rather silly moment of possessiveness on my part, I'm afraid – and regret.*

*The truth of the matter is that I long for your next home leave and to marry you as we planned on your final night before you returned to France. I can barely wait for your next leave and am already busy preparing my trousseau!*

*With all my love,*
*Your*

*Sybil*

On top of receiving the letter, the battalion were now back in reserve. Frank was out of harm's way, if only for a few days. First things first, though, Frank had just enjoyed the luxury of a bath and change of clothes. Then, to his horror, he noticed a small sore on his penis as he was drying himself.

'Good grief!' Frank gasped. 'Jimmy, man. Will you have a look at this for me?'

'Whey aye, Frankie, you're not trying to get fresh with us, are you?' replied Jimmy.

Frank didn't find Jimmy's reply amusing in the slightest.

'Don't be daft, man. I'm being serious here. There's something wrong with me, I'm sure.'

Jimmy grinned and went over to Frank.

'*Jesus!*' exclaimed Jimmy as he inspected Frank. 'Get over to the medical officer, man. I can't be certain, but I think you might have got a dose of the pox.'

Frank gasped, dressed as fast as he could, ran to Company Headquarters and reported in sick.

'Have you had sex in the past couple of weeks?' asked the medical officer once he had finished his examination of Frank.

'Yes, sir,' replied Frank, feeling a deep sense of shame.

'When?'

'During the recent four-day rest period, sir.'

'Where?'

'In the brothel, sir.'

'Bloody idiot! As we medics say – *Brevis voluptas mox doloris est parens* – *Short-lived pleasure is the parent of pain*! I'd put you down as someone who'd have known better, Dawson. But, unfortunately, I was wrong. It looks like your little visit to the brothel has left you infected with syphilis.'

Frank stood in shocked silence for a minute or two, a period of frenzy, guilt and fear.

*Oh, dear God, no! Sybil will finish with me for sure if she ever finds out! That's got to have been the worst two francs I've ever spent.*

\*

Frank had spent a couple of weeks being treated for and cured of syphilis. Embarrassing as his condition was, and however unpleasant its treatment, Frank was out of the front line for that time. Away from danger. He had dreaded returning to the front line, but he was now standing on the fire step in the torrential rain that cascaded down on him. The German artillery had already begun a barrage of indiscriminate shellfire on No Man's Land and the British communication trenches. Such a barrage invariably started in the first few hours of darkness when soldiers would be going on patrol or moving from the front line to the reserves.

That night, Frank had been detailed to go out into No Man's Land to dig an assault trench a hundred yards to the front of the British line. He waited with the other members of the digging party, soaked to the skin and freezing cold. He was in abject misery, shivering, while he continually shifted his weight from his left foot to the right and back again. But at least he was in the relative safety of the trench rather than out there in the open.

The German barrage lifted. Frank's heartbeat rocketed, and his stomach churned. He felt but managed to control an almost irresistible urge to urinate. Then the signal to move forward was given, and the digging party slithered over the parapet and began their move forward.

The ground between the front line and the assault trench was wet and slippery. Furthermore, there were shell craters everywhere. Everyone had to move with the greatest of care to avoid missing their footing and sliding down into one of the many deep craters dotted around. Each one was inevitably brimming with a cloying soup of mud, foul green water and detritus. Even so, Frank slipped and fell into a shallow shell hole, landing face down in the quagmire that filled it. Spitting out muddy water, he stifled a mouthful of obscenities. After all, he was about a hundred yards or so from the German front line. Everything was so still and quiet. Almost too quiet.

He climbed out of the shell hole and continued to move

forward. His stomach tightened. It felt as if it was twisting up inside of him. He looked anxiously about him to try and identify a point of cover if things were to go wrong – any point of cover. Finally, he noted a large, shallow but muddy shell hole as he passed by it.

*Not much – but better than nothing.*

Minutes later, heavy machine-gun fire poured onto the digging party, its intensity increasing every second. Simultaneously, the Germans began heavy shelling and trench mortar fire aimed at the party. Frank bolted towards the shell hole he had noted. He was not alone. Second Lieutenant Robinson, Frank's platoon commander, made it there just before him. They both lay in the muddy hole, with Frank hoping for the best and willing the artillery to retaliate on his behalf as bullets and shrapnel tore at the ground around him.

The two men crawled through the shell hole, trying to find an advantage point from which they could observe what was happening in front of him. However, it was impossible to do so without seriously risking life or limb. They settled back down under cover and lay there in silence until the enemy machine gun and artillery fire eventually stopped as dusk began to approach.

'Private, we'll just sit it out until nightfall and then work our way back,' said Robinson.

'Right you are, sir,' replied Frank.

The final embers of day flickered and died. Moonlight shone briefly through a rift in the clouds before it closed up. The sky then was absolutely black.

'All right, Dawson,' said Robinson. 'Time to go. We'll do this in stages. You drop back ten yards while I cover you. I'll come back to you while you cover me. We'll repeat that until we reach our lines. Got that?'

Frank gulped.

'Yes, sir,' he replied.

'Good. Off you go then.'

The two men pulled back as best they could, slithering and sliding through the thick mud, before dropping down into their own firing trench.

'Well done, Dawson,' said Robinson. 'I'm off to report to the company commander. You make your way back to your dugout. I'll catch up with you and the rest of the men later.'

In a dazed, mechanical way, Frank sat down on the fire step and watched Robinson disappear from view. As he did so, he was overwhelmed with a feeling of despondency and despair before a red mist descended. Frank sprang to his feet and, with the strength of frenzy, dashed his head and body relentlessly against the unyielding parados of the trench.

He fell back bruised, screaming and shouting indistinguishable words intermingled with noises more readily associated with a wild animal. Frank lay still, gazing up vacantly. Then, the red mist descended once more, and he threw himself at the parados a second time, sliding down it onto his knees. He remained there, pummelling the sandbags covering the wood that strengthened the parados, too demented to be still.

He moaned, groaned and screamed out foul and profane language before falling still, except for an incessant rolling and nodding of his head. He partially recovered his reason just before Robinson returned, accompanied by Corporal Dale.

Dale strode over to where Frank was kneeling.

'And just where the fuck have you been Dawson?' he barked. 'Mr Robinson and I have been looking for you everywhere!'

Frank pulled himself onto his feet, and came to attention.

'I can't go back. I can't go back,' he mumbled.

Dale's response was vehement and rapid.

'Get a grip, man!'

'I can't go back. I can't go back,' Frank muttered again.

'Corporal Dale,' said Robinson, 'I'm going to turn a blind eye to this for now. I'm heading off back to Company HQ, but get Dawson sorted out – sharpish.'

'Sir! Leave it to me,' replied Dale.

He grabbed Frank's arm, pulled him forward and made him sit down on the fire step.

'Put your head between your knees and take deep breaths,' Dale ordered.

It took a while, but gradually Frank fully recovered his composure.

'Thanks, Corporal,' he said as he stood up.

'It's Mr Robinson you should be thanking, laddie. I'd have had your guts for garters if it had just been me that found you. You can't just fucking well hide away somewhere every time you find yourself suffering from overwork, overstrain, weariness, or just because you're scared shitless. In my book, this is the second time you've fucked up in recent times when under fire. God help you if there's a third time! I'll likely fucking shoot you myself! Now get yourself back to your dugout, clean up and report back to me. I've just thought of a little job for you to do.'

# FOURTEEN
# *France, Christmas 1917*

I just didn't know what to do. Edward Bennion had written to ask me if I would like to spend a day with him in Boulogne. He was going on home leave for Christmas. The trouble for me was that it was less than two months since the horror of my trip to Paris-Plage with Jack Miller. I was habitually preoccupied with the feeling that I was powerless to stop thinking about what had happened. I had difficulty sleeping. It was almost impossible for me to sit still when I wasn't working.

I experienced frequent flashbacks, reliving that moment when Jack had grabbed me, forced a kiss on me, and groped me. I constantly imagined that he would come back and harm me again or that someone else might be lurking in the shadows waiting to accost me. I faced a constant dichotomy; I was afraid of being alone, yet I would go to great lengths to avoid people, places, things, or situations that reminded me of the assault.

Throughout, Sarah proved herself to be a true friend. She helped to arrange for me to return to my old hospital. She became an almost constant companion and confidante.

I showed her Edward's letter as we sat in the Mess having breakfast.

'What should I do?' I asked.

Sarah read the letter, then leant forward towards me.

'Not all men are like Miller, Emily,' she said softly. 'You can't let him, and the likes of him, beat you down. So the first question you have to ask yourself is whether Edward is like Miller in any way.'

I rested my chin on my hand and thought before leaning back and looking up at Sarah.

'No, he's not,' I replied.

'Are you sure about that?'

I knew the answer to that question without thinking about it.

'Yes, I'm sure. Edward has never said or done anything to make me doubt him.'

'And how do you actually feel about him yourself?'

'I think I feel the same now as when I first met him. Then, when we parted, my silent wish was: *I very much hope that we will meet again*.'

'There you are, then, Emily,' Sarah consoled, reaching out and patting my shoulders. 'Meet him in Boulogne. I have a plan for how to go about it. I'll catch the train from Étaples to Boulogne with you, and we'll meet Edward together. After that, we'll all have a cup of coffee at the Hôtel Maurice. Then, if you're happy to continue on your own with Edward, I'll leave you together and go on a shopping tour of Boulogne. You and I can arrange to meet up again later and return to Étaples together. If you're not happy to continue on your own with Edward, I'll stay with you for as long as you want me to – whether that may be five minutes or until he leaves for his ship to England.'

*

There was a distinct spring in my step as Sarah and I set off briskly towards Étaples Railway Station. It was a cold day, but the sun shone brightly in a cloudless sky. A train to Boulogne was waiting when we arrived, and we boarded and sat down.

'It never ceases to amaze me how uncomfortable these train seats are,' I sighed as I shifted back and forth, trying to get comfortable.

'I agree. Fortunately, the journey is not that long – although long enough considering we're only going about fifteen miles. So tell me, Emily, how are you feeling?'

'Nervous, for sure, but a little excited,' I replied, picking at a loose thread on the sleeve of my jacket. 'If things do turn out all right between Edward and me, have you any plans for what shopping you may like to do?'

'Oh, I never actually make any plans when I go shopping,' Sarah chuckled. 'I'm a typical "grazer", you know what I mean? From shop to shop and then counter to counter. However, I need to get a few small Christmas gifts and maybe treat myself to something.'

'Something like what?' I chuckled.

'Well, I did find a rather nice hat shop the last time I was in Boulogne. I resisted the temptation to buy a hat then, but maybe not this time.'

We continued to discuss shopping and the shops that were our particular favourites until the train edged into Boulogne Station and, clanking and hissing steam, came to a shuddery stop.

As I got down from the railway carriage, I looked down the platform. Given Edward's height, I knew that it wouldn't be too difficult to see him, and sure enough, I soon spotted him standing almost a head and shoulders above most of the maelstrom of people around him. He must have seen me too and was hurrying towards me. As he drew close, I put out my hand to shake his. He took hold of it gently, raised it to his lips and kissed it lightly.

He realised that I was not alone. A warm, almost girlish

blush momentarily coloured his cheeks at first before turning to a bright scarlet. He closed his eyes, took a deep breath, held it in, and looked up to the sky.

'Forgive me. I didn't realise you were travelling with a colleague.'

Sarah laughed loudly.

'A colleague, yes, the VAD uniform is certainly a giveaway, isn't it?' she said. 'I'm Sarah Nugent.'

Edward held out his hand.

'I'm Edward Bennion,' he said.

'Well, why don't we all go to the Hôtel Maurice for some coffee and a catch-up,' I said, rehearsing Sarah's earlier suggestion.

We headed towards the hotel and found a table close to a roaring log fire in the hotel reception area. Sarah and I sat down while Edward went to organise a pot of coffee.

'I think that I will be able to take this on my own, Sarah,' I said, as soon as Edward was out of earshot. 'That's if you're happy to make that tour of the shops.'

Sarah looked at me and grinned.

'I don't doubt that you'll be safe with Edward,' she replied. 'I'll slip away as soon as I've finished a cup of coffee. I'll come back here in a couple of hours. Good luck to you, dearest Emily.'

Edward and I watched as Sarah made her way to the hotel entrance and disappeared into the street, bound for the shops.

'Your friend seems very nice,' said Edward.

'That she is,' I replied, 'and she's become very important to me over the last month or so.'

I paused and took in a deep breath.

'I have a confession to make, Edward,' I said softly as I exhaled gently, 'I nearly didn't come to meet you today.'

Edward looked at me, his face paling.

'Why...?' he asked. 'Have I done something wrong... something to upset you?'

'No, you haven't – It's nothing to do with anything you've said or done.'

'Then, what?' he asked, his head angled down.

I felt very uncomfortable. I struggled to think of the right words to say.

*How can I explain…? It's all so difficult…*

Edward looked up at me, breathing slowly and heavily, but said nothing.

Occasionally sobbing, occasionally mumbling, sometimes expressing anger, I gradually explained what had happened in Paris-Plage; how what had happened had devastated me.

Edward rubbed the back of his neck and sighed.

'I'm so sorry, Emily. Perhaps I should go,' he said, getting out of his chair. 'I wouldn't want to be someone who caused you further hurt and upset.'

At that moment, I knew that I had not been wrong to travel to Boulogne to see Edward again. He was certainly not like Jack Miller – undoubtedly, he was not Jack Miller. I reached forward, touched his hand and looked him straight in the eyes.

'Hush, Edward. Perhaps you are meant to be the one to help me through all that has happened. I know we have only been out together once before, but I really enjoyed being with you then, and your letters have been a constant source of hope and happiness for me. Of course, I can't forget and will probably never forgive Jack Miller for what he did and what he has put me through, but I'm sure that I can trust you. You are certainly nothing like him.'

Edward smiled, the corners of his mouth upturned, and with crow's feet wrinkles forming around the corners of his eyes.

'Enough of this mawkishness,' I said before he could say anything. 'Let's change the subject – no, let's have a change of scenery. Why don't we finish our coffee and go and get some fresh air? Do a bit of window shopping, perhaps. We just need to be back here in about an hour and a half unless we meet up with Sarah in town before then.'

Without any demur from Edward, we left the Hôtel Maurice and headed towards the main shopping centre. I led the way into a side street where a perpetual market was being held. There were husbandless women and fatherless children with hungry faces, sad faces, pale faces and endless pushing and jostling around the costermonger barrows. Finally, I spotted Sarah in the distance, emerging from a milliner's shop, and called out to her. When we caught up with her, I could see from her rather red face that something had upset her.

'You look like you've lost sixpence and found a farthing,' I said.

Sarah looked at me with a half-smile.

'Don't you dare laugh,' she replied. 'I bought a hat from that shop, but after leaving, I decided I had made a mistake and went back to change it. *Madame* in there refused to take it back. There was no consolation for me when I told her she would never enjoy my custom again. I still have the hat! Here, look.'

As Sarah took the hat out of its box, I couldn't help but chuckle. The hat was not to my taste and did not suit her either. She, too, began to chuckle.

'I suppose that I could always offer it for the Christmas jumble sale at the church,' she joked.

'Did you manage to buy anything else?' I asked.

'As it happens,' Sarah replied rather cheerfully, 'one of the larger shops had a rather attractive bargain table at one end of an aisle. It contained many nice, useful items that I thought would make ideal Christmas presents to give to friends at the hospital. Little cakes of scented soap, lacquered boxes of hairpins, and so on. So, I bought a few things.'

'Has your shopping expedition given you an appetite by any chance? Lunch, maybe?' Edward chipped in.

'Typical man,' I joked. 'Thinking of his stomach before anything else.'

Sarah and I looked at one another.

'Come on, Sarah, it seems that a cup of coffee is not enough for Edward – but I guess he still has a long journey ahead of him. If it's not too much of the same surroundings, let's head back to the hotel. They do a decent lunch there.'

We soon arrived back at the Hôtel Maurice and commandeered a table that offered a view of the street outside. Poor Edward found himself subjected to intense interrogation by Sarah and me about his forthcoming leave, both before ordering and during the meal.

How I envied him. I had no chance of Christmas at home, yet he would be sitting at home with his parents, tucking into Christmas lunch with all the trimmings, sandwiched between trips to the pub with his father and visits to friends and other family members. He would also have the joy of seeing in 1918 in the comfort of his own home. He would be a universe away from the horrors of war manifest in the wards at Étaples.

All too soon, it was time for Edward to head off to his ship. Sarah took her leave and discreetly went to powder her nose, leaving Edward and me to say goodbye.

'Thank you for seeing me today, Emily. I realise that it must have been challenging for you. I could fully understand if you didn't want to see me again.'

I tilted my head slightly to the side and smiled at him.

'It's not that I wouldn't want to see you again, Edward,' I said as reassuringly as I could. 'You've become a friend – and I do need friends. It's just that what happened with Jack Miller is still raw. So I'm glad I came today. Before, I didn't think I could ever trust a man again, especially during a war that can often expose humans' latent savagery in its basest form – but now I know I can. But let's wait and see. As the saying goes: *Que sera, sera*.'

# FIFTEEN

## *France, Spring 1918*

It was coming towards the end of the morning stand-to, and Frank and Jimmy were standing side by side on the fire step with rifles fully loaded and bayonets fixed. It was very misty across No Man's Land, and Frank could hardly see anything to his front on the few occasions he peered through a gap strategically sculpted between the sandbags on the parapet.

Unusually, the battalion had not been subjected to the usual barrage of shelling across No Man's Land and British trenches that started at around dawn – the "morning hate" as it was known.

Frank turned to Jimmy.

'It's too quiet, bonny lad,' said Frank. 'I don't like it.'

'Fritz must be having a lie-in this morning,' Jimmy joked.

Frank wasn't laughing. He was becoming increasingly worried.

'I don't think so, Jimmy. That would be too much to ask for.'

'Come on, bonny lad. Think positively. I reckon we're in for a nice quiet day.'

No sooner had Jimmy finished speaking than Sergeant Bishop moved down the line, giving the order to don gas masks.

Not long afterwards, the enemy opened up a massive artillery barrage along the British front.

'It's funny how it goes sometimes,' Frank called across to Jimmy. 'As the saying goes – *he bites his tongue who speaks in haste* – and all that!'

The noise was deafening. The air filled with smoke which lit up like a vivid sunset each time a shell burst – a feast of fuchsia and orange. An increasing number of the shells fired by the Germans were gas shells, which produced an ever-thickening gas cloud. The mist, smoke and gas clouds mixed in with the morning mist, creating a near opaque fog that covered No Man's Land. To make matters worse, Frank's box respirator made it impossible for him to see the wire in front of where he was standing.

It was a terrifying time for Frank; shells were exploding all around his position, but he couldn't see anything. It would have been possible for the Germans to have launched a frontal attack at any time, and neither Frank nor anyone else in his trench would have been any the wiser.

The bombardment eased off, but the trenches were attacked by several German fighter aircraft, which began to strafe the ground with machine-gun fire. They also dropped bombs.

The German aircraft turned away and for a short while, all went quiet before the platoon came under further heavy artillery fire. High explosives and gas shells rained down on them.

It was an awful, gut-wrenching experience. Frank felt completely helpless. He knew that he was in constant danger while the shelling lasted – and in constant fear that the enemy would be on top of him as soon as it stopped.

For Frank, the bombardment was the last thing he needed or wanted. The longer it went on, the greater the sense of panic that welled up inside him. He started to shake. Then he heard Jimmy call over to him.

'Hang on in there, Franky, man. You and I are going to make

it, for sure. We're bound to get out of this together. So just stick with me, bonny lad. From now on, we'll go wherever we're told to – together.'

Frank really appreciated what Jimmy had said to him. Jimmy really was his mate – his best friend.

'Thanks, Jimmy,' Frank replied. 'I was beginning to lose it there for a moment.'

Deep down, though, there was a depth of fear, which he knew that he must conquer.

*Get hold of yourself!*

As Frank gradually overcame his fear, his heartbeat slowed. There was still an empty feeling in the pit of his stomach, his heart was pounding, but he had stopped shaking. Then his sense of panic subsided. He was back in control of himself again. He felt that he could face anything the Germans might throw at them with Jimmy by his side.

*

During the following day's stand-to, the platoon came under heavy machine-gun and artillery fire. The ground was again covered with a thick mist. However, the barrage lifted shortly after it began and enemy soldiers started to emerge, ghost-like, through the smoke and haze and pressed forward. The platoon opened fire in rapid-fire, sending out a hail of bullets. The noise of battle was relentless. From what Frank could see, the battalion appeared to be taking heavy casualties.

At that point, Lieutenant King gave the order to make a fighting retirement, and they all pulled back. Things got pretty hectic after that. The battalion became fragmented. Eventually, Frank and Jimmy found themselves in a wooded area with King, a sergeant, a corporal and about a dozen other men from various companies from the battalion.

King gave orders to pull back to Croisilles Switch North. They were to make a covered withdrawal, which involved crossing about two hundred and fifty yards of open ground. King divided the group into three sections. Frank and Jimmy were ordered to join the section commanded by the corporal.

King's group moved back section by section for about fifty yards before forming into a line again. As Frank's section got up to move for a second time, Jimmy was a couple of yards or so in front of Frank. He was hit as he turned to look back at Frank. He screamed out and pitched forward.

'Sweet Jesus, no!' Frank cried out in anguish.

Without thinking, he rushed towards Jimmy, who was lying face down just in front of the shell hole he had been occupying just before he had got up to move forward. Frank dragged Jimmy into a nearby shell hole and turned him over onto his back. He was still alive but very badly hurt. He had been shot in the stomach and part of his intestines were protruding through a gaping wound.

'Jimmy, man, Jimmy,' Frank cried out, despairingly.

Frank tried to make Jimmy as comfortable as possible, but each time he did so, Jimmy screamed out in pain. Frank reached inside the front left skirt of Jimmy's tunic and pulled out the field dressing pack he was carrying. Frank tore open the pack, took out the dressing and applied it to Jimmy's wound.

*I've got to keep Jimmy warm.*

Frank unbuckled his webbing, took off his own tunic and covered Jimmy's chest with it. Once he had done this, Frank looked back over the edge of the shell hole. He could make out the Germans pushing forward from the wooded area he had left. They were heading towards the trenches King's group had been trying to reach. Frank decided to lie still there until it got dark and then endeavour to make it back to Croisilles Switch North.

Frank lay down, placed his arm under Jimmy's head and

cradled him. He looked at Jimmy, who was now deathly pale and whose breathing was becoming increasingly shallow.

'Stay with me, marra. Please stay with me,' Frank pleaded, but to no avail. Jimmy died just before dusk.

Frank felt as if the bottom had fallen out of his world at that moment. He felt numb. He was in a state of complete disbelief. Lost. Frank cradled Jimmy into his chest and held him for what seemed an age. Then he realised that he had to get back to the platoon. First, though, he had to lay Jimmy to rest.

Frank picked up his tunic and webbing and put them on. After that, he used his entrenching tool to scrape a narrow grave for Jimmy and laid him in it. He covered Jimmy's body with earth from the shell hole as best he could. Frank took the magazine and bolt out of his rifle and threw them as far away as possible. He then drove the rifle into the ground as a marker. After that, Frank placed his helmet on top of the rifle.

*

Later that night, Frank peered out at the surrounding area. As far as he could see, the coast was clear, so he eased himself out of the shell hole and crawled away, keeping as close to the ground as possible. It soon became apparent that any German attackers had moved on, presumably pursuing the battalion as it pulled back. At that moment, Frank pulled himself up into a crouch and edged westwards in the direction he believed the battalion had probably taken. He dropped down into suitable cover every now and again, either because he detected enemy patrol activity or to rest while he carefully surveyed the area.

Frank knew that he would only be able to move under cover of darkness. His first priority, therefore, was to get as far away from where he had left Jimmy and find somewhere to hide through the coming day before dawn broke.

Eventually, Frank hit a railway line and followed it northwest until he reached the railway station at Boyelles. He found suitable cover where he could hole up until night fell again. He surreptitiously refilled his water bottle at the railway station. He still had some hardtack in his pouches and ate half of this, washed down by the water, before settling down for the day.

Frank left his position at about ten o'clock that night and made his way into Boyelles, where he saw some men from the Irish Guards who were on their way up to the sugar factory situated in the town.

'Alreet, bonny lad,' Frank called out to the first one he saw. 'Can you help me?'

A look of surprise shot across the face of the guardsman, and he raised his rifle and pointed it at Frank.

'Steady, man,' Frank shouted out. 'I'm British. My name is Dawson. I got separated from my battalion and am trying to find them.'

'Come a bit closer, mate – very slowly,' the guardsman called back.

Frank edged forward.

'All right, mate, hold it just there,' he said as Frank reached a point about five yards away.

The guardsman looked Frank up and down. As he did so, he gradually lowered his rifle.

'God – you look like a bleeding scarecrow!' the guardsman exclaimed. 'Where's your rifle and helmet?'

Frank explained what had happened and that he was desperate to find his unit; the last thing he wanted was to be thought of as a deserter. Not only that, he had a score to settle; Jimmy's death had to be avenged.

Several other guardsmen came over, but none of them could help Frank.

'We've only just got here ourselves,' said one. 'We were sent here from Boisleux-Saint-Marc. We've spent the whole day being shunted from pillar to post by Boche machine-gunners supported by field guns. We're to go into huts in and around the sugar factory. You'd better come with us and see if there's anyone there you can report to.'

Frank went with the guardsmen, but no sooner had they arrived at the huts than the Germans began heavy shelling of the area. An enemy infantry attack seemed imminent, and the order was given for the guardsmen to withdraw to a nearby line of trenches. At that point, Frank decided to resume his search for his battalion elsewhere.

'You might want to head towards Boisleux-Saint-Marc,' one of the guardsmen suggested. 'You never know – someone there may be able to help you, which doesn't look at all likely here.'

'Thanks. I'll give it a try,' replied Frank.

With that, he headed northwest.

\*

Frank arrived in Boisleux-Saint-Marc after dark the next day. It seemed to be teeming with men from various regiments of the Guards Division. At first, he didn't quite know what to do but eventually approached a small group of men from the Welsh Guards who appeared to be heading towards a line of former German trenches. As was the case the previous day, Frank told them who he was and the name of his unit. He asked them if they could help him find them, but they couldn't.

Frank was at a loss to decide what to do next.

*Do I press on? Should I try and find an officer and report to him?*

'You're welcome to stay with us for a while,' invited one of the guardsmen while Frank was cogitating. 'You never know – there may be someone around who can help.'

The suggestion seemed a sound one to Frank, but he had concerns.

'Thanks,' replied Frank. 'But my great worry is that someone might think that I'm a deserter from my own unit.'

'Don't be daft, boyo,' came the reply. 'If you're a deserter, why would you be here among all of us lovely boys? Surely, you'd be skulking away somewhere, avoiding all contact with anyone.'

*What he's saying seems to make sense. Have I really got anything to lose if I go along with his suggestion for now? I can always report to an officer if and when I meet one here.*

'Maybe you're right,' replied Frank. 'Hopefully, someone here can help – and I could use a bit of a rest.'

Frank remained with the men from the Welsh Guards throughout the day. It seemed strange to do nothing other than spend time with one group of guardsmen or another while they smoked cigarettes and swapped stories of their experiences in the trenches. Frank was able to buy something to eat at an *estaminet* which was permitted to open for an hour at midday. Eventually, he decided to head out again when it became clear to him that no one he met could help him find his own unit.

\*

Frank left as soon as darkness fell. This time, he followed the line of the River Sojeul until he arrived at the village of Boiry-Saint-Martin. However, much to his horror, the surrounding area through which he was travelling was under a heavy artillery bombardment. He was forced to dive from one piece of cover to another throughout the night, hoping and praying that no harm would come to him as he did so.

Somehow, Frank arrived safely on the outskirts of Boiry-Saint-Martin an hour or so before dawn. He found suitable cover and settled down before moving into Boiry-Saint-Martin after dusk that evening. On his arrival, Frank found the YMCA and went in, where he saw three soldiers sitting at one of the tables. He bought himself a cup of tea and a plate of egg and chips and went over to them.

'Alreet, friends,' he greeted the men. 'May I join you?'

'Of course, matey, make yourself comfortable,' replied one of them.

Frank explained his predicament, but none of the three could help him. While disappointed, Frank decided that it might be a good idea to base himself at the YMCA for a day or two in the hope of meeting someone who could help him.

'Save yourself a bit of money,' said one of the three men when Frank outlined his intention. 'Come and stay with us. We've set up camp in the woods nearby. It's quite comfortable and, more importantly, safe. We've been here a little while without having to face any danger – plus we're only a short walk from the YMCA here whenever we need to tend to our creature comforts.'

It seemed like a reasonable suggestion to Frank, so he went along with it, and later that evening, he went with the three men to a wooded area where they were occupying a somewhat dilapidated woodman's hut. One of the men lit a small fire, and Frank and his new-found colleagues stood around it smoking and chatting into the small hours before Frank took his leave and went into the hut. He made himself comfortable in one corner of it, using straw he found strewn over the floor to form a mattress. He took his webbing and tunic off and used these as a pillow. He lay down and fell asleep.

Frank enjoyed a decent night's sleep for the first time in a long while, not waking until after eight o'clock the following morning. When he did finally awaken, the three men were not around.

*They must have gone down to the YMCA for breakfast.*

He moved to the entrance of the hut and looked out towards Boiry-Saint-Martin. As he did so, an icy fear shot through his veins. He could clearly see the red cap of a military policeman striding towards the wooded area. A realisation flashed through his mind.

*The three men I'm with ARE deserters. I'm likely to be tarred with the same brush as them.*

Frank panicked and disappeared back into the hut. Barely moments later, the military policeman – a sergeant – came into the shelter.

'Well, who have we here, then?' he asked.

A startled Frank looked at him, wide-eyed.

'My name is Dawson, Sergeant. Private Dawson,' he mumbled.

'And, Dawson, what the fuck are you doing here?'

Frank could almost feel the colour drain from his face as he tried to explain what had happened. How he had become separated from his battalion, how Jimmy had died, and how he had been trying to find his unit. He became increasingly incoherent as almost gut-wrenching fear surged inside him.

'I don't believe you, laddie. I think that you're nothing more than a fucking deserter – a fucking coward!'

'No ... no,' Frank replied. 'The three men that were here with me last night will vouch for me.'

The sergeant lifted his shoulders up to his ears and opened out his arms.

'What three men? You're the only fucker here.'

Frank's stomach tightened. He felt sick. He made a move towards the hut entrance.

'Stay just where you are,' barked the sergeant.

'But there were three other men here with me last night. I just want to look to see if they are outside somewhere.'

'I've already told you that you are the only one here – there is no one else,' the sergeant replied, forcefully. 'Now, laddie, show me your paybook.'

'It's over there in my tunic pocket,' Frank whispered.

'Well, fucking go and get it then.'

Frank edged over to his tunic, picked it up, felt inside the breast pocket and pulled out his paybook, which he held out towards the sergeant. The sergeant did not look at it.

'Yeh… yeh,' he sneered. 'Right, get properly dressed, you're going back to the guardroom in Boiry-Saint-Martin for further questioning. Doubtless, my officer commanding will be interested to learn why you're here – and how you got here.'

Frank gasped, put on his tunic and webbing, and stood in front of the sergeant.

'Am I under arrest?' he croaked.

'Yes, you are, laddie. I have reason to believe that you are a deserter. Now let's get going – no monkey business on the way back, mind, or I'll drop you where you stand.'

# SIXTEEN

# *France, Spring 1918*

Sometimes, it is nice to feel wanted. Other times, it is not. Sarah and I had hoped that I would be allowed some leave and had asked Sister Bettsworth if there was any possibility of being allowed to visit home again. In turn, she saw Matron on our behalf and passed on her answer to us.

'I have some bad news for you, I'm afraid,' Sister told me. 'It's quite out of the question for you to go on leave just now. We are short-staffed, and you are both needed at the hospital. There is, though, some good news. You are first in the queue the next time leave is possible.'

My heart sank.

*Leave looks as far off as ever – perhaps the chance may not come for ages yet.*

But I was wrong.

Just a week later, and notwithstanding it was my day off, Sister called for me.

'I've good news,' she beamed. 'We will be getting three extra nursing staff in the next few days, which will relieve the staffing shortage. As a result, you may take a week's leave to start a week on Monday.'

I could scarcely believe my ears and had already started making plans for preparing to go on leave as I almost skipped back to my room. A trip to Paris-Plage was the priority for that morning. First, to get my hair washed and cut, and second, to buy gifts for Mam and Fatha. I quickly smartened myself up and then went to the tram stop.

When I arrived, my first port of call was to the Coiffure Anna Annick in the Rue de Paris. Unsurprisingly, I didn't have an appointment, but luckily, they could accommodate me at eleven-thirty, thanks to a late cancellation. I had time to do my shopping beforehand and have lunch afterwards. It would also allow me time to enjoy a couple of hours in the afternoon walking along the beach before returning to Étaples.

All went pretty much to plan to begin with. I quickly found an interesting shop offering a rather eclectic array of goods where I was able to buy the gifts I wanted, and my hair looked immaculate as I emerged from the Coiffure Anna Annick. But, unfortunately, the day, which had started so well, with clear blue skies and bright sunshine, now looked like ending with rain, as rather ominous-looking dark clouds rolled in from the northwest.

Deciding that discretion was the better part of valour, I chose to forgo the afternoon stroll along the beach. Instead, I would enjoy a quiet lunch and, to ensure my newly preened hair didn't fall foul of any downpour, I would indulge myself in the expense of a taxi ride back to the hospital. After all, I had to do everything I could to ensure I looked my best when I went home.

As things turned out, I had a most enjoyable lunch in a restaurant that looked out across the beach and then found a taxi. It was just as well that I did. It was raining stair rods long before I arrived back at Étaples.

# France, Spring 1918

*

Wild rumours had been flying around. The Germans, reinforced by thousands of troops now freed from fighting on the Russian Front, had launched a fierce attack and were advancing rapidly towards Albert, Amiens and Paris.

'We've learnt that there has been terrible carnage, with heavy British casualties,' Sister Bettsworth explained to all the medical staff in the ward. 'We have to ready ourselves for a mass influx of casualties starting today and continuing for... well... we don't know how long. Those of you who were in France during 1916 and 1917 will have some idea of what to expect.'

Sarah and I looked at one another with open mouths. At that moment, I knew what Sister was going to say next. I suspected that Sarah also did.

'I'm afraid that that can mean one thing only,' Sister continued. 'All leave is cancelled until further notice.'

This news was devastating and came just two days before I was due to return home and ten days before Sarah did so. However, there was little time to remain morose for any length of time. We had to get the wards ready.

'Harland and Nugent, get over to the dispensary immediately,' Sister directed. 'We'll need extra bandages, splints, cotton wool and gauze to be getting along with... oh, and iodine and eusol.'

No sooner had we returned to the ward than the first convoy of wounded arrived at the hospital. The ward began to fill up fast. It was a case of all hands to the pump again. By evening, no bed remained unoccupied. There were stretchers on the ward floor on which men dressed, or partly dressed, in muddy khaki were lying.

I bent down to attend to a young infantryman. His left leg had been blown off, All I could see was his thigh bone. He was conscious, but only just.

'Is there anything I can do?' I asked.

His eyes flickered towards me. He seemed strangely calm.

'Yes, please, Miss,' he whispered. 'Will you please straighten my legs?'

I did my best. I took his right foot and helped the soldier to rest it down flat. I could do nothing more than touch his left leg above the protruding thigh bone.

'Thanks, Miss,' he croaked. 'That feels so much better.'

'Is there anything else I can do?' I asked.

He closed his eyes briefly, then opened them and looked straight at me.

'Yes, Miss. Would you get me the photograph that's in my tunic pocket?'

I leant forward, undid the pocket and took out a photograph of a very attractive young woman, about the same age as me. Cradled in her arms was a baby. I went to hand the photograph to the soldier, but he was dead. Callous as it may seem, I replaced the photograph in the man's tunic pocket and moved to the next man.

Throughout the day and beyond, no one tidied the ward. My work never seemed to end. I worked my way from bed to bed, from bed to stretcher, and from stretcher to stretcher, doing whatever I could to tend to bullet and shrapnel wounds, smashed limbs bound to splints by filthy blood-stained bandages, and stumps where limbs had once existed before being blown off by an exploding artillery shell. Wounds hurriedly dressed at a casualty clearing station concealed stomach-churning visions, each awaiting me beneath a stinking wad of blood-sodden dressing packed around them. Often, in stretcher cases, a soldier's congealed blood glued him to the canvas, and I could only free him by cutting the material away. Unfortunately, there was little I could do for anyone other than to purify each wound with eusol and paint the surrounding parts with iodine before dressing it again with fresh cotton wool, gauze and a new bandage.

Convoys of men arrived. Some survived, and others died. Each survivor was hastily tended to and dispatched to another convoy, which transported him to a hospital ship and thence to Blighty. Those who died were taken from the ward, laid out after a fashion in another part of the hospital and then taken to Étaples Military Cemetery for burial.

Sister Bettsworth stood me down just after nine o'clock in the evening. The rush of work over two days had taken a heavy toll on me, and there seemed little chance of any slackening soon. I was exhausted. All I wanted was rest – utter, complete rest – so I went straight to bed.

Any chance of sleep, though, evaporated immediately. The sound of aircraft and anti-aircraft guns, apparently coming from the north of Étaples, shattered the evening quiet.

*Bombs! It can only be the sound of bombs!*

I shot up from my bed and ran outside the hut. I could see the flashes of anti-aircraft shells exploding in the distance, but little else. I could still make out the unmistakable mechanical whirring hum of aircraft engines. From what I could tell, the aircraft circled overhead until they headed off again. The noise of their engines dwindled until silence reigned again.

Around me, staff in various stages of dress were wandering about, anxiously chatting together. Then, finally, I caught sight of Sister Bettsworth and moved over to her.

'What do you think has happened, Sister?' I enquired.

'I'm afraid I don't know,' she replied, 'but it looks like the Germans have carried out a bomb attack on Étaples as part of all that is going on.'

One by one, we all drifted back to our rooms. In my case, I was trying to sleep before duty called again in the morning. In the event, I couldn't get back to sleep and ended up going for a walk around the compound that started just after dawn and continued until I joined Sarah in the Mess for breakfast.

I must have looked terrible, as Sarah gasped as I approached her.

'Good grief!' she exclaimed. 'For heaven's sake, sit down. I'll fetch you some tea and breakfast.'

'Just tea, pet,' I replied. 'I couldn't eat anything.'

'Nonsense,' Sarah chided. 'You're going to have a proper breakfast. We can't have you pass out in the ward because you haven't eaten.'

I smiled at her weakly, flopped down on a chair, and watched through bleary eyes as Sarah left to get my breakfast.

After a chaotic morning, I went to the Mess to get a cup of tea and enjoy a leisurely lunch. Sister had allowed us to take an extended lunch break. We did not have to report back until teatime, but we would be required to work until very late in the evening. As I entered the Mess Hall, I saw Sarah sitting at a table close to the tea trolley. I waved at her and moved over to her.

'Hello, Sarah,' I greeted as I reached her and sat opposite her. 'I fancy a walk after lunch. Do you want to join me?'

Sarah leant forward eagerly.

'Sounds like a great idea,' she replied. 'A bit of fresh air away from the ward would be just the tonic I need. How about going to look around the area where the bombs fell yesterday? Whatever else, it's a nice walk across the fields to the river and back even if we see nothing on the way.'

After finishing our lunch, we left the hospital and went across the green, downy countryside by the railway track to inspect any damage where the bombs had landed. As we went, I glimpsed budding trees that would soon burst into new life. I imagined golden cowslip bells and yellow buttercups permeating the various tints of green fields that swept up to the banks of the River Canche. Soon, a mantle of spring splendour would bedeck them all. But now, a sinister stillness hung like heavy fog upon the air.

We came across a crater. Then another. In each case, the

bomb creating it had upheaved the earth, flinging up masses of soil that had then become a chaos of tumbled earth around its lip. Subsoil lay scattered above the earth and grass in vast, sterile stretches of desolation. Then, finally, we found a third crater near the railway track.

'That's a bit of luck,' I exclaimed when I realised the bomb had narrowly missed damaging the railway line. 'Can you imagine the chaos if the bomb had exploded on the track? So many wounded are arriving at Étaples on ambulance trains.'

'Talking of wounded, we'd better start heading back to the hospital,' replied Sarah.

\*

I was exhausted. Ten days of working more than twelve hours a day often spent in operating theatres that were kept going day and night had taken its toll on me. I drifted wearily into the Mess for supper, expecting to hear the latest hair-raising rumour from the front. Sometimes, these originated from French families fleeing danger; sometimes, from medical staff evacuated out of casualty clearing stations. More often, they originated from the ever-increasing numbers of wounded arriving at the hospital. But almost invariably, they centred on the German advance, which appeared to be relentless.

I saw Sarah sitting with Florence Norgate and went over to join them.

'What's the latest news from the front?' I enquired.

'One corporal in the Sussex Regiment told me that Amiens has fallen,' replied Sarah.

'Yes, but someone else told me that it had been retaken,' chipped in Florence.

One of the orderlies at an adjacent table leant over.

'One of the sisters recently arriving from one of the evacuated casualty clearing stations said that Abbeville is on standby to make a complete and rapid evacuation.'

It was all so terribly depressing.

'We're very close to the front line. Are the Boche on their way here?' I asked.

'Who can say?' Sarah replied. 'I've heard a wounded officer say that we might now be about to lose the war.'

'Yes, and Matron seems certain that we, too, will soon have to get ready to leave. The Germans seem to be advancing all too quickly. So quickly, she believes, that we may all end up as prisoners of the Germans,' said a voice behind me.

I turned to see who had spoken. It was Sister Bettsworth. She came towards me carrying an envelope.

'Harland, this has arrived for you,' she said.

I took the envelope and looked at it with bleary eyes. At first, I couldn't quite make out the handwriting. I blinked hard, shook my head slightly, and gradually realised whose handwriting it was.

*The letter is from Edward!*

# SEVENTEEN

# *France, Spring 1918*

The hedges and trees bordering the fields were touched with that first shade of green that no artist has accurately captured. Men can paint many things, but the promise of the seasons escapes them; it is too subtle for a brush or a pencil. They may as well try to paint a whisper.

I looked down nervously at my watch for the third time in almost as many minutes. I had been on tenterhooks since I received the letter from Edward. I had read it and reread it. One particular paragraph kept racing through my mind.

> *I remember all too well how crestfallen I was when we last met. However, my feelings for you have never wavered. We have continued to exchange letters, and I have drawn comfort from the sentiments you have expressed in them. They have offered me hope. I shall be in Étaples for a couple of days and wondered if you would spend a little time with me when I am.*

After a great deal of soul-searching, I realised that I did want to see Edward again and agreed to do so, but with two provisos:

firstly, we would get away from Étaples; and secondly, we did not go to Boulogne.

As I approached the station, I could see Edward waiting outside. I caught my breath and exhaled in a series of short breaths as I got closer. He stood watching me, almost as if he was afraid to move towards me. Finally, as I reached a point a few feet away from him, I stopped and looked at him. As I did so, a panicked expression flittered across his face.

'Hello, Emily,' he said, holding his hand out to me.

I looked at him and smiled. Then, I squeezed his hand gently for a second or two before letting go.

'Hello, Edward. It's so nice to see you again.'

As we stood there silently, I could feel myself begin to relax.

'What treats have we got in store for today?'

To my surprise, and momentary concern, Edward told me that he had hired a small car for the day.

'I thought we might head towards Équihen-Plage with its beautiful beach and the Quartier des Quilles en l'air. It's definitely not Étaples — nor is it Boulogne.'

I felt a little rush of butterflies in my stomach, but this rapidly passed. Edward *was* a man I could trust.

'What's the Quartier des Quilles en l'air?' I asked.

'Wait and see,' replied Edward.

Our journey took us to Neufchâtel-Hardelot in the first instance. It certainly was a very picturesque place. On one side of the town was the sea, complete with a beautiful beach. On the other was a forest, where the daffodils were beginning to show. Several villas had been built around the tennis courts on the seafront. Edward parked the car and turned to me.

'This place looks lovely,' he said. 'How about having a look around?'

I was not that keen on the idea myself. I knew that while Neufchâtel-Hardelot was definitely not Étaples, it would be full of medical personnel and patients, as some of the villas and a hotel had been requisitioned when a general hospital had been established in the town the previous year. The villas were occupied by sick officers or used to billet nurses; the hotel housed administrative offices, the main theatre, acute surgical wards and a dispensary. Elsewhere, there was row upon row of tents.

'I'm not sure myself, Edward – the town is infinitely more attractive than Étaples, but there are so many reminders of it.'

Edward looked quizzical.

'In what way?'

'So many parts of the town are given over to the military,' I replied, 'but don't let me spoil things for you. Come on then, let's go for a walk, but avoid the town.'

We started to walk across the sand dunes. The only problem for me, though, was that there were a large number of patients also congregated on the beach. While most of these were predominantly skin cases, I needed a break from an environment populated by patients.

I stopped and turned towards Edward.

'I'm really sorry about this, but would you mind terribly if we continued to Équihen-Plage now? I don't need an almost constant reminder of my work in the wards.'

\*

Équihen-Plage seemed to me like a village in a children's story. Sitting on top of a clay cliff, it looked out over a large beach populated with small coves. There was nothing unusual in that regard. Nor was there anything unusual in the collection of fishing boats lined up on the beach. The fishermen had dragged up *harenguiers* and *flobarts* after returning with the daily catch of herrings and mackerel. However, what was unusual were the dwellings crafted by the poorest villagers. These consisted of the upturned hulls of abandoned boats. They were planted on the hillside on the heights overlooking the sea. From afar, they looked like mussels lining the beach rocks – thanks to the pitch paint used to seal the bottoms of the boats.

Edward parked the car, and we climbed out. I looked about me in wonder.

'This place is a Wonderland!' I exclaimed.

Edward looked at me and laughed.

'I thought you might like it,' he replied.

'Come on. Let's explore!' I called to him gleefully as I ran off.

Edward followed and caught me up, and we started to walk along the coastal path.

'They tell me that this path was well trodden by excisemen and smugglers,' Edward explained as we went.

'Smugglers – and not men from ambulance trains on moonlight working?' I asked jokingly.

Edward let out a joyful chuckle.

'No, no, Emily, I can assure you that any smugglers were not men from ambulance trains.'

I could see a flight of steps that led down to the beach.

'How about a detour?' I asked. 'It looks like we can get down those steps and walk along the shore.'

'You lead, I'll follow,' replied Edward.

*Just as well*, I thought. I had already started to descend the steps.

As we continued our walk, we could see people hunting out shellfish among the rocks. Resisting the urge to join them, we continued towards the Plage de Ningles, where a waterfall tumbled onto the beach. We watched the water cascading down for a short while before turning back towards Équihen-Plage.

I was intrigued by the *flobarts* with their wide bows and flat sterns that allowed two men to push a boat with their backs by bracing themselves to slide it on logs placed on the beach.

'Rather different from anything I've ever seen at Alnmouth back home,' I said.

'And a world away from anything I've seen in Dulwich Park,' replied Edward, with a broad grin.

We walked around several of the boats before Edward suggested we try to find somewhere to get some lunch.

'That sounds like a good idea,' I replied, 'but do let's look at the boathouses on our way. Everything seems to be going on around them.'

Trying not to stare, I watched women in black mid-calf-length dresses with an apron tied at the waist, a shawl, thick woollen stockings and clogs, all of them hard at work. They were washing baskets of mussels or scaling and cleaning herring.

'Just watching them is exhausting!' I exclaimed.

'And seeing the mussels and herring reminds me that I'm starving,' laughed Edward.

'All right – all right – lead on, Edward.'

We found a quiet café and took up residence for lunch and a tête-à-tête.

We studied the menu, concluding that there could only be one dish for us, *moules à la crème*, to be washed down with a glass of cider.

'In all probability, they'll just run over to the women we've just seen to get the mussels,' I joked.

The cider arrived. Edward raised his glass.

'Here's to more days like today, and to you, Emily, for helping make it special.'

I looked away and then back at Edward. In truth, I was a little lost for words – but I was just beginning to realise how much I was drawn to him.

*Yes, today has been rather special – so far. Let's hope it continues.*

As Edward and I tucked into our *moules à la crème*, I noticed that above his left tunic pocket was a dark blue ribbon with three white and two red centre stripes. I pressed my hand to my throat.

'You never told me you had been awarded the Military Medal,' I blurted out. 'That'll give all those who ever doubted you back home something to think about.'

Edward blushed.

'Oh, that,' he said. 'That was something I received for just doing my job – helping bring in the wounded.'

I looked at him, slightly aghast at his response.

'But you must have done more than that.'

Edward gave a half-shrug.

'My train was under a heavy shell and gas attack; nothing more. So I just got on with my job. What else was I to do? I'm sure there are others elsewhere who were and are far more deserving. But let's change the subject.'

'All right – in that case, you can do something you still haven't done. You can tell me about *Edward Bennion*, the person.'

Edward paused, took a deep breath, and began to talk about his life before the war and himself for the first time. He spoke in a calm, relaxed voice, his words drawn-out and low.

'I live in what I regard as a truly wonderful part of the world. It's near Sydenham Hill, not that far from the Horniman Museum. Dulwich Village, Dulwich Gallery and Dulwich College are nearby. London's West End is only a short train ride away, as is London Bridge. That is where I worked before joining the FAU. We've got a very nice house in a place called Rowland Grove. Number fifteen. It's where I was born.'

*Geographic details are fine, Edward, but I need to know about you; your family.*

'What about your family?' I interrupted.

'My father, Peter, is in partnership with a cousin of his. They are carmen and contractors. I had three brothers. Two older than me, one younger. They all enlisted in the Army in 1915, but the youngest, Les, was killed at the Somme in 1916. That hit my parents hard. After all, the youngest of the family is second only in importance to the eldest. The fact that my brothers had enlisted and I didn't made matters worse for me at the time – and still does. No one seemed to understand, and still doesn't, that, in many Quaker families, some siblings served at the front while others joined the FAU.'

'What about your mother?'

'Like my father, she was born near St James' Church in Croydon. Her parents came from Peckham.'

I was on a roll now. Finally, Edward was opening up as I had hoped he would. But there were still things I wanted to find out about him.

'Where did you go to school?'

I think that Edward could see where I was going and was anticipating the direction of any further questioning.

'I went to Sydenham School until I was fourteen. After that, and before you ask,' he said with a twinkle in his eye, 'I worked with my father for a while but later took a clerical job with George Vickers Limited.'

'Who are George Vickers Limited, and what do they do?' I asked, never having heard of them before.

'They're publishers,' Edward replied. He paused. As he did so, the corners of his mouth curled up in a broad grin. 'As a Jarrow escapee,' he continued, 'you may not have heard of it, but their best-known publication was the *London Journal*, which first appeared in the middle of the last century.'

\*

The afternoon flew by. All too soon for me, we had arrived back at the entrance to the hospital. Before I got out, I leant in towards Edward and kissed him lightly on the cheek.

'Thank you for a lovely day, Edward,' I said. 'Especially Équihen-Plage – and I now know that *Quilles en l'air* means "keels in the air", and why it does. I hope I can see you again before too long.'

Edward got out of the car, came round to my side and opened the door. He took my hand and helped me out, and I stood up and faced him. Edward did not let go of my hand. Instead, he raised it to his lips, and as I lifted my head, he gently kissed my forehead. A shiver of excitement passed through my whole body. Somewhat surprised, I gasped and took a half-step backwards.

'I'm sorry,' Edward whispered, letting go of my hand.

'Please don't be,' I replied. 'I just wasn't expecting that.'

I took his hand and faced him as I was speaking. He stared at me. A gentle evening breeze swept softly over our faces as he slowly bent his head towards me. I smiled faintly. My heart was beating, half in trepidation, half in anticipation. It was so new and sweet. Then his lips met mine. My brain started to fizzle.

He gently guided me towards him, gathered me in his arms and kissed me. I lay my head on his shoulder and turned my face towards his. I felt his breath on my cheek. I sighed, a sigh of joy and contentment. I had always understood that life takes unexpected twists and turns, sometimes the result of making a deliberate choice, sometimes through happenstance. But, until that moment, I hadn't realised what it felt like to meet a person and know without a doubt that the whole part of my life until then – every twist of fate along the way – was just a journey to get to that person. Now, I knew that Edward was mine and I was his. Now, I realised that I had fallen in love with him and would give myself to him if he asked.

# EIGHTEEN

# *France, Spring 1918*

As the newly appointed brigade chaplain, Henry Sheldon had several battalions to minister to, plus many other units and arms. All of them were scattered across an extensive area. Today had been the first opportunity he had had to officially report to the brigade commander. Not that the meeting had yielded anything of real note. Most of the time spent had been given over to a rant by the brigadier about the accommodation occupied by him and the Brigade Headquarters staff. Eventually, though, the conversation turned to Henry's duties.

'You'll have to spread yourself pretty thinly, Padre,' the brigadier warned. 'One other thing, and by way of a heads-up, I am not a great admirer of army chaplains. In my opinion, they should only be seen in the trenches if and when asked to do so. At best, they should be found in first aid posts or at coffee stalls for the walking wounded – in either case, at the rear of the trenches. Generally, though, I expect them to only carry out duties more consistent with their calling.'

Henry winced. The brigadier's attitude was one he had experienced before, all too often.

'I'm sorry to hear that, sir, but with respect, your view runs contrary to my own. I believe I have a role to play at all times, be it behind the front line or as close as possible to the men on the front line. I'm no Woodbine Willy, but I share his view that it is a betrayal of the men we are supposed to support if we aren't in the thick of it with them.'

The brigade commander looked at Henry and raised his eyebrows.

'I admire the sentiment, but I remain unconvinced that the men in the brigade necessarily welcome a chaplain in their midst.'

'I am convinced that they do, sir,' replied Henry.

'Well, we shall see, Padre. In the meantime, we have a church parade this Sunday. I hope I can look forward to hearing a thought-provoking sermon from you – not one like some of those I heard from at least one of your predecessors.'

'I'll do my best,' Henry replied. 'I learnt my lesson about church parades and sermons a while ago when a soldier spoke with me after one church parade. "Forgive me for saying this, Padre," he said, "but these church parades are all a fucking joke. First, they take us out of the trenches for a rest. Then they tell us we've got to attend a church parade, where some fucking Bible-basher like you tells us we've got to turn the other cheek – then fuck me, the next day they send us back up to the trenches again with orders to kill like there is no such thing as tomorrow." It struck me then just how right he was.'

The brigadier looked around his office with seeming indifference and then to Henry.

'Well, I guess the man may have had something there,' he said in a markedly bored tone. 'Well, off you go then, Padre. I dare say you've got one or two things to do between now and Sunday.'

Henry gritted his teeth.
*Pompous arse. I can see that you and I are going to get on!*
'Indeed, sir,' he replied, saluted, left the brigadier's office and immediately headed towards the trenches. He knew that an advance was to take place the following morning.

\*

It was zero minus ten. The battalion were formed up in the fire trench, waiting nervously. Henry was making his way along the firing line, trying to exchange a few friendly words with men enduring the stress and anxiety in front of an advance. As he did so, he could hear someone say, 'Here comes that bloody God-botherer. I wish the bastard would fuck off back to wherever he came from.'

Henry couldn't see who had spoken, but he would not let things pass.

'Yes, here I come – yes, I am also a bloody Bible-basher,' he shouted back, 'but I have no intention of going anywhere just yet. So get used to the idea!'

Precisely at "zero", whistles sounded, and Henry watched as the men climbed into No Man's Land in near daylight. He took a trench periscope and, standing on a fire step, continued to watch them as they advanced steadily, heading for the enemy line in extended order. However, they appeared to be in full view of the enemy's machine guns and snipers, who immediately opened fire on them.

Many advancing troops were killed or wounded before they went fifteen yards. Soldiers dropped down everywhere. Henry saw an officer fall forward in a heap before he had moved forward thirty yards. At first, Henry thought that the officer was dead, but he crawled a dozen yards to his front and slid down into a shell hole.

Henry watched, feeling helpless, as the attack ground to a halt and the men pulled back. The survivors struggled and scrambled their way back into their fire trench. Henry stacked the periscope against the trench wall and hurried to give what help he could to the returning soldiers. He remained there for the remainder of the day, readying himself for when it would be safe for the stretcher-bearers to go out into No Man's Land and recover the wounded and dead.

As daylight surrendered to darkness, Henry was standing on the fire step. Above, a pale moonlight was obscured from time to time by scudding clouds. He watched a steady stream of pairs of men with a stretcher between them as they eased over the parapet and out into No Man's Land. A shot rang out as one of the pairs began to climb out of the trench, and one of the stretcher-bearers screamed out and slithered backwards. Henry sprinted towards the fallen man without a second thought and joined the surviving stretcher-bearer.

'Come on, man,' he shouted. 'No time to lose!'

The pair worked tirelessly backwards and forwards, retrieving one wounded or dead battalion member after another. The officer Henry had seen fall early in the attack was one of the wounded they recovered. He had lain in the shell hole he had slid into for more than twelve hours. Each time Henry returned, he could feel the stretcher sway and pitch behind him as he picked his way between one shell hole and another.

As dawn approached, the recovery of the dead and wounded had to cease, and Henry returned to the British lines.

'Well done, Bible-basher,' came a voice behind Henry as he was eventually manoeuvring through the fire trench on his return. 'Sorry for what I said this morning, sir. It's just that most of the chaplains I've met in France were completely fucking useless.'

Henry gave a brief laugh before making his way to Brigade Headquarters.

On his way there, he met the brigade major.

'Ah! Padre,' said the brigade major. 'You've saved me part of a journey. I was on my way to find you.'

The two men made their way back into the Brigade Headquarters hut.

'Make yourself comfortable, Padre,' invited the brigade major.

They sat on either side of a large trestle table in the hut's centre. The brigade major took out a silver cigarette case from his jacket pocket, opened it, and held it out towards Henry.

'Cigarette?' he asked.

'No, thank you, sir.'

The brigade major took out a cigarette and closed the case. He tapped the cigarette on the table before putting the case back in his pocket. He lit the cigarette, drew on it deeply and inhaled before exhaling slowly, taking care not to blow the smoke in Henry's immediate direction.

'About a week ago,' he finally said, 'a soldier was found in a wooded area outside Boiry-Saint-Martin. He was some way from his battalion nearly a week after it had withdrawn from the area around St Leger at the start of the Boche "Spring Offensive". He faces a charge of desertion.' The brigade major paused to draw on his cigarette again. 'I believe he will be found guilty,' he continued. 'I probably shouldn't say this, but I am concerned that several members of the brigade have faced a court-martial for desertion or cowardice in the past few months and are under sentence of death. None of the soldiers in question had benefitted from any representation at their trial. I do not want a recurrence of that state of affairs.' He paused again, looking straight at Henry. 'I believe someone should be there to represent this man at his trial, someone who will speak on his behalf. As his brigade chaplain, I believe that you are the most appropriate person to do so. I also understand that you have appeared as a prisoner's friend several times before. Would you help the man if he wants you to?'

'Of course I will, sir,' replied Henry, without giving a moment's thought to the request.

The brigade major paused to take yet another draw on his cigarette.

'Thank you, Padre. Would you be available almost immediately?'

Henry raised his eyebrows at the brigade major in surprise.

'Immediately, sir? How soon is *"immediately"*?'

'The court-martial has been listed for hearing in four days. Will that give you sufficient time to get some idea of what will be involved?'

Henry drew in a stuttered gasp.

'From the sound of what you were saying, sir, I guess that it will have to be. Why the hurry, may I ask?'

The brigade major shrugged his shoulders.

'I guess that this is one of those occasions where High Command wants to see justice carried out sooner rather than later.'

Henry paused to think of a diplomatic response to the brigade major but could not.

'Justice, sir – or no justice?'

The brigade major sighed and took another draw on his cigarette.

'You must appreciate, Padre, that I cannot answer or comment on your question.'

'No, sir,' replied a somewhat resigned Henry. 'I will need to see this man as soon as possible – now, perhaps.'

'Yes, of course, Padre. The man's name is Dawson. He's being held in custody in a guardroom about ten kilometres from here.'

Henry left the brigade major and hurried on his way to see the accused soldier.

*There's much to do and little or no time to do it!*

# NINETEEN

# *France, Spring 1918*

Sandwiched between two military policemen, Frank was marched into a large room in a farmhouse. The three men halted in front of a large trestle table behind which three officers were sitting: a major, a captain and a lieutenant. Another captain stood next to a chair to the table's left. Henry Sheldon stood to the right of the table.

A steady trickle of sweat dribbled down the small of Frank's back. A mixture of nausea, apprehension, uncertainty, misery and terror consumed him. He had been brought before a field general court-martial. He was on trial for his life.

With eyes flickering, Frank looked nervously around the courtroom. He was scarcely conscious of the Order convening the court-martial being read out, of the subsequent marking and signing by the major, or of it being placed next to the Charge Sheet and Summaries of Evidence which lay on the table.

'The Court is satisfied that Rules Twenty-Two and Twenty-Three of the Rules of Procedure have been complied with,' said the major. 'My name is Major Tuck, and I have been appointed as President of this court-martial.' He looked at Frank before he continued. 'The accused, Private Dawson, is brought before the Court. Captain Ryder appears before us as Prosecutor. Padre Sheldon appears before us to assist the accused.'

Tuck introduced the captain and the lieutenant as the two other Members of the court-martial hearing the case with him and then looked at Frank again.

'Private Dawson,' he said, 'do you object to being tried by me, as President, or by either of the officers sat by me?'

Frank swallowed hard. He was blinking almost incessantly.

'N-no, sir,' he mumbled.

Frank's eyes flitted nervously from one Member to another, his anxiety mounting as they were each sworn in. The captain and the lieutenant by Tuck and Tuck by the captain. Tuck then looked sternly at Frank.

'Private Dawson,' he began. 'You are charged with whilst on active service deserting His Majesty's Service pursuant to Section Twelve One (a) of the Army Act Eighteen Eighty-One. This case involves a capital offence. Accordingly, a plea of "Not guilty" is automatically entered. Do you understand, Dawson?'

'Yes, sir,' Frank answered, almost inaudibly.

'Please be seated, Dawson,' said Tuck.

A dazed Frank walked like a somnambulist to the two chairs in front of the Members and sat down on one. Cold sweat glued his shirt to his back. Henry Sheldon then sat next to him.

Tuck turned to Ryder.

'Captain Ryder, do you wish to make an opening address?'

'No, sir,' replied Ryder.

'Thank you. In that case, please call your first witness.'

Sergeant Inglis of the Military Police was to be the only witness for the prosecution. He entered the room and was directed to a small table beside the Members' table. He stood behind the chair placed behind it and was sworn in.

'Thank you, Sergeant Inglis. Please be seated,' said Tuck.

Inglis sat down and readied himself to give his evidence. Frank shuffled somewhat uneasily in his chair, his brow furrowing as he became increasingly worried about what was about to happen.

Ryder consulted his notes and then began to question Inglis without looking at him at first.

'Sergeant Inglis, please tell the Court of the circumstances leading to your arrest of the accused.'

Inglis cleared his throat, took a sip of water from the glass on the table in front of him and looked up at Ryder.

'Well, sir, I was on duty when I received a report that smoke had been seen rising from a wooded area along the Cojeul River about two or three hundred yards northeast of the village of Boiry-Saint-Martin. I couldn't think why there should be any smoke in that area, so I went to investigate. I was making my way along a footpath leading to the wood when I caught sight of the accused standing next to a smouldering fire outside a hut which was just inside the treeline—'

'What time was this?' interrupted Ryder.

'It would have been between eight and eight-thirty in the morning, sir.'

'Thank you, Sergeant Inglis, please continue.'

'I started to approach and was about twenty yards away from the accused when he bolted inside the hut. I immediately chased after him.'

'What did you see when you entered the hut?' asked Ryder.

Inglis paused as if trying to recollect before answering.

'I saw the accused, who was about halfway inside. As far as I could see, there was some straw in a corner of the hut that had been heaped up to form a mattress. There was a can of corned beef —maybe two, and an opened tin of jam.'

'Did you say anything to the accused then?' asked Ryder.

'I asked him what he was doing there.'

'What did he say?'

Inglis grimaced before replying mockingly.

'He gave me some cock and bull story about a mate being killed, about getting separated from his battalion and ending up in Boiry-Saint-Martin where, he claimed, he met three soldiers who took him to the hut. However, there was no sign of anyone else at the hut – and nothing to indicate that anyone else had been there.'

'What did you do then?' asked Ryder.

'I asked him for his paybook, but he did not produce it, so I placed him under arrest and took him to the guardroom at Boiry-Saint-Martin for further questioning.'

'What happened when you got to the guardroom?'

'On arrival at the guardroom, I searched the accused, found his paybook and ascertained which regiment and battalion he belonged to. I knew that neither his battalion nor the regiment had been in Boiry-Saint-Martin.'

Ryder consulted his notes once more, wrote something on them, and then looked up at Inglis.

'Thank you, Sergeant – to your knowledge, were there any units or outposts stationed in the woods in question?' asked Ryder.

'No, sir. A line of trenches four hundred and fifty yards long ran from southwest to southeast and almost due south of the town's southern boundary, but there were no units in the woods.'

'Was the accused in uniform?' asked Ryder.

'When arrested, the accused was jacketless but wore his uniform trousers, puttees and boots. His jacket and webbing were on a pile of straw. He had no headgear – cap or helmet,' replied Inglis.

'Did the accused have his rifle with him?'

'No, sir.'

Ryder turned towards the Members.

'I have no further questions for this witness.'

'Thank you, Captain Ryder,' replied Tuck before looking at Henry. 'Padre Sheldon – do you wish to cross-examine the witness?'

'Yes, sir,' replied Henry.

Henry looked briefly at Frank, smiled at him fleetingly, and began his cross-examination of Inglis.

'Remind me, Sergeant, at the time you arrested the accused, apart from his rifle and headgear, was the accused fully uniformed?'

'Yes, sir.'

'It will be the accused's evidence that you did ask him for his paybook – and that he showed it to you, but you did not look at it. That is the case, isn't it, Sergeant Inglis?'

'No, sir. The accused is wrong there.'

'I put it to you that you are mistaken *there*, Sergeant – or lying.'

'No, sir. I am neither mistaken nor lying.'

'That's as may be, Sergeant, but you did find the accused's paybook when you searched him after you reached Boiry-Saint-Martin, didn't you?'

'Yes, sir.'

'Then will you accept that the accused had his paybook with him at all times?'

Inglis hesitated before answering.

'I suppose so, sir.'

Henry turned towards the Members.

'I have no further questions for this witness.'

Frank looked across at Henry quizzically.

*Why hasn't the Padre asked Sergeant Inglis more questions – about the three men from the YMCA?*

Frank shuffled uneasily on his chair. Henry nodded and smiled at him. Frank guessed that the smile was intended to reassure him, but it didn't.

Tuck looked at Ryder.

'Do you wish to re-examine, Captain Ryder?'

'No, thank you, sir.'

Tuck looked at each of the two other Members, who gave no indication that they wanted to question Inglis.

'The Court has no questions for you, Sergeant. Thank you, you may go,' he said.

After Sergeant Inglis had left the courtroom, Ryder turned towards Tuck.

'That concludes the case for the prosecution, sir.'

'Thank you,' replied Tuck. He then turned to look at Frank.

'Private Dawson, do you apply to give evidence yourself as a witness? Please be aware that you will be subject to cross-examination if you do.'

Not knowing what he should say in response, Frank looked anxiously at Henry, who discreetly nodded his head.

'Yes – sir. Yes, I do,' mumbled Frank.

'Do you intend to call any other witness in your defence?'

Frank again looked at Henry, who shook his head.

'N-no, sir.'

'Thank you, Dawson. Please go to the witness table.'

Frank stood up and glanced nervously at Henry before making his way to the witness table somewhat uncertainly.

'Do you swear that the evidence that you shall give before this Court shall be the truth, the whole truth, and nothing but the truth, so help you, God?'

'Yes... I mean... I do, sir.'

'Please sit down, Private Dawson,' said Tuck.

Frank sat at the witness's table and looked around, wide-eyed. His mouth was dry. He picked up a glass of water that stood on the table and took a sip before looking at Henry, as ready as he could be to answer Henry's questions.

'Private Dawson, when you give your evidence, please address it directly towards the Members, not me.'

'Yes, sir,' croaked Frank before taking another sip of water.

Henry went through Frank's evidence in a slow, methodical

sequence, gradually taking him from the morning when the German offensive first began to the moment he was searched in the guardroom in Boiry-Saint-Martin.

'Thank you, Private Dawson,' Henry said when he had finished questioning Frank. 'I have no further questions for you, but Captain Ryder may have.'

Ryder shuffled some papers set out in front of him, looked at Frank without expression and started his cross-examination.

'Private Dawson, you say that you used your rifle as a marker for the body of Private Prentice. Why didn't you use his rifle?'

'He'd dropped it on the ground when he fell,' replied Frank. 'His helmet also fell off his head at the same time. So they remained there when I pulled him into the shell hole.'

Ryder looked straight at Frank. The corners of his mouth turned upwards into a sneer.

'A likely story, I must say. I put it to you that you didn't just throw the magazine and rifle bolt away – you threw away your whole rifle and helmet and then fled.'

Frank could feel his nostrils flare.

'No, sir. It was as I said.'

'You say you met some men from the Irish Guards in Boyelles. How many?' asked Ryder contemptuously.

'Three or four, sir.'

'Oh – *three or four*,' Ryder retorted sarcastically. 'And just what were their names?'

'I didn't ask, sir.'

'What was their rank?'

'They were all privates, sir.'

'Why didn't you ask them if they would take you to their NCO or officer?'

'I just didn't think to ask them, sir.'

Ryder looked at Frank, looked away, chuckled, and looked back, tut-tutting.

'The truth is that you never met anyone from the Irish Guards, did you?'

'I did, sir. I did meet them,' Frank protested.

'I simply don't believe you, Private Dawson. I put it to you that if, as you say, you met the men and you were looking to rejoin your unit, you would have gone with them to the sugar factory in Boyelles and made further enquiries there.'

Frank was beginning to become flustered.

'But... as I have already said, sir,' he spluttered, 'there was... considerable confusion generally, and...I decided I needed to... er... move on by myself to try... umm... and find my unit.'

'You said that you went to Boisleux-Saint-Marc from Boyelles and met a number of men from the Welsh Guards in some old German trenches there and that you remained with them throughout the day before heading out again. Is that right, Private Dawson?'

'Y-y-yes, sir,' Frank stuttered.

'And, just how many men did you meet?' asked Ryder.

Frank said nothing at first. He just sat there, slightly open-mouthed, and looked around the courtroom.

'I don't know for sure, sir, maybe eight or nine,' he replied eventually.

Ryder lifted his shoulder in a half-shrug and stared at Frank.

'Were these all privates, or were some or all NCOs or officers?'

'There was one lance corporal, I think – and a sergeant. The others were privates.'

'So there we are – a lance corporal, a sergeant and some privates. Did you press the NCOs for their help?'

'No, sir, it didn't cross my mind to do so.'

'Tell the Court their names.'

'I don't know, sir. I didn't ask them.'

'Private Dawson, do you expect this Court to believe you

spent a full day with them without asking them for their names?' Ryder snorted with derision.

'It's what happened, sir,' replied Frank, his heart racing and his stomach tightening.

'I put it to you that you did not spend time with any men from the Welsh Guards. Rather, whilst you may have reached Boisleux-Saint-Marc, you simply hid out of sight until making your way to Boiry-Saint-Martin because you had absolutely no intention of returning to your unit. You were simply *en route* to Calais or Boulogne hoping to sneak on board a boat to England when you got there, weren't you?'

'No, sir. I swear that I had every intention of returning to my unit.'

'Let's move on. Apart from the three men you allege you met at the YMCA, did you meet anyone else in Boiry-Saint-Martin?'

'No, sir.'

'Remind me, Private Dawson. Were you *actually* looking for your unit at the time?' Ryder asked, each word edged with sarcasm.

'Yes, I was, sir,' Frank replied, dropping his voice slightly.

Ryder lifted his head and looked up at the ceiling. He shook his head, tutted as before, and looked back at Frank.

'Then, Private Dawson, why didn't you ask anyone else?'

'I would have done so at some stage, but I got on well with the three men, and they had invited me to join them in their hut. I thought it would not cause a problem if I went with them. It would not prevent me from continuing my search the following day.'

'Ah yes – the mythical three men. So tell the Court, what were their names?'

'I don't know, sir. I didn't ask.'

Ryder lifted his shoulders to his ears and spread out his arms.

'Well, that seems to be a common failing with you, doesn't it, Private Dawson? You never actually asked anyone their name in any of the three towns you say you stopped at. The truth is, you didn't meet anyone, did you?'

Frank could feel himself beginning to shake.

'I did, sir. I promise you I did.'

'With respect, Private Dawson. That is patent nonsense. The truth is that the three men you allege you met in Boiry-Saint-Martin and all the others in Boyelles and Boiry-Saint-Marc are just figments of your imagination.'

With that, and without waiting for a reply from Frank, Ryder turned to the Members.

'I have no further questions for the accused.'

'Thank you, Captain Ryder. Please be seated. I have a question – no, two questions for you, Private Dawson,' said Tuck.

'We have heard that there was a Military Police presence in Boiry-Saint-Martin. Why didn't you look for the guardroom and report in?'

Frank tensed. Panic began to swell up inside him.

'Er… umm… I wasn't thinking straight, I guess, sir.'

'Tell me, why was the first thing that you did at the YMCA was to buy yourself a cup of tea and a plate of egg and chips?'

'I was famished – In any event, I could see that there were soldiers in the YMCA who I could ask about my unit.'

Tuck leant forward, his fingers laced before him on the top of the trestle table.

'I see. Fascinating explanations – thank you, Private Dawson,' he said. He smiled, but no mirth was showing in his eyes. He looked at his fellow Members who gave no indication they had any questions, before looking back at Frank. 'The Members have no further questions for the accused. Do you wish to re-examine, Padre?'

'Yes, sir.'

'Private Dawson, how did you feel when Prentice died?' asked Henry.

'I was devastated,' replied Frank. 'He was my best friend.

When he died, I felt completely drained and empty at first. Then I became angry and determined to return to my unit and avenge him if I possibly could.'

'So would it be true to say that it never crossed your mind to desert?'

'Yes, sir, it would. All I wanted to do was to return to my unit – and avenge Jimmy's death.'

Henry turned to the Members. 'Thank you. I have no further re-examination.'

'Thank you,' Tuck replied before turning to Frank. 'Thank you, Private Dawson. You may return to your seat next to Padre Sheldon.'

Frank rose unsteadily from the witness table, returned to Henry and sat down next to him. Tuck looked towards Ryder.

'Captain Ryder, do you wish to address the Court?'

'Yes, sir. Thank you,' he said, rising to his feet. 'The evidence the Court has heard shows without question that the accused is a deserter. Firstly, he was arrested in Boiry-Saint-Martin, about six miles from where he had last been present with his unit – and several days later. It is axiomatic that his absence from his unit was unauthorised.'

Ryder paused, looked at Frank, then back to the Members.

'The accused alleges that he was trying to rejoin his unit throughout his absence,' he continued. 'In support of that allegation, the accused claims that he met men from the Irish Guards in Boyelles and men from the Welsh Guards in Boisleux-Saint-Marc and sought their help to find his unit. My primary contention is that no such meetings took place; the accused never actually went into either town. However, even if the Court is not with me in this regard, the accused's account of what happened must establish his guilt. If he met the men in question, he had ample opportunity to formally report to an NCO or an officer about his predicament but singularly failed to do so – as he says himself.'

Ryder paused again.

'The accused also alleges that he met three soldiers in the YMCA at Boiry-Saint-Martin and went with them to the hut where he was arrested. The evidence of Sergeant Inglis brings that version of events into question. In any event, the President himself questioned the accused as to why he didn't look for the guardroom at Boiry-Saint-Martin and report in but received no satisfactory answer.'

Ryder looked at each Member one by one before continuing.

'Had the accused any intention of returning to his unit, it was perfectly feasible for him to have made that state of affairs known to an appropriate authority in Boyelles, Boisleux-Saint-Marc, or Boiry-Saint-Martin and to have insisted on being given further orders. He singularly failed to do so. The truth of the matter is that all he did was move continuously away from any battle action, finally skulking away in a hut in a wooded area outside Boiry-Saint-Martin. The only conclusion that can be drawn from the accused's conduct is that he was intent on deserting.'

'Thank you, Captain Ryder. Padre, do you wish to address the Court?'

'Yes, sir,' replied Henry.

He stood up, holding a notebook in which he had listed the points he wished to make to the Members on Frank's behalf. Henry looked briefly at these and began to make his submission.

'In simple terms, the Court will know that to establish whether a man deserts or not, it is necessary to prove that he intended to do so – or to show that a circumstance exists or circumstances exist to justify drawing the inference that he intended to do so. Therefore, *intent* is crucial – and distinguishes desertion from the lesser charge of absence without leave.'

Henry paused for a moment or two to allow his point to register.

'I respectfully contend that no evidence has been adduced to prove intention on the part of the accused or that could justify the inference that the accused intended to desert.'

Henry took a deep breath before turning the page of his notebook.

'The Prosecutor relies on what happened in Boyelles, Boisleux-Saint-Marc and Boiry-Saint-Martin,' he continued. 'But, the accused's *sworn* evidence was that he met with men in all three locations intending to return to his unit. The Prosecutor has produced no evidence that can rebut that evidence. Accordingly, I contend that the Court should accept the evidence of the accused when making its decision.'

Henry looked at each of the Members in turn.

'There is a conflict between the evidence of Sergeant Inglis and the accused concerning the accused's paybook. But what is not in dispute is that the accused *had* his paybook when he was arrested. Furthermore, whilst he was not carrying his rifle and wore no headgear – and there is a perfectly acceptable reason for that – he was otherwise in full uniform. All of this supports the accused's contention that his sole *intention* throughout the time he was separated from his comrades was to return to them – not to desert.'

Henry paused and put his notebook down.

'The accused may have made errors of judgement by not formally reporting to an officer or NCO in Boyelles, Boisleux-Saint-Marc and Boiry-Saint-Martin,' he continued. 'However, that did not evince any intention on his part to avoid his duty.'

Henry paused once more. He cleared his throat and looked at Tuck.

'The accused accepts that if the Court finds he did not desert, it will then consider whether he is guilty of the lesser charge of being absent without leave. In that regard, I respectfully contend that the Court should also acquit the accused on that charge. The accused's *sworn* evidence is that, at all times, he was trying to get back to his unit. It is true he got separated from them, but that separation was accidental.'

'Thank you, Padre. That concludes this stage of the court-martial. The Members will now retire to consider their verdict.'

The Members left the room, and Henry turned to Frank, who stood there feeling totally disconsolate, and placed his hand on his shoulder.

'I don't know how long the Members will take to arrive at their decision, Frank,' he said softly. 'But hopefully, they will take their time and give proper in-depth scrutiny to what they have heard. At the end of the day, though, the reality is that this will come down solely to whether the Members are actually prepared to believe what you have told them – rather than seeing this as an opportunity to use you to send out a chilling message to the other men serving in the brigade.'

\*

A perfect silence reigned when the Members returned to the courtroom.

'May we have any evidence as to the character of the accused?' asked Tuck.

*Why are they now asking for evidence about my character?*

The significance of the President's question was lost on Frank completely. He had no idea that the Members would only consider character evidence if they had found him guilty of desertion.

Second Lieutenant Robinson came forward and was sworn in. He handed a document to Tuck.

'I produce a certified true copy of the accused's Army Form B One Two Two concerning the character and previous services of the accused,' he said. 'The accused is the person named therein. The extracts are true copies of the entries in the regimental books.'

'Thank you, Mr Robinson,' replied Tuck, stony-faced. 'Is there anything you would like to add about the accused's character?'

Robinson answered without hesitation.

'Yes, sir. I have been the accused's platoon commander for more than a year. His general conduct has been good, and I have never had any trouble with him. He has always done whatever I have ever asked him to do.'

'Thank you, Mr Robinson,' said Tuck. 'Do you wish to cross-examine this witness, Padre?'

'Yes, sir,' replied Henry.

'Mr Robinson, have you ever noticed anything unusual about the accused's demeanour whilst you have known him?'

'Well, Padre, I have noticed on occasion that he appears to suffer from nerves,' replied Robinson after a brief pause, 'but this has not been sufficient to cause me any concern about his performing his duty at any time.'

'Mr Robinson, do you think the accused is a coward?'

'No, Padre.'

'Do you think that he is a deserter?'

'No, Padre.'

'Thank you, Mr Robinson.'

Henry turned towards Tuck.

'Thank you, sir. I have no further questions.'

'Thank you,' said Tuck. 'We will now retire again to make our further deliberations.'

With that, the Members withdrew from the courtroom, returning barely ten minutes later. They sat down. Frank stood facing them.

'Private Dawson,' said Tuck, looking straight at Frank. 'This Court finds you guilty of the offence of whilst on active service deserting His Majesty's Service pursuant to Section Twelve Paragraph One (a) of the Army Act of Eighteen Eighty-One. Do you have anything you wish to say before I pronounce the sentence of the Court?'

Frank gasped audibly. He wrung his hands in front of his body.

*What do I do? What do I say? What can I say?*

He looked around at Henry, who mouthed, 'Plead for leniency. Tell them about your service in France.'

'Yes, please, sir,' said Frank, almost in a whisper.

'You may continue,' said Tuck.

Frank took a deep breath.

'Please, sir, I plead for leniency,' said Frank as he began to address the Members, struggling to speak slowly and clearly, hoping that what he was saying would resonate well with them. 'I have served in the trenches in France almost continuously since I arrived from training in Nineteen Fifteen. I have only been home on leave twice in all that time, the first leave period being cut short by illness. I have only been in trouble once during my army service. I deeply regret and have served my punishment for my transgressions at that time. I am not a bad soldier. All the time I was away from my unit, my sole intention was to rejoin them. It was the only way I could make the enemy pay for killing Jimmy. I ask the Court for the chance to prove that I am a good soldier. I only ever wanted to do my bit when my country called me. I still do.'

Frank looked down at the floor as he finished, his heart pounding, his body shaking uncontrollably.

'Thank you, Private Dawson,' said Tuck. He turned to face each of the two Members. Neither gave any sign to him that they had any further contribution to make. Tuck turned back to face Frank.

'Private Dawson, it now falls upon me to pass sentence on you. The sentence of the Court is that you shall suffer death by shooting.'

Completely stunned, Frank took a slight step forward before steadying himself again. He looked towards Henry and then back to the three Members. He was in a state of utter despair. He could neither believe nor adequately take in what he had just heard.

## France, Spring 1918

'Take him away,' ordered Tuck.

Moments later, Frank's escort formed either side of him, and he was marched out of the courtroom, handed over to the Assistant Provost Marshall of the Division and taken to the Brigade Guardroom.

\*

Frank was in a sparsely furnished cell in a brick building in front of a courtyard, The only furniture in the room was a trestle table, two chairs and a straw mattress on an iron bedstead. There were some pencils, writing paper and a copy of the *New Testament* on the table.

Frank was lying on the mattress, his head spinning and heart pounding. He was expecting a visit from Henry, but he wasn't sure when Henry would arrive – or what he would say to him. Frank was still trying to take in that he had been sentenced to death.

The door to Frank's cell opened, and Henry walked in. Frank jumped up to his feet and looked pleadingly at Henry.

'What happens now, Padre?' he asked.

Henry stood and looked agonisingly at Frank. Then, finally, he lowered his head and fastened his hands behind his back.

'I'm so sorry, Frank,' he said in a hushed voice. 'I feel I failed you.'

'No, Padre, you did your best. I couldn't have had a better prisoner's friend. I am also most grateful to you for taking the trouble to come and see me now.'

'Frank, believe me, it is no trouble – I am your brigade chaplain, but I hope I am your friend also. To answer your question, your case will now be the subject of a review process. Firstly, Brigade will review it. After that, it will pass up the chain of command until it reaches the commander-in-chief, who will make the final decision. Then, all being well, he will commute your sentence. I will do everything I can for you throughout the process and come to see you at every opportunity.'

'Thank you, Padre,' said Frank as he moved back to his bed and sat down. Henry moved across the room, sat next to him and put his arm around Frank's shoulder.

'It will be difficult for you now,' he told Frank, 'but don't just lie on the bed stewing. Make the most of the coming days. Use the paper on the table. Write home. Set out a plan for your future, your hopes, your dreams, and how you'll achieve them. Remember what I said, the commander-in-chief may well commute your sentence. Hang on to that thought. While you're writing home and making your plans, I'll be doing what I can for you – starting right now.' Henry got up from the bed and turned to leave. 'I'm off to see the battalion commanding officer and discuss your case. Hopefully, I can convince him that it is appropriate to recommend mercy for you.'

Frank stayed sitting on the bed, looking blankly at Henry.

'Thank you, Padre,' he mumbled.

'I'll come back and see you again as soon as possible, Frank.'

Henry left Frank and went back through an inner chamber, an outer room, and into the courtyard outside the Brigade Guardroom where Frank was being held. He crossed the courtyard and got into a waiting Daimler.

'Battalion HQ, please,' he said to the driver.

When he arrived at Battalion HQ, Henry got out of the car and walked to the commanding officer's office. He entered.

'Good afternoon, sir,' he said as he saluted. 'May I please speak to you about Private Dawson?'

Lieutenant Colonel Carr looked up at Henry and nodded in greeting.

'Good afternoon, Padre,' he replied. 'Please take a seat.'

Henry sat in front of Carr's desk.

'Sir,' he said. 'Dawson has been found guilty and sentenced to be shot. I've come to ask you to do everything you can to save his life. I've got to know him over the past few days and believe that he is a man to whom mercy can and ought to be extended.'

Carr looked at Henry. He hesitated for a minute or two, seemingly deep in thought.

'I didn't think so at the time I carried out my investigation before committing him for trial, Padre. In my view, it was only right and proper that he should face a court-martial – and his guilt be established. However, I am inclined to agree that actually imposing the death penalty on Dawson would be extreme; far better, in my view, to commute the death sentence to a lengthy term of imprisonment.' Carr paused to clear his throat. 'I don't know whether anything I might say will help, given what has been happening on the front since the German offensive began,' he continued, 'but I am willing to try. You will be aware that I must write a report, which will go to the brigade commander when he reviews Dawson's case. Of course, my report has to be fair and honest on all fronts, but I will make a case for mercy in this case.'

Henry heaved a sigh of relief.

'Thank you, sir,' he replied.

'I should finish my report and send it off to Brigade by this afternoon. I would expect a response in the next couple of days. I'll let you know when I receive it.'

'May I see you again once you do?'

Carr looked at Henry and smiled warmly.

'Please do, Padre.'

\*

Henry stood nervously in front of Carr as he looked down at the copy of the brigade commander's recommendation handed to him.

*... I have considered the report submitted by Lieutenant Colonel Carr with great care. He makes a strong case in favour of not inflicting the extreme penalty. However, I cannot concur with him in this case.*

*As the commanding officer of this brigade, I urge in the strongest possible terms that the sentence is proceeded with.*

*This man's previous character has not been good, and from a fighting point of view, he presently demonstrates that he is of little or no value. An earlier court-martial convicted him of drunkenness. Additionally, he spent time in hospital with syphilis. Drunkenness and contracting a sexually transmitted disease are wholly prejudicial to good order and military discipline. I also believe that his courage whilst in the line may be questionable. I do not doubt that this crime was deliberately committed for the sole purpose of avoiding personal danger.*

*Taking all these attributes together, they suggest to me that an example should be made in this case. Kill two birds with a single stone. Remove a bad soldier and set an example to the brigade members at the same time.*

Henry could scarcely contain a deep feeling of disappointment and despondency.

'But there must be something more we can do to try and save this man,' he pleaded.

'I'm afraid I don't think there is anything more than I can do, Padre – even if I was inclined to attempt to in the first place. However, as you know full well, ultimately, it falls to the commander-in-chief whether to confirm or commute the sentence. This, of course, is something he may well do in this case – as he has on many other occasions.'

## TWENTY

# *France, May 1918*

Frank half sat, half lay on the straw mattress on his bed, his back and shoulders propped against the metal bedhead with the two pillows that came with the two rough blankets issued to him when he arrived in the cell. He had been trying to read the *New Testament* that had been on the table in the room. It now lay closed next to his right leg. The door to his cell opened and Henry Sheldon and a major entered. A cold shiver ran through Frank's body as he sprang to his feet.

'Good evening, Frank,' Henry greeted him. 'The major with me is an assistant provost marshal.'

The assistant provost marshal nodded towards Frank but said nothing.

The words *Sweet, Jesus, No!* flashed through Frank's mind. Panic welled up inside him. He had a premonition that he might only have a short time to live. Why else would the assistant provost marshal come to see him so late in the evening?

The assistant provost marshal looked at Frank and cleared his throat.

'There's no easy way to say this, Private Dawson,' he said sternly, 'so I won't beat about the bush. I bring bad news. After due consideration and having carefully taken into account the representations made to him, notably by Padre Sheldon, the commander-in-chief has confirmed the sentence of your court-martial. It will be carried out at dawn tomorrow morning.'

A cold shiver had run through Frank's body and his stomach was tied in knots well before the assistant provost marshal finished speaking. He crossed the room in a near trance, pulled back one of the chairs in front of the trestle table and sat down. Frank shuffled the chair forward, put his elbows on the table and buried his head between his hands. He began to shake uncontrollably as the assistant provost marshal left the room.

Henry moved over to Frank and placed a hand on his shoulder. He did not know whether to say anything – or what to say even if he did. Frank gradually began to control his breathing, and the shaking stopped. He looked pleadingly at Henry. Then, finally, a desperate gasp clipped the silence.

'Is there any hope, Padre?' he whispered.

'I'm afraid not, Frank. The battalion commander and I have done everything we possibly could, or felt we could do, to save you, but to no avail. Therefore, despite all efforts, the decision was taken at the highest level to carry out the sentence as you heard.'

Frank was silent for a moment.

'Thinking about everything, Padre, I never had a chance, did I?'

'I fear not, Frank. Someone, somewhere, demanded a sacrificial lamb, and you were it.'

A series of bitter and angry thoughts tumbled inside Frank's mind. His lips moved in time with his thoughts, but he uttered no sound until he turned once more to Henry, having reflected on his silent outburst.

'They will have to answer for what they have done!' he cried out in a strangulated voice. 'They will!'

Frank fell silent again for several minutes. Then a half-smile hovered across his lips.

'But I do at least have a real advantage over them all.'

Henry sat down on the other seat placed in front of the table. He looked at Frank with a puzzled expression on his face.

'How do you mean, Frank?'

Frank gave an ironic chuckle.

'I know when, where, and how my life will end. But, they do not – and probably will not know it until it happens.'

Henry couldn't think of what to say to Frank.

Frank broke the ensuing silence.

'I should prepare myself for my end. Will you pray with me, Padre?' he asked.

'Of course, Frank,' replied Henry. 'I have brought my communion vessels with me. Would you like to take communion?'

Frank gave a wry smile.

'Yes, please, Padre.'

Henry cleared the table, took out a small white altar cloth and the communion vessels from his bag and placed them on the table. Frank knelt, and Henry gave him communion. Henry then knelt beside Frank and prayed with him.

'Thank you, Padre,' said Frank quietly after he and Henry had finished reciting the *Lord's Prayer*.

'I need some time alone now to write home and then try and collect my thoughts, but will you come to see me in the morning before it happens?'

'Of course, Frank. I've brought some writing materials with me in case you needed them and there were none here. I'll leave them on the table for you.'

'I'm grateful for the chance of a well-prepared death and will pray for you,' said Frank as Henry left him. Henry could find no words of reply as he walked away. Frank went over to the bed, lay down and looked at the ceiling. He closed his eyes. His mind was racing, his heart pounding in his chest. Panic swelled inside him.

'Pull yourself together,' Frank chided himself.

He got up from the bed, went over to the table, sat down and began writing home. The words came slowly to him at first.

*Dear Mam, Fatha and sisters,*

*Just a few lines to let you know that I am in the best of health, and I hope you are too, Mam.*

   *I am sorry to tell you that I will be shot at dawn tomorrow. I hope you take it with a good heart and won't upset yourselves. I shall die like a soldier, so goodbye, Mam, Fatha and sisters. I am writing my last letter to you all at home.*
   *So Mam, don't be angry with me, for I am going to my rest. Pray for me, and I will do the same for you.*

Frank paused, his pencil held upwards as he thought of what to write next. Then, moments later, he scribbled words to convey his seething sense of angst, his smouldering sense of outrage.

*Think how men like me were being slaughtered at the beginning of the war for* their *cause. You'd think they would have a bit of mercy and pity for those of us who are still living and who have continued fighting for their stupidity, their lack of regard for anything besides their own worthless ambition, and their almost insatiable bloodlust.*

Frank paused again and took a deep breath. He calmed his inner anger before setting down a brief conclusion.

*Goodbye to all at home,*

*Goodbye,*

*Goodbye from your son, dearest parents – and from your brother, dearest sisters.*

*Frank*

Once he had finished the letter and a similar one to Sybil, Frank went back to the bed and lay down. He shivered in the chillness. His anxiety levels began to increase as time marched on. Exponentially. A myriad of thoughts rushed through his mind, but he couldn't snatch and hold on to any single one – apart from a terror of what would be.

\*

Moonlight shone directly into the cell as Frank sat bolt upright on the bed. Footsteps approached, and Henry entered the room with the guard. Every muscle in Frank's body went rigid momentarily. He held his breath and tried to control himself.

Frank turned and sat on the edge of the bed. At first, his chest raised and fell with rapid breaths before he gave out a desperate gasp. Frank said nothing at first, just staring blankly at the wall. Then he seemed to gain inner strength. He took in a deep breath.

'Guard,' he called out, 'may we have a mug of tea?'

The guard left and returned with two mugs of tea. Twilight was creeping fast into the cell.

'Whatever else, Padre, I believe I must go out and meet my death as fearlessly as possible. I'm sure a mug of tea will help steady my nerves,' said Frank quietly.

Henry sat down and picked up his mug of tea.

'Do you know when they will be coming for me?' asked Frank.

'No, I don't know, I'm afraid,' replied Henry.

'It's twenty-five minutes past five now,' said Frank. 'So, I guess it won't be long now.'

He finished his tea. A few moments later, the guards entered. Frank sighed as they put a hood over his head. They fastened it loosely below his chin so he could not see anything. Then they handcuffed his hands behind his back.

Frank started to hyperventilate. He experienced a flashback to the time a blast had thrown him onto the lip of a deep shell hole. As the hood covered his head, Frank imagined he was again slipping back into a dark muddy morass below him, which seemed to be reaching up to clutch him, drag him into it, and drown him. The hood moved in and out with each breath he took.

'Keep calm! Keep calm!' Frank hissed before he regained control of his breathing.

\*

Henry's mind turned back to the conundrum the Chaplain General presented to him in his interview when he volunteered back in 1914: '*A soldier is lying in the field of battle, mortally wounded in the stomach. He has no more than ten minutes left to live. What would you do?*'

He remembered the answer he had given then. But a different one was needed now. He took Frank's arm and led him gently through the inner chamber, and, as he did so, he started to recite *Psalm 23*.

'*The Lord is my shepherd; I shall not want.*

The two men walked into the outer room.

'*He maketh me to lie down in green pastures: he leadeth me beside the still waters.*'

They went out into the courtyard.

'*He restoreth my soul: he leadeth me in the paths of righteousness for his name's sake.*'

They crossed the courtyard.

'*Yea, though I walk through the valley of the shadow of death, I will fear no evil: for thou art with me; thy rod and thy staff they comfort me.*'

They stopped outside the ambulance.

'*Thou preparest a table before me in the presence of mine enemies: thou anointest my head with oil; my cup runneth over.*'

Henry guided Frank into a parked ambulance.

'*Surely goodness and mercy shall follow me all the days of my life: and I will dwell in the house of the Lord forever.*'

'Amen.'

'Amen,' Frank repeated.

\*

Frank sat down, his head leaning forward. He was trembling uncontrollably. He felt Henry sit next to him on one side and someone else on the other. Frank sat bolt upright as the ambulance door slammed shut. He could hear his teeth chattering as the vehicle lurched forward almost immediately afterwards.

After a short but bumpy journey, the ambulance came to a halt. Frank felt his stomach knot as a blast of cold air burst into the vehicle as the door creaked and then thudded. Frank realised that it had been opened. The man who had climbed into the ambulance after Henry started to get out. He took Frank by the arm and guided him out of the vehicle.

'Stand there,' Frank was told.

He heard Henry get out of the ambulance and approach him. Frank felt Henry stand next to him and take his arm. Someone stood on the other side of Frank. Moments later, the three men started to walk forward. After they had gone about ten yards, Frank stumbled and fell to his knees. He felt a sharp pain as he struck a large stone. Helped by Henry and the other man, Frank staggered back up.

'Give Private Dawson a moment or two,' he heard Henry say.

'I'm all right, Padre,' Frank called out. 'Let's just get this over and done with.'

Frank felt Henry and the other man each take one of his arms, and they all moved forward again. Not long afterwards, they stopped. Frank felt himself being pulled forward, turned around and guided backwards until he felt something with his back. He was guided half a pace forward. His handcuffs were undone at one wrist, and his arms pulled back behind what he now realised was the execution post. That was what he had felt with his back. Frank let out a sharp gasp and shuddered as he felt the handcuffs being fastened again.

Someone stood in front of Frank and began to wrap what he realised was a rope around his chest and tie it behind his back. Next, another rope was tied around his knees. Finally, Frank felt his left breast pocket being pulled and twisted slightly before being let go.

Frank was in a state of near-complete emotional shock. It felt like nothing around him was real, or if it was, it was happening to someone else. Not him.

Henry went up to Frank and pronounced the Benediction. After doing so, he could just make out Frank's last few whispered words.

'*Have no fear! Have no fear!*'

Henry turned and walked away from Frank. He looked towards the firing party as they came into line, the officer in charge standing to their left. Henry walked to a position to the rear of the firing party. He stood next to the doctor ordered to officiate at the execution.

Henry saw the officer commanding the firing party, a lieutenant, raise his stick to his waist. Then, each member of the firing party raised his rifle.

The lieutenant raised his stick to his shoulder. All rifles waved about unsteadily as the firing party tried as hard as possible to take aim. Henry could see that they were all shaking.

As the lieutenant dropped his arm, there was a stuttering volley of shots. It sounded like a firecracker going off. Henry saw Frank shudder. Once. Twice. His head slumped forward, his body held by the ropes tied around his chest and knees.

A sickened Henry and the doctor both went back to Frank. The doctor felt Frank's pulse.

'He's still alive,' he gasped.

The lieutenant's face went white as the doctor looked at him and shook his head.

Henry sighed and started to whisper the *Lord's Prayer* as the lieutenant took out his revolver. He hesitantly approached Frank and put a bullet into his head. After that, the lieutenant moved quickly away to the side of the thicket and vomited. Henry saw that several firing party members had tears streaming down their faces. One broke down completely.

Once they had all collected themselves, the firing party marched off and returned to the prison's courtyard. Henry joined them and comforted them as best he could. He then returned to the thicket.

Frank's body had been taken down and placed in a pinewood coffin by the time Henry returned. He helped lift the coffin into the ambulance and climbed into the back of the vehicle. He pulled the door shut and sat beside the casket throughout the journey to the military cemetery where the dead from recent battles in the surrounding area had been laid to rest. Once there, Henry conducted a service as they buried Frank. He wept as he did so.

# TWENTY-ONE

# *France, November 1918*

I was feeling unwell and nauseous. I was sweating profusely and my head felt like it had been packed with a massive wad of soggy cotton wool. Every other part of my body ached.

'I'm afraid that it's influenza,' was the diagnosis I received when I reported sick. 'You will have to remain in your room in isolation. I'll let Sister Bettsworth know.'

Wearily, I returned to my room. I undressed, got into bed and fell asleep until I awoke with a start early the following morning. Someone else was in my room, a shadowy figure shifting in the half-light. I gasped.

'W-who's there?'

'Sorry to startle you, Harland. It's Sister Bettsworth. How are you feeling today?' a voice called out.

I breathed a short sigh of relief.

'I wish I could say I was feeling a little better, but I feel awful,' I replied.

Sister put her hand on my forehead.

'You feel hot – and you're sweating. I'll check your TPRs,'

she said. She popped a thermometer under my tongue, took my pulse and checked my breathing.

'Temperature, a hundred and three point four,' she said after removing the thermometer and checking the mercury level, '... pulse, one hundred... respiration, thirty.'

I knew that these were not promising signs.

'I'll get someone to look in on you during the day to keep a close eye on you,' said Sister.

I drifted into a fitful sleep, a sleep often disturbed by spasmodic but short-lasting fits of coughing. I was aware that Sarah was in the room with me from time to time, that she had wiped my face and forehead with a cool, damp flannel.

I was in a bad way for several days but gradually started to pull through. Slowly, my cough subsided, my temperature fell and my pulse rate slowed, as did my respiration. Finally, I was able to sit up in bed. I was still feeling unwell, but I was on the mend.

Sister Bettsworth called in to see me every morning and check on my progress. Eventually, I could report to her that I thought I might be well enough to return to the ward.

'Maybe, Harland, maybe not,' she replied. 'We miss you, but I think another few days in bed yet.'

Sister was right. I slept most of that day and the next; the extra few days worked wonders. First, I was well enough to get up and about. Then I was well enough to take some light outdoor exercise – a short, gentle walk with Sarah. Finally, I was able to return to my ward.

As I returned for duty, Sister greeted me with a welcoming smile.

'It's terrific to see you again, Harland. But I'm throwing you in at the deep end. We've got a ward full of "fluers". A word of warning, though, they are all incontinent, so you are likely to find yourself continually changing beds and washing.'

\*

The numbers falling victim to a deadly strain of influenza that became known as "Spanish Flu" or the "Spanish Lady" continued to increase sharply. I had to cope with an ever-growing flood of corpses, dark blue and putrescent, within hours of death. At the same time, rumours started to spread that the war was about to end.

'We can't afford to waste time speculating about the war ending,' was Sister Bettsworth's mantra. 'We've far more pressing priorities to think about – and one of them is that young man in the bed over there. He has a persistent, intense headache and is frequently delirious. His delirium is sometimes quiet, sometimes violent, and sometimes he is almost maniacal.'

The soldier in question was barely twenty years of age. He looked gaunt and exhausted. I sat with him, holding his hand and bathing his forehead with cold water. He was in a terrible state.

'Miss,' he croaked, 'it feels like they've taken out the lining from my lungs.'

The soldier was coughing up mucus streaked with blood. Each time he did so, I washed his face. There was a peculiar tinge to his lips, one that I found chilling – the mark of the Spanish Lady in its deadliest manifestation.

'Thank you, Miss. Sorry to be such a pain,' he gasped.

It made me ache to see the soldier's head shift from side to side, to listen to him struggling for breath. His condition worsened rapidly to the point where he no longer felt he could stay in bed and insisted on being propped up against the wall. Then the reaction came, and the young man slept. But not a healthy, restful sleep; it was more like the dying stupor of exhaustion. He remained where he was until he finally drowned in his own sputum in the early hours of the following morning: the morning that the Armistice was signed.

The news that the war had ended triggered mixed emotions.

There wasn't a single man among the patients in my ward who understood its meaning. They were all delirious, not conscious enough to realise. All of them were too ill. I felt no joyous exultation, just relief that the war was over, mixed with sadness at the thought of the many who had died and those who were still dying. The death of the twenty-year-old sapper that morning was very much a reminder to me of that. Elsewhere, there was a sense of elation. There were shouts of joy. People hugged and laughed and rushed around the wards to break the news. Some tots of medicinal brandy were poured and drunk in celebration.

*Won't we all be able to return home shortly?*

\*

But while the Great War had ended, the war against the Spanish Lady had not. The strain on the hospital's resources became increasingly intense. There were forty-three cases in my ward alone. Elsewhere, three doctors fell victim to the Spanish Lady. They recovered slowly. Two orderlies also contracted the disease, but they died. The very severe cases were sent to a ward allocated to provide intensive care. Outside, the weather took a turn for the worse. A stark reminder that winter was nearing fast. The temperature plummeted.

While the hospital continued to treat soldiers suffering from other illnesses, the vast majority now were flu victims. At least, though, there were no more victims of bombs, bullets or shells. There was no set pattern to the epidemic. Some victims were only mildly affected. Others developed a savage form where severe complications set in at a frightening pace.

I still had a great deal to do. More was still needed of us all. This masked, but did not obscure, that I would remain separated from my family for yet another Christmas. There was no prospect of home leave, whether over Christmas or otherwise, and no talk of any early termination of a VAD's contract. However, Christmas would be celebrated in Étaples, even if this celebration was a mixture of enjoyment and duty.

*

I lifted the top of the hospital's "*A. Bord of Paris*" oak harmonium to reveal the twenty-six black keys sitting proudly above thirty-six white keys. I had practised playing it whenever I had any free time. I was to provide the musical accompaniment during an afternoon of music and singing in the ward on the Saturday before Christmas. Sarah and Sister Bettsworth stood behind the harmonium, facing me as I sat on the piano stool in front of it. I brought down the two foot pedals and readied myself. I took a deep breath and started to play as the three of us opened proceedings with our version of *Three Little Maids From School*.

We gave an acceptable performance, and it seemed to chime well with the audience. We were followed by one of the convalescent patients who gave a rousing rendition of *Gilbert the Filbert the Knut with a "K"*, the song made famous by Basil Hallam. Everyone joined in raucously with each chorus.

> '*I'm Gilbert, the Filbert,*
> *The Knut with a "K",*
> *The pride of Piccadilly,*
> *the blasé roué.*
> *Oh, Hades! the ladies*
> *who leave their wooden huts*
> *For Gilbert, the Filbert,*
> *The Colonel of the Knuts.*'

He and I then duetted *Brindisi* from *La Traviata*. He was no Enrico Caruso and I am no Alma Gluck, but we did our best.

Others contributed to a most enjoyable afternoon, culminating with everyone joining together for a selection of Christmas carols.

The festivities continued that evening when Sarah and I joined the audience at a concert held in the hospital complex. Again, some rousing music, a good orchestra, some good singers and an accomplished violinist provided a further welcome distraction from the horrors of the Spanish Lady.

As we walked slowly from the concert, I heard a voice behind me call out.

'Emily! Emily!'

I turned and started as if stunned by a flash of lightning. Before me stood – Edward.

'Emily, my dear Emily!' he cried.

I momentarily clasped my hands to my face. I nearly fainted.

'Goodness me!' I exclaimed. 'What are you doing here?'

I threw my arms open as Edward strode towards me with a smile that widened with his every step.

Edward reached me and threw his arms around me. He embraced me so warmly and passionately that my head started to spin. I lifted my head towards him.

'I can't believe it – you're here, now. What a surprise. What a wonderful surprise!' I gasped.

He kissed me lightly on the top of my head.

'You know perfectly well that all the fun of Christmas is in surprising people. Wouldn't you rather have a plain and simple present, and have the joy of being astonished over it, than get the most beautiful gift you could ever wish for and know all about it beforehand?'

'And I suppose you are that plain and simple present?' I said, pressing a hand to my mouth to stifle my giggles.

'Who knows,' he laughed.

I turned to see Sarah hurrying away.

'Sarah!' I called out. 'Sarah, wait! Look who's here! Sarah…!'

Sarah stopped and looked back at me, saying nothing at first.

'You need to be with Edward,' she eventually called back.

'Don't be daft, Sarah. Come and join us,' Edward shouted.

Sarah picked her way through a small group heading towards the hospital and joined Edward and me. He moved to her and embraced her.

'Hello, Sarah,' he said, 'and where did you think you were scuttling off to? I don't bite, I promise you.'

He started to laugh. Sarah and I also.

'Hello, Edward,' Sarah said. 'I just didn't want to play gooseberry.'

'You can stop that,' Edward chided gently, linking arms with Sarah and me. 'We're all friends.'

On the way back to the Mess, poor Edward was bombarded with questions from either side of him.

'What are you doing here in Étaples?'

'I'm on my way back to England – I'm being demobilised from the Friends' Ambulance Unit to return to civilian life.'

'How did you know where we'd be?'

'I called at the hospital. Sister Bettsworth told me how to find where the concert was being held.'

We continued the interrogation of Edward until we were standing at the entrance to the hospital.

'Here's where I leave you,' said Sarah diplomatically. 'This really is a case of *"three's a crowd"*.'

Edward shook Sarah's hand and kissed her lightly on the cheek.

'I hope that we meet again one day,' he said.

Sarah looked at me, smiled, winked and went to her room. I took hold of Edward's hand and gently squeezed it.

'Come on, Edward, I could use a cup of tea – and there are still questions I have for you – and an invitation.'

'Hmm – *"an invitation"* – that sounds intriguing,' Edward replied with a distinct twinkle in his eye.

'Not that intriguing,' I giggled. 'There's a dance in the Red Cross hut close to the hospital tomorrow evening. If you were still here, perhaps you'd like to be my guest.'

Edward looked at me, smiled, and nodded gently.

'Wild horses and all that,' he replied. 'I'd love to go to the dance with you. I don't leave Étaples until the day after tomorrow. I couldn't think of a better way to spend my last evening in France –umm – and now for that cup of tea – and your questions.'

\*

I opened my eyes in the cold grey dawn to see the air outside filled with occasional whirling snowflakes dancing and scurrying this way and that, propelled by a whistling wind. Such a tempting morning to pull the blankets over my shoulders and snuggle down for another forty winks! But there could be no such luxury for me. I had a job to do.

I dressed hurriedly and made my way to the Mess for a welcome breakfast of bacon rashers and hot rolls before reporting for duty. A long, hard, often heart-wrenching day tending to victims of the Spanish Lady lay ahead. But at least there was the prospect of seeing Edward again.

We arrived at the Red Cross hut just as the convalescent camp orchestra, booked to provide the music for the evening, started to play *The Memphis Blues*. I could see that a space had been cleared for a dance floor.

'Come on, Edward,' I said excitedly, taking his arm. 'Our chance to shine! Let's show them we are very much *à la mode* by dancing a foxtrot.'

We made our way to the dance floor.

If I'm honest, neither of us was particularly adept at the foxtrot, but we tried. Edward stood directly in front of me and took my right hand in his left hand. As he placed his right hand, loosely cupped with fingers and thumb together, on my left shoulder blade, he started to tremble.

'Edward – are you all right?' I asked as I placed my left hand lightly on his right shoulder.

'Just a little nervous. I've been on ambulance trains too long.'

I giggled. Edward moved his left foot forward; I stepped backwards with my right. We moved in time to the music – as softly and smoothly as possible, taking a step to every count of the music.

I readied myself for the next dance as soon as the band had finished playing *The Memphis Blues*. This was to be a one-step. I was certainly more at home with that dance, but I'm not so sure that Edward was comfortable with any dance except the waltz. So, as the music started, we moved forward again.

We eventually called it a day shortly after midnight. I was feeling ecstatically happy but physically tired when I left the Red Cross hut with Edward. Then came the moment I had been dreading. It was time to say both goodnight and goodbye to Edward. He had to leave just three and a half hours later to go to Boulogne to catch his boat home.

What happened next shocked me into total silence. Edward took my hand, kissed it lightly and looked into my eyes.

'Emily,' he whispered, 'I love you so much that I hardly know what to say.' He took a deep breath. 'I can think of just six words – Emily Harland, will you marry me?'

Taken totally by surprise, it took me a long time to say something, because I couldn't quite think of the right words, even though I was sure what to say. A simple "yes" somehow didn't seem enough.

'Emily Harland, will you marry me?' he asked me again. He looked so anxious.

I hugged him and kissed him.

'Is that a yes?' he asked.

'Oh yes,' was the only reply I could manage.

## TWENTY-TWO

# *France, Spring 1919*

The year 1918 had ended on such a high note for me, but since then my life had been in a constant state of flux. My return home seemed as far away as ever. All sorts and kinds of rumours were flying about the hospital, some uplifting, others depressing. We were all about to pack up and return home one minute. The next, we were staying put and would be required to continue our duties at the hospital for the foreseeable future. No one could think of just what might happen or when it might happen if it did. The only certainty was that the Spanish Lady continued to heap misery on most of those she touched.

We were still taking a large number of cases into the hospital. Some became very sick and died as complications developed before you knew it. In contrast, there were others, like my own, where those complications did not materialise, and the patients survived. No one, though, knew how or why this difference existed.

We tried our best, but our efforts, whether those of doctors or nurses, appeared ineffective. We felt wholly inadequate, consumed with a feeling of hopelessness in the face of the virulence of the disease at its worst. It seemed to me, other medical staff and the patients that we were travelling the same never-ending journey. We all shared a common thought: *The war is over, but we are still here. When, oh when, will this nightmare end?*

For me, though, the nightmare was to get worse when Sarah was taken ill. I was concerned that she hadn't appeared in the Mess for breakfast one morning and made my way back to her room to find her still in bed. She was asleep but looked rather pale.

I rushed over to Sarah and felt her forehead. It felt slightly warmer than usual, but not unduly so. She came to as I touched her, drew a long breath, then slowly passed her hand across her eyes, lips and mouth. Sarah looked at me and seemed about to speak, but no sound came from her lips at first. Then she smiled weakly.

'Hello, Emily,' she whispered. 'I fear that I may have overslept – have I?'

'You look pale, Sarah,' I said. 'How are you feeling?'

'Not so good, I'm afraid.'

'In what way?'

'I've had an upset tummy during the night – slight diarrhoea – feeling sick – and some pains.'

I took Sarah's temperature. It was slightly above normal.

'It may be that you ate something yesterday evening that has upset you. I'll go and see Sister Bettsworth and tell her you're not well. In the meantime, stay in bed. I'll call back and see you as soon as I can.'

The day seemed to drag by. Things in the ward were relatively quiet. There was little to take my mind off Sarah and how she might be faring. As soon as I finished my shift, I rushed back to her room. She was still in bed but feeling better than she had in the morning. Her temperature was still slightly higher than normal, but the nausea was gone. She felt well enough to have some tea and toast and was feeling better except for a headache. I left her with a glass of water and a couple of aspirin tablets and went to have something to eat myself.

The following day was my day off, and I spent it with Sarah in her room. I helped her get up, bathe, and wash and arrange her hair. After that, I sat with her and played several games of draughts until she again started to suffer tummy pains. These became more severe as the afternoon progressed. Sarah's temperature rose to 100.8, and she began to vomit. Her heartbeat increased rapidly. I called the doctor, who thought that Sarah might have pancreatitis.

I was allowed to stay with Sarah through the night. Then, after a short sleep and a quick breakfast, I stayed with her during the day. Unfortunately, her condition deteriorated almost continuously. She became increasingly confused. Her speech often became slurred, and she made little or no sense. Then, she became cogent and asked me to write to her parents to tell them how much she loved them.

'I've got a bad feeling about all this,' she told me.

'Don't be daft, pet,' I replied. 'We're going to come through this together.'

Sarah looked at me, her eyes starting to glaze over.

'Promise me that you will write,' she whispered.

'Of course I will,' I replied.

'Thanks, Emily,' she said, her voice trailing off as she drifted back to sleep.

Worryingly, her condition worsened. Her skin became blotchy and turned a light blue, and a rash appeared that did not fade when I rolled a glass over it. She began to experience breathing difficulties. One moment, she suffered breathlessness; the next, she was breathing very quickly. Her temperature was now 101.4. I summoned the doctor again. He told me that he feared that Sarah's pancreatitis had triggered sepsis. Things were becoming dire.

There was, though, little or nothing I or anyone could do for Sarah as septic shock set in. Then, horror-struck and distraught, I witnessed her body gradually shut down. I sat by the side of her bed, holding her hands in mine as she slowly lost consciousness.

I struggled to stay awake as Sarah lay there. I dozed, then woke with a start a short while later. There was an air of tension in the room, and I knew something was seriously amiss. I shot up from the chair on which I was sitting. There was an eerie stillness. I looked at Sarah's face, translucent white on the pillowcase, and knew what it was. Death had come to her. At that moment, I felt numb.

'This can't have happened,' I sobbed. 'The world has just stopped making sense.'

Numbness turned to anger and guilt; for not being able to do anything that might have saved Sarah's life. Finally, anger and guilt gave way to deep, heartfelt grief as Sarah was buried in the military cemetery the following day.

*

After the service, my mind returned to the night before Sarah's death and the promise I had made at her bedside. I went into the chapel to think about what I should say when I wrote to her parents. A spirit of peace seemed to brood over the pew where I sat down, and the words seemed to flow so easily – both then and when I later put pen to paper.

*Dear Mr and Mrs Nugent,*

*There aren't sufficient words to truly express my sadness and shock at the tragic death of Sarah.*

## France, Spring 1919

*I have just returned from the military cemetery, where Sarah is now at rest. It was a most moving ceremony, fitting for such a unique and caring person. There were so many beautiful floral tributes and wreaths from her colleagues, friends and patients.*

*I am one person who is lucky enough to have known Sarah. I first met her when we both travelled from Victoria to Étaples. We became friends. Then good friends. Then the best of friends. I was with her at the end. Her last thoughts expressed to me were of you, her parents. She loved you with all her heart.*

*With her passing, I have lost a good friend, but the sense of loss I feel can be nothing to the loss you must feel and the heartbreak you must be suffering.*

*Sarah was loved and respected by everyone who knew her, worked with her, or was cared for by her. Her loss is a bitter one for us all.*

*She loved her job. She died while doing something where she believed she made a difference – and did make a difference.*

*I will miss her and her friendship forever.*

*With my most sincere sympathy and good wishes,*

*Yours, very truly,*

*Emily Harland*

As I went to post the letter afterwards, all I could think of was the question I'd heard repeatedly: *When, oh when, will this nightmare end?*

Slowly, the number of victims of the Spanish Lady began to dwindle. Finally, the pandemic seemed to have run its course. One by one, the military hospitals were starting to close down. My hopes of returning to Blighty grew day by day. But fate held one final twist to the story of my time in France.

## TWENTY-THREE

## *France, Spring 1919*

I looked hard at the letter Sister Bettsworth had just handed to me.

'It looks like a letter from home,' she remarked, 'judging by the postmark.'

I looked at the envelope, postmarked Jarrow.

'Thank you, Sister – but not from home, though,' I replied. 'I don't recognise the handwriting.'

I opened the letter and began to read it.

Dear Emily,

I've thought long and hard about writing to you – and what I might say if I did.

I received your letter so many months ago and feel very guilty that I never replied – and indeed not to thank you for what you said. Your letter made such a difference to me then, and I shall be forever grateful to you that you did write.

But I digress.

*I am not writing about that letter. I am writing now to see whether you might be able to help me once more, especially since the help I seek concerns Frank.*

*You probably do not know, but I received the saddest letter about nine months ago. I haven't and probably never will get over the shock of receiving it. It was a letter from Frank to tell me that he was about to be shot for desertion.*

*Since then, I have tried desperately to piece together what happened. It has not been easy, I can tell you. The military authorities have been entirely unhelpful, but I have managed to unravel some of the mystery.*

*In this regard, I had a lucky break when I contacted the chaplain who represented Frank at his court-martial and was with him at the end. His name is Henry Sheldon, and through him, I have discovered the whereabouts of the cemetery where Frank is buried. In addition, Henry has agreed to help me as best he can to try and clear Frank's name. He is sure that Frank was the victim of a miscarriage of justice.*

*I have also found out that other families and friends of men shot for desertion are trying to launch a campaign for justice for them. The process has begun, but heaven knows how long it will take. In the meantime, I am hoping to travel to France to see if I can find Frank's last resting place.*

*With Henry's help, I have managed to contact a group of former soldiers making a tour of the battlefields. They have helped me to arrange for a car to take me the ten kilometres or so from Albert to the cemetery where Frank is buried and back.*

*However, I am more than a little fearful of making the journey on my own and wondered if you would be willing to accompany me if you could take time off from your work.*

*I am planning to arrive in France in a couple of weeks and was thinking of taking a train to Étaples once I arrive in Boulogne. If you can join me, perhaps we could meet there and carry on* to Albert together. We could then travel back to Étaples before I continued to Boulogne and then back to Jarrow.

It's a lot to ask, but I really feel that I need to have a travel companion in France – and you are the only person I can think of I could turn to, even though we barely know one another.

Yours hopefully,

Sybil Oakes

I read the letter and reread it. I was stunned. Firstly on learning of Frank's death and the reason for it, and secondly that Sybil should ask me to help her.

*What am I to do?*

Half of me wanted to join Sybil; the other half was unsure. I remembered all too well her attitude towards me that time near Henry Street after Frank had chased after me when he had seen me from the Albert Road Post Office. I felt I needed to talk to someone about the letter, but the one person I would have turned to automatically was no longer a part of my life.

I returned to the Mess and sat down with a cup of tea. I had Sybil's letter with me and read it through again.

'Are you all right, my dear?' a familiar voice asked behind me.

I turned to look at Sister Bettsworth.

'I think so,' I replied tentatively, 'but I would appreciate some advice on this.'

I held up Sybil's letter.

'May I read it?' she asked.

'Of course, Sister, please do.'

Sister took the letter, sat next to me and read it before looking back at me.

'What a tragedy,' she whispered.

'What should I do, Sister? It's not as if I really knew Frank –

or know Sybil for that matter. And there is so much I should be doing here rather than taking time off to go with her.'

Sister looked at me – a little pensively at first, then her eyes widened, and she lifted her eyebrows.

'What do you think Sarah would have said to you?' she asked.

I looked down at the floor.

'I think she would have told me to go with Sybil,' I replied, looking back up at Sister.

She smiled.

'Yes, and I think she would have been right, not just because Sybil has reached out to you. I feel you need to get away from here for a day or two. Get away from things so close to Sarah and her death.'

I looked down again, then around the Mess, unable to find the words to reply.

'B-but can I be spared from the hospital?' I sputtered eventually.

Sister reached out and put her hand over mine.

'You would have at least a few afternoons free in the coming days. Even we don't expect you to work non-stop,' Sister replied. 'I'm sure I can arrange the necessary cover while you are away. Leave that to me – and leave it to me to clear things with Matron.'

\*

I couldn't sleep. Urged by the impulse of sheer necessity to be doing something, I rose and dressed. Then I sat on the edge of my bed, my hands folded in my lap. What should I do next? Was I any better off up and dressed rather than thrashing about restlessly in bed – my mind racing with thoughts about meeting with Sybil?

*Am I doing the right thing in agreeing to go with her? What might I say to her? How might she feel towards me?*

My mind continued to churn throughout breakfast and during my walk to Étaples Railway Station to meet up with Sybil.

I took a small basket containing a packed lunch with me, although I couldn't help thinking that it seemed as frugal as an anchorite's fare – some boiled ham, a variety of cheeses, half a loaf of brown bread and some apples. I also took an army water bottle filled with cold milkless tea.

Sybil was waiting for me outside the station. She had arrived in Étaples the previous evening and, by coincidence, had stayed at the same hotel that Edward had just before I saw him last. I felt a rush of butterflies in my stomach when I caught sight of Sybil.

She wore a white blouse and a dark brown skirt under a beige-coloured linen duster finished with silk moiré cuffs and collar and facet cut jet buttons. Until then, I had not taken in that Sybil was a tall, striking-looking woman with full wide-open dark eyes and a mass of wavy auburn hair turned back from her brow. Her lips were firm, her features well formed, but the deep lines of sadness under her eyes and round her lips bore testimony to what she must have been going through.

I hurried towards her, holding out my hand to her as I did so. She moved towards me and took my hand.

'Hello, Emily,' she gasped. 'I don't know how to thank you for what you are doing.'

I don't think that either of us knew what to say next until Sybil gushed out: 'Come on, Emily, the train will be here any minute now.'

Still holding my hand, she turned towards the ticket hall and onto the platform. A short while later, the train puffed its way along the platform and came to a shuddering halt. As it did so, we both headed towards a carriage and prepared to board the train.

The carriage was almost full. Sybil opened the door and started to head for two vacant spaces next to the window on the far side of the carriage. As she did so, she tripped over the feet of a corpulent, red-faced man sitting by the door, plunging forward towards a woman on the opposite seat before regaining her balance and poise and easing herself into the vacant seat by the window. She giggled, adjusted her coat about her and settled back as if nothing untoward had occurred. Feeling slightly sheepish, I followed her into the carriage and sat next to her. Sybil nudged me gently with her elbow. Little lines of humour crinkled about the corners of her mouth as I turned to face her.

The train pulled out of Étaples and moved through the French countryside at a leisurely pace along grass-grown tracks, passing level crossings guarded by horn-blowing women. At first, Sybil and I sat in silence. I felt awkward, not knowing what to say to her. So instead, I gazed pensively out of the window. Houses, farms, villages and hedged fields beginning to sprout green moved in and out of my view. Lines of poplar trees fled away amid the continuous fanning of the air by the train as it continued its journey, occasionally stopping at stations with no platforms. People got off. People got on.

Sybil was the first to break the silence.

'It can't have been an easy decision for you to come with me,' she said. 'Especially after the way I behaved when we met that time in Jarrow and the fuss I caused about your meeting with Frank. I feel so ashamed about that.'

She seemed genuinely upset about what had happened then, first looking downwards momentarily and then directly at me. I smiled at her, realising that my earlier doubts and misgivings about meeting Sybil and travelling with her had begun to fade away.

'If I'm honest, I did wonder whether I was doing the right thing in agreeing to go with you.'

'And yet you did agree.'

'Yes, after much thought, it seemed to me that it was the right thing to do. You see, I was grieving when your letter arrived – I had just lost a very good friend to sepsis. I showed your letter to the sister in charge of my ward and talked it through with her. She thought that our being together might somehow be of help to both you and me. So she arranged for me to have a couple of days' leave to do so.'

'I'm so glad she did – and that you are here today.'

With the ice broken, so to speak, I began to ask about Frank and his parents.

'As you can imagine, Frank's parents were distraught when they received a letter from him telling them he was going to be shot. It was worse still when they received the official notification from the Army that Frank had been executed. Frank's mother had a nervous breakdown, and his sister Isabelle ran away from home. The Dawsons have heard nothing from her since other than a short letter sent about three months ago and posted from Canada.'

I could see the tears welling up in Sybil's eyes.

'What about you?' I asked, realising almost immediately afterwards how clumsily I had put the question to her.

Sybil bowed her head, moved her hand to her temple and started to twist a wisp of hair between her thumb and forefinger. Then she looked, blinking back her tears.

'My heart was so stunned,' she said eventually, with a sigh. 'I didn't know whether it was broken or not. I could not take it in that I would never see Frank again. I couldn't sleep. For much of the night after I read the letter, I stood with my face pressing the windowpane, shuddering at the slightest sound outside, expecting every moment to wake up from what had been nothing more than a terrible nightmare. But, of course, I never did. It was all too real.'

The journey to Albert seemed to take an eternity, but eventually, we pulled into the station and alighted. Then, rather wearily, we made the short walk to a hotel close to the station and booked in for the night.

*

The following morning, we returned to the railway station to meet up with the driver of the car to take us the ten kilometres or so to the cemetery where Frank was buried.

We climbed into the car and headed out of Albert. As we drove, we saw groups of graves scattered here and there, recalling the terrible battles fought throughout the area during the war. Debris littered the countryside. Barbed wire entanglements, twisted and cut about by artillery fire, were still there. I also saw wrecked German pillboxes and a landscape pockmarked by shell holes and scarred by zigzagging trenches. Saddest of all were the crosses we passed, scattered about the fields in ones and twos and occasionally small groups of four, five, six or more in out-of-the-way corners.

The villages we drove through lay in ruins, all of them almost completely destroyed. Little or no trace remained of the houses, the sites of which were now virtually indistinguishable from the surrounding fields. The whole area was devastated, strewn with wreckage of all kinds – stones, bricks, beams, agricultural implements and household furniture from the shattered farms and houses. The trees had been hacked to pieces by artillery barrages, while among the stumps, I could see trenches, shelters, blockhouses and small forts.

About five kilometres outside Albert, we turned towards our destination, and a short while later, we were driving through the ruins of another village. Fragments of walls and half-burnt beams marked the site of the old houses. Some of the inhabitants had returned and were living in huts erected near the ruins of the church. Of the church itself, only the bases of a few pillars remained. Some graves in the churchyard showed signs that they had been torn open by the bombardments that had devastated the whole area.

Outside the village, I could see a large cross erected by the British in memory of their fallen comrades. A little further on, we arrived at our destination; the British cemetery on the same side of the road as the cross.

'I think that that was the most soul-destroying journey I have ever taken,' I gasped as I got out of the car. 'What Frank and his comrades must have gone through,' I sighed. 'And let's not forget the kind of hell the inhabitants have gone through also – both then and now.'

We walked together to the entrance to the cemetery, which seemed to stretch out either side of us, and forward almost as far as we could see.

'How should we do this?' I asked.

'Let's each walk down alternate rows where these exist and then make our way across the remainder of the cemetery together once the rows stop,' Sybil replied.

As we began our quest to find Frank's grave, it became clear that this would not be an easy task. Other than those set out in rows, there were graves everywhere. Occasionally, grass and weeds had grown around them, covering them and partially hiding them. Some crosses with names echoed the men who had given up their lives nearby, but far too many simply carried the words *Unknown British Soldier* or *Unknown German Soldier*. Sadly, a few of the crosses had become victims of the ravages of nature and time. Some of these had been turned black by the wind, weather and rain, and others were now green. In all such cases, any record or detail that had been there was now gone. Some of the crosses were lying about haphazardly. Originally marking specific graves, they had since been scattered from the spot they were intended to mark, a consequence of the battles fought throughout the area after the beginning of the Spring Offensive. There were also a few headstones marking the victims of earlier battles. Two graves recorded a kind of gallows humour that must have existed at the time their headstones were erected. One carried the words: *Here lie two Huns who met a Tommy*, and near it was another on which was inscribed: *Here lies the Tommy*.

Try as hard as we could, we found no marker that carried Frank's name. Eventually, we both realised that we would not be able to.

'I'm not giving up,' whispered Sybil as she took my hand. 'Someday, somehow, I will find Frank's grave.' Tears dimmed her eyes, and I could feel her hands begin to tremble. 'Someday, somehow, I'll clear his name.'

'And I'll do everything I can to help you with both your quests when I return to Jarrow,' I promised.

# TWENTY-FOUR
# *France, Spring 1919*

As spring edged into summer and just as I was beginning to fear it might never happen, I finally received the news I had been longing for. At last, the nightmare I had been living through for almost three years was at an end. I *was* going home.

I collected my luggage from my room and, making two journeys, placed it next to the pile of cases and trunks already left by my fellow passengers – a small group of other VADs waiting expectantly for the bus that would take us to the railway station. I then stood looking in the direction of the expected bus, not engaging with anyone in the group.

I looked anxiously at my watch, then down the road, then back to my watch. The bus was late, and I feared I would miss my train to Boulogne. Then, to make matters worse, it started to rain; not much heavier than a light drizzle, but an aggravation, nevertheless. Eventually, the bus lumbered into view, rumbling along the street until it came to a halt.

*Thank heavens – about time!*

An orderly appeared from the bus, helped load our baggage and guided us on board. Somewhat relieved, I climbed in, took a seat in the front and settled down. I was the last of the group to board, and a moment later, the bus moved into life and rumbled down the road. We were on our way. I began to relax a little.

When the bus reached Étaples, it was met by two rather elderly porters, who worked as best they could to help us all alight from the bus and unload our luggage. One carried mine onto the platform, for which I handed him a franc coin.

'*Merci beaucoup, Mademoiselle,*' he said, his mouth widening into an appreciative grin.

All I had to do now was wait for the train, which, as inevitably was the case, was late. But fortunately, it had stopped raining, and I began to pace backwards and forwards along the platform. As I did so, I noticed a board on which the words of a rhyme were painted.

*A wise old owl lived in an oak,*
*The more he saw, the less he spoke;*
*The less he spoke, the more he heard;*
*Soldiers should imitate that old bird.*

I laughed as I read it.

*So, a warning to soldiers that careless talk could cost them their lives.*

Still, a rather more novel way to say it than when you tell a secret to a friend, remember that your friend has a friend and your friend's friend also has a friend. But the war had ended. Many soldiers had already returned home, and yet the board remained.

*Still, all that is needed is to rewrite the final sentence back to the one I recognised;* 'Why can't we all be like that wise old bird?'

At last, the train crawled into the station, hissed and puffed, and came to a halt. I handed my luggage up to a grey-suited man who offered to help me. Then I climbed into a carriage and took my seat for the journey to Boulogne.

I studied the people around me. Several VADs, including those who had travelled on the bus with me, chatted excitedly about the first things they would do once they'd returned home. Other passengers had dulled, tired faces.

*Perhaps people going home from work in Étaples?*

None of them paid any attention to me. All sat quietly, sunk in their seats, jiggling with the train's motion.

The man who had helped me with my luggage reached into his briefcase and took out what looked like a file of papers. He selected a document and read it, his lips moving but uttering no sound.

*Perhaps a lawyer on his way to see a client?*

Across the aisle, a young woman about my age gazed absently ahead.

*Perhaps on her way to see her fiancé or husband?*

If anyone was looking at me, would they suspect that I was on my way to see Edward before we were both to travel to Jarrow? –That he was taking time off from work and would meet me at Folkestone Station? That we were then to go to Jarrow, meet my parents in the first instance, and set the wheels in motion for our wedding?

\*

After leaving Boulogne Station, I walked towards my steamship to the accompaniment of bells of trams journeying to and from the town. I picked my way through an untidy mass of goods and other items that littered the quayside until I reached the gangway. I showed my travel papers to the guards stationed there and headed towards the deck.

When I reached the top of the gangway, I looked back at the town and closed my eyes. A memory of the Boulogne of nearly three years earlier returned to me in an instant. The Boulogne that had already come to know the horrors of war. The Boulogne I had first seen with Sarah after I first met her on the steamer taking us and other members of the Voluntary Aid Detachment to France.

As my thoughts turned to Sarah, tears welled up in my eyes. She had died so near the time we could have returned to Blighty together; she would have been my bridesmaid.

I remained on deck until the gangway was hauled in and we began to inch away from the dockside. A cheer rang out as we did so. The sun sank low, tinting the buildings and lighting their windows with fairy-like colours. I took a last look at the town and turned away. My mind was a swirling mix of emotions. I was haunted by the cries of the dead and dying I had cared for. I regretted that I was leaving the work I had come to love. I looked forward excitedly to seeing my parents again. I looked forward to meeting up with Sybil and helping her as I had promised I would. But, above all, I was filled with hope and expectation for my future with Edward.

From having travelled home on leave eighteen months or so earlier, I knew that the journey from Boulogne to Folkestone on board a troopship was nowhere near a pleasant experience for a woman. Unfortunately, little seemed to have changed this time around.

The decks were a heaving mass of people, so I headed towards the ladies' saloon as soon as we were underway. Fortunately, this time it had not been commandeered to serve as an officers' sleeping compartment, and I could find a place to settle down in relative comfort rather than suffer the inclemency of the upper and lower decks.

After we had been sailing for about an hour, I went down to the ship's buffet area, where I bought a pot of coffee and a bun. I sat at a small table with these and looked around me, discreetly tuning in on occasion to the conversations of other passengers around me. I saw one officer holding a large, oddly shaped parcel.

'It's for my daughter,' I heard him say to his travelling companion. 'A few toys I bought for her on my way through Paris.'

*Now there's a lucky young lady!*

It was a relief when the boat sailed calmly and approached Folkestone. I stood on the upper deck with many fellow travellers to watch the English coastline draw closer. As we did so, another steamship passed by so close that when we waved our handkerchiefs, we could see the faces of passengers on the other ship waving back. I could sense the excitement felt by us all. The deck remained crowded as the shore loomed larger, and the steamship edged into the harbour and tied up at the dockside.

Everyone prepared to disembark as the gangplank was lowered to the quayside. I stood waiting with growing impatience, nervousness and expectation. It seemed to take forever before I was heading towards Folkestone Station, where Edward and I had arranged to meet.

As I neared the station, I saw a tall man striding purposely towards me.

*Is that Edward?*

I scarcely recognised him. His beard was gone. His face was clean-shaven, revealing a finely-chiselled mouth with thin lips and a well-marked chin and jaw. His grey-blue eyes were bright and sparkling. The upper part of the face was darker and more weather-beaten than the lower, from which it seemed to me that he had only recently shaved off his beard, one I knew he had worn for a considerable time.

He looked so smart. Resplendent in a dark grey suit, white shirt with starched collar and burgundy tie with white polka dots. Highly polished shoes. He was wearing a brand new fedora

—with its soft brim and indented crown, which had been creased lengthwise and pinched near the front on both sides.

As Edward approached, I dropped my luggage and ran towards him. He caught hold of me and lifted me clean off my feet and up to his chest as we met. He kissed my forehead and gently lowered me down. I looked up at him, tears of joy streaming down my face.

He raised his hat to show his close-cut black hair with a straight middle parting above his forehead, leant down, put his arm around my shoulder and kissed me. A quiver passed through my entire body. I caught my breath for moments of pure joy. The kiss was a long one, twenty seconds or more, but it ended all too soon for me. I rested there in his clasp, my eyes gazing up into his. A fierce passion swept me to be held by him like this, always warm, close, and secure. I trembled at the thought. My eyes closed, and then I kissed him, yielding utterly to the swirl of mad impulse. We clung together. Time seemed to stand still.

*This is happiness. True happiness.*

I eased my head back and looked at Edward.

'I love you, Edward Bennion,' I whispered.

\*

We were on our way. The train had left Folkestone well behind, and we were rumbling through green English countryside towards Victoria Station. We had the luxury of a railway compartment to ourselves. Then Edward stood up from his seat, put his hand into his jacket pocket and took something out I could not quite see. He turned to face me. I looked up at his smiling face, wondering what he was doing.

He lifted his right hand, and, as he did so, I could see what looked like a small red box between the thumb and index finger of his right hand. Then, steadying himself, he opened the box with his left hand.

'Something I've wanted to give you since I left Étaples before Christmas,' he said softly, handing the box to me.

I gasped. My mouth gaped open. I was looking at the most beautiful ring I had ever seen.

'It was Great-Grandmother's ring. My Great-Grandfather gave it to her when they became engaged nearly ninety years ago,' said Edward.

I was speechless and sat there mesmerised.

'Well, aren't you going to try it on?' Edward asked, a broad grin spreading across his face.

I eased the ring out of the beige velvet cushion it sat in and looked at it in awe. It was a glorious oval-cut ruby set in gold surrounded by twelve diamonds. The ruby was an enormous stone. I could almost warm myself by the red in it. The diamonds dazzled and sparkled.

'Here, let me,' said Edward, gently taking the ring and easing it onto the third finger of my left hand. 'There,' he said, 'it fits perfectly. You were destined to wear it!'

'Oh, Edward. It's so beautiful,' I whispered. 'I just don't know how to thank you enough.'

'That's easy,' Edward laughed. 'Don't ever take it off.'

He sat down, leant into me and kissed me again. Blissfully happy, I drew in close to him, rested my head on his shoulder and started to shed tears of pure joy. Outside the train, the countryside gradually gave way to the suburbs of London. The sight of green fields was replaced with that of red-brick terraces as they came into view. Finally, the train entered the tunnel that formed the final stretch of our journey before coming to a screeching halt.

Edward called a porter, who unloaded my luggage onto a trolley and came with us to the left- luggage office, where Edward also collected his suitcase and placed this on the trolley. We then went outside the station before taking a cab across London to catch the train to Jarrow for the final leg of my journey from Étaples.

\*

As we stood in the corridor as the train finally trundled into Jarrow Station, I was apprehensive. My parents had promised to meet us, but how might they react to Edward? How would Fatha respond to him? Finally, the train slowly came to a halt. Edward leant out of the window, turned the handle and pushed the door open.

'Out you go, Emily,' he said. 'See if you can see your parents. I'll fetch the luggage down.'

As Edward unloaded our luggage, I stepped onto the platform and saw Mam and Fatha materialise from the steam billowing out from the locomotive. I held out my arms and ran towards them. I reached Mam and, sobbing, threw my arms around her neck. She eased me away, put her hand under my chin and kissed me.

'Thank God you're finally back with us,' she said.

I turned and ran to Fatha. He lifted me off my feet, gently swung me around, put me down again and kissed me on the top of my head.

'Now, where's your young man?' he asked.

'Right here, sir,' said Edward as he reached the three of us. 'I'm Edward Bennion. It's an honour to meet you and Mrs Harland.'

'I'm delighted to meet you, my boy,' replied Fatha. 'I can't wait to formally welcome you into our family – even if you are a "southern softy"! I bet you're even a Chelsea supporter.'

Edward smiled, a quick movement of his lips.

'Sorry to disappoint you there, sir,' he replied. 'I'm The

Arsenal through and through! You'd better watch out for us in years to come!'

'We'll see, bonny lad. We'll see. Let me take one of those cases and get you and Emily home.'

We emerged from the station hall to face a very light drizzle that had sprung up from virtually nowhere but was scarcely noticeable. The sky was grey, but the clouds drifted high above. It looked like it was likely to brighten up through the afternoon. We quickly made our way along Railway Street and into Albert Road towards home. As we did so, all the horrors I'd experienced through the previous two or three years seemed less dreadful with every step.